ANDREW C.F. WHITEHEAD

INTO THE

DIGITAL

ETHER

ANDREW C.F. WHITEHEAD

INTO THE
DIGITAL
ETHER

MEREO

Cirencester

Mereo Books

1A The Wool Market Dyer Street Cirencester Gloucestershire GL7 2PR
An imprint of Memoirs Publishing www.mereobooks.com

Into the digital ether: 978-1-86151-187-4

First published in Great Britain in 2014
by Mereo Books, an imprint of Memoirs Publishing

A CIP catalogue record for this book is available from the British Library.

The address for Memoirs Publishing Group Limited can be found at
www.memoirspublishing.com

The Memoirs Publishing Group Ltd Reg. No. 7834348

The Memoirs Publishing Group supports both The Forest Stewardship Council® (FSC®) and
the PEFC® leading international forest-certification organisations. Our books carrying both the
FSC label and the PEFC® and are printed on FSC®-certified paper. FSC® is the only
forest-certification scheme supported by the leading environmental organisations including
Greenpeace. Our paper procurement policy can be found at
www.memoirspublishing.com/environment

Typeset in 12/18pt Plantin
by Wiltshire Associates Publisher Services Ltd. Printed and bound in Great Britain by
Printondemand-Worldwide, Peterborough PE2 6XD

ABOUT THE AUTHOR

Andrew Whitehead was born on 5th March 1951 in Brighton General Hospital. He attended local schools up until 1966 when he left school at the age of 15. Years later he studied "O" Levels and "A" Levels at Brighton Technical College and in 1974 he left Brighton to go to the University of East Anglia. Having graduated, he completed a PGCE course at the University of Keele and began lecturing at Buckinghamshire College of Higher Education in 1979.

In 1996 he ceased lecturing to become a carer for his newly-born child, working part time in various sales jobs before moving into supply teaching. He slowly built a positive reputation with various schools as a supply teacher, which allowed him to be available for his daughter early morning, late afternoon and all school holidays. However, in 2007 he was forced to give up teaching by malicious, lying, corrupt, self-serving police.

Since then he has maintained himself and his family through a combination of sales and now owns and runs a small private hire company.

My thanks to all those who have given encouragement and constructive criticism but, most of all, to Megan.

CHAPTER ONE

BIRTHDAY PARTY

It is Thursday 16th and I am sitting in the exam hall near the end of the allotted time. I've read through my exam paper and made a few minor corrections which should earn me a couple more marks, and I've even checked that I've spelt my name correctly: 'Edmund Decovny' stares back at me. Good! At least I've managed to get that bit right. So I walk out of the exam hall at 4 pm knowing I'll have no more school work for nearly three months, having just finished my final AS exam. This one was English and I feel pretty confident, as it is my best subject and the right questions came up. Thank you, God!

Tomorrow is my 17th birthday but, more importantly, it is also the day I take my driving test. In anticipation of my passing – at least, one day – my parents have bought me an old Mini for my birthday. When I say old, I mean it's so old they don't even make them anymore, but I just love the image of the old Minis. Yes, they are leaky and very unreliable, but riding around in one looks so cool. This one is plain blue but once I've finished doing it up, it will have a Union Jack on its roof and wing mirrors. I must get a 'BMW free' sticker too!

The date for my test has been booked long since and I am lucky that my uncle has a small business on a private industrial estate where I have been able to practise driving before I reach the legal age to drive on the public highway.

I approach the test centre with a mixture of confidence and trepidation. My instructor says he is pretty confident, but he probably says that to all his students who are about to take their tests. Even so, I'm very nervous and think about how my birthday present will go to waste if I fail.

My father has taken me around the test course a few times, so I know the layout and what's expected of me. The first pull away is fine and I'm sure I checked the mirror and looked behind me. Soon I am told to stop on a hill and then pull away again.

No problem! Then I am reversing around a corner. I manage to do it without going into the other lane or clipping the curb. On we drive, turning left and right, and suddenly I realise I'm doing more than 30 miles per hour. Oh Christ! Has he noticed? Of course he has. That's his job. But there's nothing to be done now. I just have to concentrate on what I need to do: an emergency stop. Easy! Finally, once we are back at the test centre, we stop, and so does my heart, whilst I await the verdict.

"You have made two minor errors, but I am pleased to say you have passed your driving test."

Wow! Yes, yes, yes! At this very moment, my life is complete. The exams seem like a lifetime away and my 17th birthday, along with the party tomorrow, seems so unimportant. Never again in my life will I have to take a driving test. There may be many more academic exams, but this is something I will only need to do once and it is behind me.

This evening, I go out with my friends to celebrate the end of our exams and, of course, I am the driver. Being the second youngest in my year, there are others who could have passed their test, but only one other has. I'm not going to miss the opportunity to be the driver on my first night of legal driving, even if it means I won't be able to drink alcohol. Yes, I am still under age when it comes to drinking in a pub, but we all know it's possible. Anyway, I have a party arranged for Saturday night to celebrate my birthday, the end of my exams and, now, passing my driving test.

I drive around to Josh's house, where he and David are waiting to be picked up. I'm so proud as they get in and shower me with congratulations on passing my test.

"Waahay! Well done, Edmund," exclaims Josh.

"Knew you would pass," adds David.

Once I've parked, our legal drinkers go through the front door of the Catherine Wheel pub whilst a couple of us slip around the back and wait till our friends come and sit at a table at the end of the beer garden. Now we can join a few other young people and, hopefully, not be noticed. I have been here a couple of times before and I'm never sure if the staff don't know we are under age or if they just don't want to know. Either way, a couple of hours drinking orange juice can get a little boring and all I really want to do is have the pleasure of driving us back.

"Last orders!" comes the call from the bar.

"Your round, I think," Helen says to David, and he duly gets up and goes to the bar.

When it's my round, I have to give money to Helen's big brother, Mario, who goes to the bar for us all. Trying to get a group of not too sober young people out of a pub at closing time is no easy task, even for experienced bouncers – sorry – stewards. Eventually we are out and off to the Kebab House. Here is an unexpected problem. "Hey guys, please get lots of napkins to wipe your hands so you don't get grease all over my car."

They all do, but I'm sure I still get grease on my new pride and joy. First I have to drop Helen and Mario off at their house before taking Josh and David home. Then I head home for a very contented night's sleep. It has been a good day.

Saturday morning, I awake to a noisy house. My parents and my younger brother and sister are preparing for their ten-week holiday to Australia. I'm not going with them. Yes, I have been invited, but, as much as I would like to see Australia, I think now is the time to stop going on family holidays and to start living my own life. I come out of my bedroom to see my Mum dragging a large trunk. She drops it, throws her arms around me and tells me what she has told me so many times before. "I will miss you, my darling boy, and I so wish you were coming with us."

I too am going to miss her, my father and both of my annoying little siblings, but a summer without my parents watching me will make it all worthwhile. In all fairness, they cannot be described as particularly controlling parents and they have done everything possible to enable me to pass my driving test at the earliest possible date, but the thought of ten weeks doing whatever I want is more inviting than going to Australia. That can come later in life.

It is half past seven in the evening and I arrive at the Minster Lovell village hall to help get everything ready for the party. The DJ, Clive, is waiting to get in and set up and my friend, David, is also waiting to help me arrange the tables and chairs. We have virtually all of them set up when the caterers arrive.

It is nothing very flash, just a simple meal for the 30 friends I have invited. I know some may not turn up, but I also know there will be a few who will ask to bring a friend at the last minute. I just hope the numbers will balance out. The invites say 8:30 for 9.00 and as a few guests have arrived, they help with the final set up. By now the music is playing, so already there is a party atmosphere. Soon after nine the caterers start to serve us and by ten we are moving the tables back so we can dance.

Since I don't currently have a girlfriend, I'm hoping my luck might be in, as there are a couple of girls in our year that I fancy. Jade knows I fancy her and is always friendly but she never seems to want to be anything more than just friends. Serene may be a better bet, so I chat her up. She's responsive but it might be just because I'm the host. I try my luck once more with Jade and get the usual reaction. She's very flirtatious, but there's no follow-through, so I turn my attention back to Serene. She's much more responsive this time, maybe because she's seen me dancing with Jade. I think I'm winning her favour, but by the end of the night all I get is a kiss. Even though there are tongues involved, she is clearly intent on leaving with her friends. By now Jade is also saying goodbye to her friends as her parents are waiting for her outside in the car. It seems I've blown it! I've played it far too long and tried to play one off against the other. My wonderful post exam experience has come to an end.

CHAPTER TWO

COMPUTER ERROR!

It is half past nine on Sunday morning and I am the last to get up. The house is buzzing as there is only an hour to go until my family leaves for two and a half months. Between snatching mouthfuls of cereal I help load the car. Soon it is half past ten and the hugs, kisses and long goodbyes begin.

"Bye, son. Look after yourself."

"Yeah, bye, Dad. Have fun!" I reply as Dad slaps me on the back.

"Goodbye, my darling little boy."

"Bye-bye, Mum. I'll miss you." I struggle to free myself from her embrace.

There is a brief period of no talking as an aeroplane takes off from the RAF base a few hundred yards from where we live, but it only lasts about 30 seconds. We hardly notice the planes now that we've got used to the interruption to our conversations, even though it doesn't happen very often. "Bye, Connor."

"Yeah, bye." He moves away.

"Oh, give your brother a hug, Connor; you won't see him for nearly three months."

"It doesn't matter, Mum." "Hey, Connor! Don't do anything I wouldn't do. And if you do – don't get caught!" I say, trying to lighten the situation.

"Pfft," Connor mumbles.

"Goodbye, my little sister."

"I'm not little!"

With that, they all get into the car. I don't give a great deal of thought to their departure, really, as it feels like they're all off for a day out, but soon the car is disappearing down the drive and into the road amidst much waving and honking of the horn.

My Mum is a Neuro Linguistic Programming Practitioner, so a part of our house has always been used as a place of work where she meets her patients. She says they aren't "patients", but never seems too sure what word to use to describe them either. She usually calls them "clients". When we were young, Mum would never see clients outside of school hours, as she would need complete silence, but as we've grown older, we've just had to learn to keep quiet when we are home and she is working. It's not easy, but she does have a separate room near the front door that she uses, so the rest of the house is okay. However, no music or shouting is allowed for half an hour or so after we get home from school. Mum says it's inconvenient having to work from home, but it pays some of the bills and for a few extras like my 17th birthday party.

Dad is a pharmacist and owns a chemist's in our small town of Carterton. He has arranged for the shop to be looked after by the manager for the ten weeks he is away. My sister, Lynsey, is 15 and in year 10 at the same school as me. She has no exams this year and is supposed to be in school for another few weeks, but is going to Australia anyway. Connor, my younger brother, is 13 and in year 8 at the same school, so really should also still be in school, but Australia is a once in a lifetime opportunity and he's not going to miss it to spend the last month at school just mucking about. I don't know if either of them got permission to take the time out of school, though. What irresponsible parents we have!

I go back into the house, finish my breakfast and have a cup of tea. Suddenly it hits me that I'm alone with nothing really planned and nothing much to do .Of course I knew I'd have to look after myself for ten weeks and that's not a problem, but the thought of not seeing my parents or my silly little brother and sister until September seems an unbearably long time. I feel an immense sense of loss and abandonment. Our school is a semi-boarding school and, although I am a day pupil, I remember at the beginning of year seven how my friend, Josh, tried to explain how he felt when his parents left him in a boarding school. His father is a diplomat in some far off place I can't pronounce – probably that place Borat comes from – and moves around a lot, so Josh has to be dumped in a boarding school. Josh had been 'dumped', but I've chosen to be left behind, so it's not quite the same, but now I do have a better idea of how he must have felt. The thought that I have another ten weeks of hell to live through… What am I to do?

There's only one thing to do. It is now 10:57 and in three minutes the first ball will be bowled in the first Ashes test. We don't have satellite television, as Mum and Dad are on a tight budget, so we always listen to Test Match Special online. I don't mind, really, as it's a five day event and if I sat in front of the television, I'd never get anything done, whereas listening to it is as exciting, but leaves me free to do other things.

I open the laptop and switch it on. There are two minutes to go and the desktop comes into view as the icons establish themselves. Now there's only one minute left and just enough time to put in the web address and hear the voice of Jonathan Agnew. Who's won the toss? Will the winner choose to bat first or field first? Here there is brilliant sunshine but what's the weather like where they're playing? If I were England's captain, I'd choose to bat first, get a good score on the board and then hope the skies cloud over tomorrow.

The egg timer disappears and it's exactly 11 o'clock as I move the pointer to the address bar and start typing 'bbc.co.uk/cricket'. I never bother with the 'www' bit. The computer's quite capable of putting that in. As I type the 't' of 'cricket' the last seven letters of the web address seem to swirl around and become indecipherable. Is this a 'lysdexic' address bar? Clearly this is some sort of computer error. I notice that I am now surrounded by the same mist the last seven letters were immersed in. I know it's impossible, but the laptop appears to be lifting off my lap, so I automatically grab it and pull it down onto my lap again. Or that's what I think. Although the laptop is once again on my lap, it seems I am more attached to it than it's attached to me. I'm following it as it moves. What to do? Let go? Will that mean I'll fall? Hang on and go with it? To where? Of course I hang on.

What feels like minutes is probably only a few seconds. Bump! I feel as if I've fallen off my seat. The mist starts to clear and the last seven letters settle back into 'cricket'. My heart slows and I ask myself if this has really happened. As I lift my eyes from the screen, I realise I'm no longer sitting on the sofa in my house, but on the ground in a field. How could this be? Am I imagining this as well? I remain motionless as it dawns on me that I've moved through space. I am definitely no longer sitting on the settee in my house. My Dad used to play an old Kinks song called 'Sitting on my sofa' and I long to hear it and be there. I look around. I'm in a field! It's pretty flat and I can't see any people, just hundreds of sheep. In the distance is a church, at least a mile away. I pick up the laptop and stand up. Now I can see a road about half a mile off leading to the church. Another road bisects it going what I think is south, by the position of the sun. There is no traffic on the road at all.

My desire to see where I am and to explore is overtaken by the understanding that I'm somewhere I haven't chosen to come and I need to get back to where I was. But how? Obviously this has something to do with the computer error. I sit down again and look at the keyboard. First I press the 'home' button. It seems logical! Nothing happens. Then I moved the pointer to the address bar and think hard about what to write. I try 'home', 'reverse', 'back' and 'return'. Then I press the seven key with the word 'home' on it. All to no avail. I look at the screen and randomly begin clicking all over it. I'm not giving a lot of thought to what I'm doing, but the mist reappears. Am I moving again? Will I go back home or just go somewhere else? Will I go anywhere? Will I die? Once more the laptop begins to lift and I know what to do this time. I hold on tight. This time I measure how long it takes by counting. 1, 2, 3, 4... Suddenly the mist begins to clear again. Bump! I feel as if I've fallen off another chair. Yes, yes, yes! I'm back in my house, sitting on my living room floor. All praise be to Ray Davis. But how have I got back? I'm not sure, but I think I clicked on the 'undo' button. That would make sense. I look around and realise I'm sitting just in front of the sofa I had been sitting on before the adventure started. So, yes, I have fallen off a seat. Perhaps I was a little further forward when I came back than when I left, so I just missed the edge of the seat. That explains the bump when I came back. I was sitting on a sofa at home but there was no seat in the field. Anyway, I'm very relieved to be back in the security of my own home and my own world.

More to the point, never mind how I got back, where have I been and how did I get there in the first place? My mind is racing. Perhaps I dreamt it all? I'm pretty sure I didn't. What happened? How long was I gone for? I have no idea at all and feel a mixture of excitement and fear. I just don't know how to make sense of it all. Of course it's impossible, but the fact is, it happened. I travelled to a different place which was completely empty except for hundreds of sheep. I was filled with fear of never returning, yet had – by chance – found the way back. Perhaps I didn't find a way back. Maybe I just returned by chance and it had nothing to do with clicking on the 'undo' button or anything else to do with the computer. I've had a very lucky escape and I should be thankful for that.

CHAPTER THREE

CONVALESCENCE!

I try to fill my time with trivial activities such as reading the newspaper, watching television and making more and more tea. I cannot even concentrate on the most important thing: the first Ashes test. Who won the toss? Are the openers still in? How many runs have they got? How many are down? How many overs have been bowled?

I realise it is only half past twelve and they are still in the first session. Not much time has gone by when I take away the time I must have spent trying to do other things to take my mind off what happened. Perhaps my time away was no time at all in the 'real' world. It might be like what happens in a dream where a whole lifetime can be dreamt but only a few minutes of sleep have passed. Oh, how I wish my Mum and Dad were here. Even my little sister and brother would be welcome now. I know I have to be with other people to take my mind off it and settle back to normality.

I pick up the phone to call Joe and begin dialling, but cancel it as I know I won't be able to speak. He's only half a mile away and I could cycle there in three minutes. Then it dawns on me that I've completely forgotten I passed my test on Friday and could drive to him. I'm so disturbed by my experience that I'm forgetting who I am and what's going on in my life. Am I becoming schizophrenic or psychotic? Certainly my assessment of reality is not what it should be. How could it be? I've just had an unreal experience. Or have I? I really don't know - which is worse? I need to get out but really don't feel up to talking to people so I decide to walk into town.

I turn on the special cricket radio I bought last year at Edgbaston and slip it over my ear. The man I bought it from at the cricket ground said it was a good fashion accessory and, although I like to think I am above such childish fashion needs, I have to admit I think it looks cool. It's set to Radio 5 Live Sports Extra and I hear Blowers' voice as I go to the door. It is now 12:55 and England are 92 for 1. Not a bad start. Or 1 for 92 as the Australian commentator calls it, which is only really confusing if a team loses wickets in the first over. It seems ironic that I'm listening to an Australian commentator's voice talking about the Australian team when my family are on their way to Australia. I get to the end of the drive and turn left towards the town as my phone rings. I answer it automatically and then remember I don't want to speak to anyone. It's too late now. It's Mum calling from Heathrow.

"Hello, Mum."

"Hello, darling. We're in the departure lounge. We just called for a final goodbye. I'll just pass you over to Dad"

"Hello, son."

"Hello, Dad."

"Bye! Here's Connor."

"Bye, Edmund."

"Yeah, bye, Connor."

In the background, I hear Mum say, "Come on, Lynsey."

"I've said goodbye to him!"

"Oh come on, Lynsey."

"No!"

I shout down the phone, "It's alright, Mum. Bye, Lynsey!"

"Sorry, Edmund, she won't talk to you."

"It's alright, Mum. Bye then."

"Bye-bye, my darling, Edmund."

"Yeah, alright, bye, Mum," I say and switch the phone off.

To my surprise, I found it quite easy to talk. Perhaps all I need is a bit of normal life to bring me back to my senses.

By now, I'm at the shops and decide to check my bank account to see how much Mum and Dad have deposited into my account to get me through the next 10 weeks. I put my card into the hole in the wall and punch in the numbers. My balance is £1,065.32, so I assume they've put in £1,000 for me. It seems a fortune, but I know if I'm not careful, it will all go soon. I don't really want to do the prodigal son bit to my parents, so I withdraw £50, fold it and put it in my pocket. As I walk away from the cash dispenser I look back at the Chinese take away next door and think I'll probably be one of their best customers over the next few weeks. I look at the flowers outside the greengrocer and then pop into the DVD shop to have a look around. I really don't want anything and am just filling time. Then I walk around the corner and into the cycle shop. This seems the natural thing to do as I often pop in there at the weekend, but I have to remind myself again that my cycling days are almost over now that I can drive. Anyway, it fills a few more minutes and helps bring me back to normality; whatever that is, I can't be sure any more.

Next, I cross over the road to the very useful shop and had a look around. I need a coaxial male to male connector for my friend's television but can't find one on display, so I have to ask. The assistant comes over to have a look and soon shows me where they are – just where I have been looking.. Oh well, that's why it's called a very useful shop, I think, and buy it before going around the corner to the newspaper shop to buy a chocolate bar. It seems so long ago now, but it was only really a couple of years ago I was doing a paper round for this shop. I did not get off to good start as I preferred the American idea of newspaper delivery – chucking it into the front garden. Pete, the shop owner, was most miffed and insisted the conventional method of actually putting it through the letter box was a better method of delivery. Better for whom? Certainly not for a young teenager in a hurry. Anyway, no sooner had I got used to this unreasonable expectation than my Mum and Dad made me give it up at the beginning of year 11. General Certificates of Secondary Education and all that, they said. Still, they did compensate me by giving me nearly as much pocket money as I had earnt delivering newspapers and I didn't have to get up at five o'clock any longer.

By now, the second session of play is in full swing and England have moved on to 121 for 1. At this rate, they should get over 400. Then another wicket falls at 125. Now they're only heading for about 300. It's not nearly enough to give them something to bowl at when the Aussies are in.

I walk to Dad's chemist shop before I remember he won't be there, and as I stand looking across the road at St John's Church, I remember how, just a few years ago, I was so bored I joined a Christian youth group and went through a religious stage just to be able to have something to do. They entice children into doing things like that. It reminds me of the man with sweeties at the school gate. How life has changed. Then I would not have believed that my computer would transport me to another place. I'm not too sure I believe it now. I walk back across the traffic lights and into the Co-op. Mum has left me plenty of food, but I know I need some milk. I fill a bit more time looking around and then have a strange desire to buy some vintage cider as I've heard it's very strong. It seems that cider has an image of not really being alcoholic like wine or beer, yet the alcohol content is much more than that of beer.

I'm just about to pick up a flagon when I remember I'll be asked for ID, so it's a waste of time and I put it back. Even though I feel much more grounded, I'm clearly still not thinking properly. At least I've saved myself the embarrassment of being challenged at the checkout and having to put it back then. It's better to just get the milk and go home.

As I leave, I hear a voice say, "Hello, Edmund!" It's Jenna's Mum, Hermione, and she asks me the usual. I feel okay to chat now, but what can I say? Then she asks me how I am. I think about telling her that I've just been on a trip to a strange empty field surrounded by sheep and didn't know if I would ever get back again, but it's not very likely she'll believe me. The men in white coats would be here in no time. Even all the chemistry in Dad's shop couldn't cure that one. So I tell her, "I'm fine, thank you. And yes, I will look after myself properly while they are all in Australia", I pre-empt her with a laugh. My family hasn't even left the country yet and already I have had the shock of my life.

"Oh good! Bye, Edmund."

"Bye, Hermione!"

It's time to walk home. I did think that once I could drive, I would never walk again, but I needed the exercise and fresh air and I feel much better for it. If I had driven, I would probably have crashed the car and wouldn't have been able to explain to the police why I was incapable of driving along a straight road. Like all children, I've been taught to always tell the truth. I don't think so! As I turn off the road and into our driveway, it doesn't seem the frightening place it was a couple of hours earlier. Not only that, but England have moved on to 187 for 3.

I walk in through the back door and take my shoes off. Even when Mum is not here, I'm still conditioned. Anyway, I will have to clean the place before they get back, so I may as well try to keep it reasonably clean. I open the fridge to put the milk in and take out some coleslaw, a packet of bread rolls and some spread. I get a plate out of the cupboard and make myself a coleslaw sandwich. Then I eat it, drink some orange juice and put the dirty stuff in the dishwasher. Without thinking, I walk into the sitting room and look at the settee. There is my open laptop. It seems to be calling me to log on and go back to where I was before. I feel like Gollum being called by the ring. Am I being taken over? Will I be able to resist?

In the background, I hear, "197 for 3."

CHAPTER FOUR

CUDDLES IN THE KITCHEN

I close my laptop and put it away in my bedroom. Mum's always telling me to put it away and not just leave it lying around, and now I'm doing it to avoid being continually reminded of what I think happened and what I might feel the need to do in the future. What am I going to do with the rest of my day? Nothing's been arranged, but I know a night out could be sorted with a phone call.

My mobile rings and I look at the caller's name. It's Serene. I answer with excitement. "Hello, Serene!"

"Hello, Edmund. How you doing?"

"Fine, thanks. You?"

"Yes, me too."

A long pause follows as I try to think of what to say. Clearly we're both finding it difficult to talk to each other, which is strange as we never had that problem at school.

"Er, Edmund, I was wondering if you liked bowling."

"Well…" There is a roar in the background and I realise the opening batsman has got his century. "Yes! Yes! Yes! He's got a century. Whoopee!" My excitement seems to dispel my nerves and I talk over Serene saying, "Oh, you're not a cricket fan, are you? Yes, I'd love to go bowling with you." It suddenly occurs to me this is a little presumptuous as she hasn't actually asked me and she may be suggesting a gang of us go bowling. Anyway, it's too late now.

"Oh great! Can you make it tonight?"

"Yes, of course. Shall I pick you up at 8?" For years I've wanted to be able to say I'd pick a girl up in my car, rather than being driven around by my parents, or somebody else's, and now I'm living the dream.

"Oh no, Edmund, I live just around the corner from the bowling alley! I'll see you outside at eight."

"Okay. If that's alright with you I'll see you there and then."

"Cool. Bye till then, then."

"Yes. Bye, Serene."

Oh well. I'll have to wait for another opportunity to say, "pick you up at eight and don't be late!"

What excitement! All thoughts of computer errors evaporate and I rush upstairs to have a shower. How things have changed. There are no more worries of psychosis. As I'm getting out of the shower, play closes with England on 284 for 4. It hasn't been a bad day's play.

As I'm drying myself and still feeling positive, I make the inevitable decision – I have to go back to wherever it was at some time. What else can I do? I'll never know for sure if I don't, and I want to know for sure and find out where it was. From the number of sheep, it could be Australia. Did I get transported to where the rest of my family were flying? It looked too green for Australia, but it is their winter season and it is a big place. Actually, I have no idea at all where it was and that's the main reason I have to go and check. I want to tell Serene but where would I start? I expect that would put her off completely. How could I start to explain, but I really need to share this with someone. I'll have to see how the evening goes.

I leave in plenty of time to park and be outside by eight and at five to I approach the entrance to Hollywood Bowls. Serene is already waiting and looking very attractive in a knee length dress that clings to her figure. I park as quickly as possible and try not to run to her so as I casually walk up and say 'hello', I lean forward to kiss her mouth. I'm pleased by her response and we walk in. I haven't been here in years and had no idea how much everything has changed. As we discuss how many games we should play Serene pushes a tenner into my hand and asks me to book two games. I pay for them and find we have a few minutes to wait. As we sit chatting, she doesn't seem like the girl I've spent six years at school with. That girl was a mate and just another school girl. This Serene is a gorgeous young lady. She looked attractive at my party but now – wow! I can't tell if it's because she really does look better or if I view her differently now that I'm on a date with her. It doesn't really matter as I think she also likes me.

When the game starts, I get off to a good start and Serene gets off to a bad one. Should I try to beat her or make her feel good by losing? Would that be patronising? I don't have long to think about it before getting a foul for overstepping the line and Serene gets a spare. Now we were about even. My competitive nature takes over and I go for a win. The best laid schemes of mice and men often go awry! Five minutes later the game's over and I've lost. Oh well, one game left. Off we go and I am soon in the lead. Serene gets a couple of noughts and I get two strikes, so not only do I win, but I score nearly twice as much as in my first game. It feels good and Serene doesn't seem to mind. When she asked for two games, I thought about what would happen if we each won a game and there was no winner, but now I realise it's better this way as no one looks like a loser. Honours were shared and I had no need to patronisingly lose to her. Or perhaps she patronised me by losing? Who cares?

Without thinking, we have a very natural cuddle at the end of the game and then there's a pregnant pause. What now? I stumble over my words and ask, "How about a drink?"

"Sure," she says and we walk over to the bar. There are signs all over the place saying that it's a bar for over 21 only and I know neither of us will get away with it, so I order two orange juices. At least there's no loss of face at being too young as we are both in the same boat, but I can't help feeling I look like a schoolboy and Serene looks like a sophisticated young lady. Still, she doesn't seem to have a problem with it, so we sit and chat. After a while, the nerves of our first date seem to disappear and we both chat as if we were still at school. I can't really remember what we talk about, but it's mostly insignificant stuff. It doesn't matter though, as I'm constantly thinking that I have an empty house at home but don't know how to raise the issue.

We chat on and our glasses are empty as it approaches 9:30. There's a short silence and I ask, "Would you like another drink?"

"Okay," she says.

As I get up, I blurt out, completely out of the blue 'Would you like to come back for coffee?' I believe that amongst university students, that is a euphemism for 'would you like to come back for sex'. Serene just looks at me for what seems like a whole minute. I start to mumble, "Er, later… If you want to. I mean, you don't have to, I just thought…" I am digging myself in deeper. Why can't I just shut up?

Serene looks me straight in the eye and says, "Okay, but I need to be home by 11 or 11:30 at the latest." Oh my God! What is she saying? Once more I start to mumble, but then get control of myself and say rather quietly and sheepishly, "Well, perhaps we had better leave now." Serene just picks up her jacket and stands up. Keep calm, keep calm, keep calm! Don't let her think you are desperate or counting your chickens. I can't believe it, but manage to prevent myself from clicking my heels.

We walk out a lot faster than we walked in and get into my car. As Serene had walked to the bowling alley, because she didn't live far from it, I need to get her back here later. I try to drive home slowly, calmly and serenely, but the only sort of serene I can think of is the one sitting next to me. We hardly speak as we drive, but what is there to say? Eventually we turn into the driveway and I park the car. We walk around the back and into the kitchen. I feel the need to go through the motions and put the kettle on as I ask Serene how she likes her coffee.

"One sugar and lots of milk," she says quickly. As I stir the coffee, I turn around to find Serene standing close behind me. I'm not sure what to do, so I put my arms around her and squeeze her as she responds. I will always remember cuddles in the kitchen to get things off the ground. We kiss and I disentangle myself as I pick up both cups and say, "Come on." I'm pushing my luck here a bit but it's no problem as she follows me upstairs.

At five past eleven we leave our driveway and head towards her home and a quarter of an hour later I stop at the end of her road before giving her a quick goodbye kiss. It isn't really late, so I don't think her parents will ban me from seeing her again. Apart from anything else, they have known me for six years now. As I turn into my driveway, I have a great sense of tranquillity.

What a turnaround from a few hours ago. I wanted to tell Serene about my little adventure but didn't know how to raise the matter. Anyway, I have to admit, I had better things to talk about and do. If I go again and return, I can always tell her next time.

I walk into the house and go straight to bed, but cannot get to sleep straight away as I think about what adventures await me tomorrow. Should I go back there and walk around? Should I take something to drink? Something to eat? How long will I be there? Should I have a test run and just go there and come back to make sure I can? Next time I must check the time before I go and when I come back to see how 'real time' relates to 'dream time'. From the fact that I plopped onto the ground when I arrived, and missed the settee when I returned, I guess there's a direct correlation between a position here and a position there. I can't believe I'm thinking like this. There? Where is 'there'? I'm still not too sure if 'there' actually exists. What if I can't come back? What will my family think has happened to me? There will be no trace. If I can't get back, would that be because I'm dead or because I'm alive elsewhere? Which would be worse for me? Either way, it would make no difference to my family as they wouldn't know. Am I being selfish? Definitely, but what is adolescence for? I know that by this time tomorrow I'll know, and eventually I drift off to sleep.

CHAPTER FIVE

ANOTHER TIME

As soon as I wake up I'm completely conscious and fully aware of what I have resolved to do today. My eyes spring open and focus on the clock. It is 7:09.

I get out of bed and dress much more quickly than when I have to go to school. Mum made me promise I would not just get out of bed and leave it unmade for ten weeks, and as this is just the first day of those ten weeks, I don't feel I'm breaking my promise by leaving it unmade. I go downstairs and immediately pick up my laptop. Then I pause. I need to slow down. I must do this rationally, calmly and make sure I don't forget anything. I've given a lot of thought to how I will do things this time, but I'm still not sure about some aspects of how to play it. Mainly I'm wondering whether I should go and then immediately return, just to check if it has worked.

I try to calm down and leisurely eat a big breakfast of cereal followed by three pieces of toast. After all, I don't know when I'll be eating again or when I'll be coming back – if ever! With these thoughts running through my head, I switch on the laptop, log on and open Internet Explorer.

When I've finished breakfast, I clean my teeth and prepare a litre bottle of squash to take with me. I also remember to get out my laptop case so I can easily carry the computer around if I need to. Having worked out that space is similar in the other place, I know it's important to come back to exactly the same spot or I may have some serious difficulties. For example, six feet further forward will put me in the middle of the house wall. It's probably best to avoid that! I'm really very frightened about what might happen. Not so much for myself, but for my Mum, Dad and younger siblings who will never have the faintest idea of what has happened. Now, of course, there's an extra person to consider: Serene. I wanted to tell her last night, but how would I have started? The truth is, I was so involved in the here and now of last night that I hardly gave any thought to what I had planned today. Now I wish I had at least said something, in case I never see her again. But what? Should I have mumbled something like, "If you never see me again don't take it personally" and hope she didn't ask any questions? That's just silly. Eventually I console myself with the thought that if I had said anything, things would not have panned out as they have.

I'm all ready: clean and tidy with the laptop case and a bottle of squash. I've combed my hair whilst thinking how I probably have my priorities wrong in wanting to look good when I have no idea what I'm getting into. Suddenly I realise I've nearly forgotten something vital. I rush into the garden and look around for Lynsey's old plastic windmill. She's far too old for it now, but she planted it in the garden years ago where I hope it will still be. It's not in the back garden. I go round to the front, and there it is, sticking out of one of the flower beds. It's a bright blue windmill on a white stick and will be perfect for marking any spot I arrive at so that I can come back to exactly the same spot and avoid that wall. Then I load the dishwasher with my breakfast things and start tidying up the kitchen, realising that I'm making excuses not to get on with it. I need to gather my resolve and apply myself to what I have to do. I dry my hands, take the bottle of squash out of the fridge, take a deep breath and walk into the sitting room where the laptop is on the sofa waiting for me. It really does feel as if it is waiting for me! As if it has been calling for me to return to the other place. As if I am its tool, not it mine.

Eventually I sit on the sofa and place the laptop case on my lap, followed by the laptop with the windmill and bottle of squash tucked in between the laptop and my tummy. My hands are shaking as I move the pointer to the address bar and begin to type in the URL 'bbc.co.uk/cricke…'. At this point, I pause to look at the clock so that I can check my time away. The clock on the DVD reads 8:37 and I check my watch to see if it's the same. It is. I look at the keyboard and suck in as much air as I can hold in my lungs as my shaking finger touches the last letter of the website address – 't'. My hands grasp the laptop as I see the last seven letters of the address swirling.

It is happening again. The mist spreads and is all around me now as I'm counting my time of 'travel': 4, 5, 6, 7… 19, 20, 21… Bump! I know I have landed again and look around. It seems like the same place: An empty field, except for hundreds of sheep. I look at them and they look at me. They don't seem to be surprised to see me and I have to remind myself that sheep are not known for their powers of wonderment. Looking at my watch to check the time, I'm pleased to see it's only 8:38. It seems time is not bending – even if space is. As I stand up, I'm overwhelmed by fear and immediately sit down again and move the pointer to 'undo' and click it. The mist swirls and I count: 3, 4, 5… 20, 21… Bump! I'm back home. The mist clears and I look around just to check it's my sitting room. It is, and this time I'm sitting on the sofa with my legs half on and half off it. Not comfortable, but successful. As I slip my legs to the floor, I look at the DVD clock to see 8:38. My watch says the same. Time in the other place is the same as time here, even if I have no idea where the other place is. My fear disappears immediately. It seems the travelling is controllable.

What now? Should I thank my luck stars that I've been able to return and just be satisfied with what I've discovered? That would be the sensible thing, but I've never been praised at school, or by my parents, for being sensible. This time, with more of a sense of excitement rather than trepidation, I move the pointer to the address bar and start typing 'bbc.co.uk/cricke…'. I stop, not out of fear but just to look at the clock. It reads 8:40. I press the last key – t'. Once more the letters swirl and the mist spreads all around me as I count. 4, 5, 6… 18, 19, 20, 21… Bump! I'm back in the same place with the same sheep. Well, I think they're the same sheep but I have to admit, they all look the same to me. It's clearly the same place, but it feels like a different world. I feel no fear; just excitement and anticipation.

I put the laptop on the ground with the windmill and the bottle next to it and open the case. Then I pick up the laptop, put it into hibernation, put it inside the case and zip it up. Now to pick up the windmill and stick it in the ground where I've been sitting. I have one last look around and by the position of the sun I try to establish north, south, east and west. But is it 8:41 in this place? The sun is low in the sky, so it seems quite early in the day, but is it summer? If it's midwinter, the sun would be low any time. It's quite warm for early morning and I can see a few chewed bushes in full leaf, so I assume it's summer. I think this must be what the South Downs looked like before they stopped sheep farming in that part of the country and it all became scrub. I've read about how terrible it is that that this type of countryside is being lost because of the change in farming. I can't see how the bare fields are better, but who am I to judge? I wonder if this is the Sussex Weald. There are hills to the north but nothing really to the south. It's pointless wondering really. It could be absolutely anywhere in the world. Or maybe another world?

Once more I look towards the distant church which I saw the first time and it appears to be to my east. As it is the only land mark I can see, it seems logical to head towards it. Off I stride and I think it looks about a mile away, so I expect to get there in about 20 minutes if I don't hang about. Before I get there, I arrive at the road I saw the first time and find it isn't a proper road but just a mud track. When I say mud, it's actually more dust than mud. I look to the north and can see the other road crossing it is also only a track, but it does seem to be heading towards the church, so I walk towards the junction. Then it strikes me that even allowing for the fact it is only a mud track, there is no traffic around; vehicular or human. At the crossroads, I turn east towards the church and take a swig of squash.

Up ahead I can see a man in the distance just before the church, so I assume I can get some information as to where I am. I speed up in case he walks off the other way. He doesn't move at all, except to lean against a tree, and watch me as I approach. He's on the side of the road and surrounded by sheep.

When I get close enough to see his garb, it strikes me as strange. By now his gaze is changing into a stare and I can see his clothes are not made of summer cotton, but some rough looking material which is torn and very dirty. His jaw drops as I get closer. Hasn't he seen a clean man before? I'm now only a few feet away and realise the smell of the sheep is being greatly added to by his personal smell. He continues to stare and I say, "Hello?" He says nothing, so I ask, "Could you tell me where I am?"

His mouth moves but nothing comes out. Eventually he makes some sounds, but nothing I can understand. I repeat, "Could you tell me where I am?"

The man speaks again and I realise he's not speaking English. Is this man a foreigner, perhaps, or am I in a foreign country where I am the foreigner?

"Sorry, could you say that again?"

Silence. Then, once again, his jaw moves but nothing comes out. I stand there, looking and feeling confused, embarrassed and uncomfortable. Once more he speaks, and I think I recognise a few sounds. It reminds me of Chaucer's work, which makes me smile. I loved studying Chaucer for English AS and enjoyed seeing how the language had changed from a form of German/Dutch/Frisian to what we now call English. Shakespearian English is just about intelligible to our ears, but two hundred years before Shakespeare, Chaucer's language was drastically different and meaningless to most people in the 21st century. Is this man German? Am I in Germany? I learnt a little German in school, so I ask him the same question in German. He continues to stare and speaks again. This time I think I recognise a few sounds and once more am struck by how much it sounds like Chaucer's English. It's worth a try! I put my question into what I think would sound like 14th century English. His face relaxes a bit and he says something that sounds like St. Petter. Petters? Petter? Better? What's better? Britus? Then I ask, "St. Britus?"

The man gives a vague nod. St. Britus? St. Britus? St. Britius!

Is he saying St. Britius, the name of the only old church in our area? It should be about a mile from where I live, but it is a lot older looking than this church. However, as I turn to look at the church, I think that it does look very similar to that church, apart from it not being nearly as old. I've not studied the church before and only ever driven past it, but it does look similar. The road I am on runs alongside it and there is another road at the T-junction that runs down the other side of the church. I look at the man and ask again, "St. Britius?"

The man nods. Looking at him again, I can't help but think he doesn't look very healthy. I'm not surprised considering all that dirt. I take a step towards him and he steps back. It's not me that's stinking, I think. Then I ask, "Brize Norton?"

He shrugs and says, "St. Petter."

He must be saying Britius, just with a different accent. This is the only church in the country dedicated to St. Britius, so it couldn't be any other church. But where is Brize Norton, the village around the church? It's not a big village, but a village nevertheless. There's nothing here except a couple of shabby sheds a few hundred yards away. Then I notice a more substantial building in the distance behind the man. Is this St. Britius in Brize Norton? What else could it be?

The man still stands there and stares unsubtly, looking me up and down. I do not return the insult. At this point, he looks over my shoulder and I turn around to see what has caught his eye. A man in long black clothes is standing by the church. A monk or a priest? Perhaps the vicar? He looks a lot cleaner and I think I'll get further talking to him, so as I walk towards him, I call out, "Excuse me!"

When I get closer, he steps back as the other man did. I've learnt that in very sparsely populated places personal space is much greater than it is in crowded cities, and assume this is the reason why they both stepped back as I got close. I say, "Sorry to trouble you, but is this St. Britius' Church?"

The vicar looks at me blankly and once more I try the same question in what I imagine to be Chaucerian English. The vicar answers in the same strange tones and I'm sure he's saying that it is. Then he says something like, "Where are you from, sir?"

Oh my God! What am I to say? This is not my St. Britius, so how can I say I come from over there, a mile back. If he's the local vicar and the population is that small, he would know me or at least know there's not a house over there. Thinking quickly I say, in my best medieval English, that I come from a far off land. This seems to satisfy the priest and I realise we're able to have a conversation even if things are not perfect. As I said I come from a far off land, this is enough for him to accept my strange use of his language. He ushers me into his church and I follow him in somewhat reluctantly. What else can I do? I can hardly run off. Although I'm reluctant, I want to find out more about this place.

Inside, the vicar offers me a drink of water from a rough mug and I accept it to be polite. We begin to chat and he seems happy to tell me about the place. After all, I'm a stranger in his land so he probably wants to tell me about his world as he knows I am a 'foreigner'. He tells me the local people are very rich, and I think about the man in the dirty, torn, rough clothing. If they are rich, what do the poor look like? This priest is relatively clean, but his hands are dirty and so are his finger nails. I think he says something about the plague and I ask for more detail. He looks confused and says, "It landed in the south a few days ago." What is this? A different strain of flu? Smallpox? Cholera? Oh no, cholera is caught from dirty water and could not be described as a plague. He goes on to talk about the spread of the disease and the speed at which its victims die, and how he feels for the people and especially his fellow priests who seem to be disproportionately stricken by the illness. He keeps repeating how he prays to God for deliverance and that he is sure the good Lord will save the children of his Holy Church. By children, I assume he means Christians and not young people. He's clearly frightened of the plague but I have no idea what he's referring to.

As he is talking, I'm thinking. The plague that landed in the south, Chaucerian English... Oh no! Is he referring to the Black Death? St. Britius, the rough roads, the lack of buildings? Am I where I live but not in the same period? In the same place but not the same time? Had I got three dimensions right and the crucial fourth one wrong? Am I in medieval England? In the 14th century? I become aware that I'm gawking and the priest has gone quiet. He asks, "Did you not know?"

I say something about knowing but not realising the severity of the situation. Now I understand why he and the other man stepped away from me as I approached. So why has this priest asked me into his church? Probably out of Christian kindness and because I look foreign and a lot cleaner than the locals. Maybe another reason is that in a strictly organised social structure I would appear high in rank as I am clean, well dressed, if rather strangely, probably educated and I have the confidence of the upper echelons of society. Things are falling into place as I understand what's happening, but the gravity of the realisation that I am in a different time begins to dawn on me.

The priest offers me some more water and I instinctively say, "No, have some of mine." I pick up the bottle I had put on the floor and proffer it. Realising I'm offering a plastic bottle, I withdraw my hand but the priest's eye has caught the bottle and he raises his mug. I remove the top, now remembering it's orange squash, and pour some into his mug. The priest raises it to his mouth, sniffs and sips.

"Mmm! Beautiful, is it a honey concoction?"

"Yes," I say, thankful for the way out.

Then he says, "That is a strange bottle, sir. May I look at it?"

Tentatively, I pass over the bottle which he takes and studies. Excuses run through my brain and eventually he asks, "What is it made from?"

"It's a leather material, dried in a special way that makes it look like that."

"Mmm… May I?" he asks, touching the top.

He has obviously seen me open it and twists the top off himself as I nod. "Ingenious!" he says and hands me back the bottle. I have survived another awkward situation.

The priest's body language indicates that he wants to end the conversation. Maybe he's bored or maybe he has other things to do. Either way, I'm pleased to have the opportunity to get away and rise to my feet. I offer my hand and remember physical contact is a no-no in times of plague. He flinches a little but shakes my hand. I'm now wondering if hand shaking is a social ritual in medieval times. I think it had been a Roman thing, so probably yes. Anyway, it indicates my equality with a priest, so I am not regarded as a peasant like that poor man outside. This makes me ask, "Who is the peasant outside?"

"Ah, him. He's not a peasant: he's a serf to the monks in Black Bourton. He's called Edric." I know the Domesday Book used the words 'serf' and 'slave' interchangeably, so I have an idea of his status and that he has no right to anything, including his clothes, which are the responsibility of the church. He is obliged to work for the Priory. I can see who is getting the better side of the deal. Little has changed! All doubts that this is where I live, only in a different time, have now been dispelled. Black Bourton is still a little village about two miles from Brize Norton.

"Thank you for your hospitality," I say as the priest raises his hand and blesses me.

I'm not sure how to respond to this, not being religious let alone Catholic, which of course everybody is in the 14th century. After all, that is what the word Catholic means. I give a little bow and make my way towards the door. I'm tempted to ask him what the date is, but I know this would be pointless as the calendar has changed since then and the answer would be rather meaningless. However, I studied medieval history along with Chaucer and know the Black Death landed at Bear Regis in the south near Poole in 1348, having spread from somewhere around the Russian Steppes only a few years earlier. It was probably brought to England on a ship. This was the main way in which it had made its way west over the previous few years.

Once outside, I take another look around and wave to Edric who is now staring at me again. The priest probably wanted to do the same, but he has more social graces than poor Edric. I stare back at him. Never mind, mate. Even if this plague does get you, it will hasten the end of this terrible socio-economic system. The transition to capitalism will not be smooth or easy but, even if capitalism is far from perfect, it has to be better than what gives you this life. I would like to have a conversation with him about the Marxist concept of the process of history, but feel that even if we could understand each other perfectly, he would not have the faintest idea what I was talking about. Neither would I had it not been for my mother's years of telling me we only live in a period of history known as capitalism, but that there is nothing permanent about it. With this thought I turn and walk east towards the crossroads.

As I walk, my thoughts are racing. How has this happened? Has it happened at all or am I still in a very long dream? Either way, I have to deal with it as a reality. It reminds me of the philosophy concept of phenomenology. Whether or not the table is still there when I do not perceive it, if I perceive it by banging my leg against it, it will still hurt, so I have to accept this world as if it is real. Walking back I look at my surroundings differently from when I was walking to St. Britius.

As I approach the Carterton crossroads, I'm thinking that for another 700 years into the future this scene will not change much at all. There will be no houses here and the land will still be used for grazing sheep. What else can one do with marginal land? Until other forms of employment emerge in later years, there is no choice other than to farm in a subsistence manner. So, standing at the crossroads I stop and look around. There is no Co-op, no pub, no charity shop and no estate agents. Oh well, not all things are better now than they were in the Middle Ages!

I walk down the road towards Black Bourton and a few hundred yards further on I stop and look into the distance towards that village thinking how, from the 1950's onwards, no one will be able to walk through to Black Bourton because the Americans will close that road to extend the air base when they hold it after World War II. What would Edric and the priest think? Not a lot probably, as it will be hundreds of years after their deaths.

I turn right off the road and cross the field towards the point which I think should be about the beginning of what would be Milestone Road. I look around for the milestone and cannot see one, so I assume that it must have been put there years after the period I am in now. I walk on and soon pick up the sight of the blue windmill blades. I had guessed well and approach the place as fast as I can. Nothing has gone wrong, and nothing has frightened me, so why the hurry? It's probably just because I'm in an unbelievable situation; in another time. I need to get back to a sense of security. As I reach the blue windmill, I pick it up and try to sit exactly where I placed it. I open the laptop case and put the computer on my lap. I open it up and have to wait for it to come back to life. When it has, my finger moves towards the 'undo' button and I click it with a slight sense of fear, but more with a warm sense of homecoming and security. The letters in the address bar swirl and the mist spreads all around me as it did before. I don't know if it is forgetfulness because my head is full of what has happened, or faith that it will work, but I do not count this time. No sooner has the mist started swirling than it begins to clear again.

CHAPTER SIX

BURFORD

"Burford! Burford! My Lord Burford!"

"Lechlade, what is all the excitement?"

"The King has news of the plague. The word is it has reached Clanfield."

"Oh, dear Lord. It must have been brought down the Thames and landed at Radcot." "Or up the road from the south coast", opines Lord Lechlade

"Yes, that's possible. Has the Earl of Gloucester been informed?" Lord Burford asks.

"I don't know, but I expect word reached him before it reached us here at Windsor."

"I am just back from collecting my younger son, Stephen, from school in London, but I must return to Burford to be with my household and rally the people. Where is my elder son, Henry?"

"I do not know but believe he is still within the castle."

Burford dismounts and calls to a servant, "You, man, find my son, Henry, and tell him to prepare to return to Burford."

"Yes, my Lord."

"Are you going back to Lechlade?" Lord Burford asks of Lord Lechlade.

"Yes, we are already packed and ready to leave. This may be the last we see of each other for a while as we will all have to stay in our homes till the plague passes."

"You are right. Give my blessings to your wife and family and tell them we shall meet for a celebratory meal once this horror has passed."

"I certainly will, Burford. Give my felicitation to your family and may the Lord be with you all. Good day and good luck."

"Good day, Lechlade, and may the Lord be with you also."

"Scabbard!" Burford calls to his manservant, who is continuing to unload the boat on the river which has just brought them back from London further downstream. "Stop unloading the boat. We must gather all our belongings and reload the boat, plus another two, and return to Burford. Everything must be gathered as we do not know how long it will be before we are in Windsor again. I must see The King and beg his leave."

The herald announces, "The Lord Burford."

Burford enters and genuflects before the King.

"My Liege, I beg your leave to return to my family and the people of Burford to prepare for the arrival of the plague."

"Of course, My Lord, and please feel free to take anything you or the people of Burford may need in these terrible times."

"Thank you, Sire, we will need some food for our journey. I shall instruct Scabbard to visit the kitchens before we leave."

"I wish you Godspeed and may he watch over us all."

"Thank you, Sire. I remain your true and trusted servant." Burford walks backwards and turns to leave the royal chambers.

Two hours later the boats are loaded and ready to leave. All three boats are low in the water, being laden with belongings, provisions and people. It is now an hour past noon and progress is fast as the convoy makes its way upstream through

Maidenhead. Here it is necessary to land as they make progress through the rocks under Clivedon towards Marlow. As it is necessary to land again, this is a good place to spend the night, but it is still light and the cox thinks the party could make Henley before midnight, so they press on. Time is important as families may be distraught awaiting the arrival of their loved ones, and because the people of Burford need to be rallied to the challenge as soon as possible.

By the time Henley is in sight, it is completely dark, but the party lands and makes its way into the town to find a bed for the night. Henley, being full of inns, provides a good choice for the discerning traveller, but quality is not the main deciding factor, so the first inn is adequate for the Burfords and a few others, whilst the rest of the party find rooms further up the town.

A quick meal is requested and questions asked as to the plague's progress. The innkeeper says, "Yes, the people have heard of the sickness upstream, but there is no evidence of it in Henley, though the people, especially the lower orders, are very frightened." The innkeeper tells Lord Burford that many of the lower orders still worship the pagan Gods, so they have more to fear as they do not have the protection of the one true Church of God. It is no surprise to hear that many have recently become baptised into the Church of Rome.

Lord Burford agrees with the landlord and opines, "This may protect them and, even if they were to die, at least they would know their souls have been saved and they will live forever in the Lord Jesus Christ." In normal times, there would have been much merrymaking and quaffing of ale, but these are not normal times, so once everybody has eaten, they retire to bed for a good sleep before rising to continue the journey home.

Soon after dawn, the Burford family are breaking their fast

and gathering their belongings before messengers are sent around the town to ensure all arrive at the boats as soon as possible. It is another bright morning as Lord Burford walks to the boats and boards. There is a little early morning mist but the sun is quickly burning it off and the floodplain and surrounding hills look beautiful in the early morning sunlight. Burford asks if everyone is there, and is informed that only two men are still in the town but will be there soon. Five minutes later the laggards arrive, giving their excuses, and the three boats move off upstream.

Having negotiated various rocks and shallows that force them to land again, the party approaches Abingdon by early evening. Now a similar decision to the previous night is necessary. Should they stop here for the night or press on to Oxford? Lord Burford decides that it would be better to land and rest at Abingdon to be able to rise early and reach Burford the next day. Soon the boats are alongside the steps and, boat by boat, the crews unload to go into the town to find lodgings for the night. Once more the party is split between more than one inn, and some request of their Lord to be allowed to make merry. Permission is granted, but only on the proviso that *all* are aboard again by the time it begins to get light the next morning. Lord Burford is aware of the times ahead and that this may be the last night the crew may have to relax for a long time.

In the town the innkeepers and others are questioned about the progress of the disease, but there is no real evidence that it has progressed further or even that it is definitely in Clanfield now. That village is only 30 miles further upstream, but it seems that over the last couple of days there has been a flood of people out of the area. All claimed, however, they were merely passing through and did not come from any plagued village. What else could they say? All travellers downstream are treated with suspicion and anyone who says they have been in Clanfield or Radcot will have been forced out. As for those going upstream, there are very few, but those who are all have family reasons to do so, like Burford and his party. There are even inns that say they are running out of provisions because the flow of food around the area is being cut drastically, as most traders are staying in their homes and villages to try to avoid contact with strangers. However, enough food can be found for those with the money to pay for it, like Lord Burford. So his party eat and drink their fill and take to their beds early in preparation for an early rise.

As the skies begin to lighten, Scabbard approaches his Lord and tells him that everyone is ready at the river. It is only a few yards from the inn, and five minutes later the first boat is pushing off from the bottom of the steps. The final leg of the journey has begun and the convoy is soon passing through Oxford, where the 19-year-old Henry Burford has been studying at Balliol College for the last two years. It is unlikely he will be returning this autumn, as all colleges are expected to close until the pestilence had passed.

There is much bustle on the riverside and most traffic is going downstream. Oxford, being a large city, is already draining of people running for the supposed safety of the countryside, as the plague is expected to arrive any moment. At Eynsham, the party stops to eat and rest and a man is dispatched to hire a horse and ride to Beamtune Castle to request horses and carts to meet them at Tadpole. Had they been travelling in smaller boats, they would have gone up the Windrush, as it flows into the Thames at Standlake and straight past Burford House where the Burford family resides.

By early evening, the first boat rounds the bend to see men

and horses waiting for them. Steam is rising from the horses, so it is clear they have not long arrived. The baggage and the rest of the party can now be left for Scabbard to bring on to Burford, whilst Lord Burford and his two sons, Henry and Stephen, ride on to Burford as fast as possible. Within minutes, all three are astride their horses and heading towards Chimney on their way to Beamtune. The fields on either side of the road are virtually flat and full of barley waiting to be harvested. This shows the four-year farming cycle is in its third year and the next year will be fallow.

Lord Burford looks at the fields and says to his sons, "It is just as well the next year will be fallow as no planting may be done next spring anyway."

Henry replies, "Let's hope they can find men fit and willing to harvest this year's crop before it rots in the fields or we shall all starve."

On they gallop and as they approach Beamtune, they can hear the bustle of the market. As they ride into the village, they find it full of people but there are many empty places where stalls would normally be set up. What stalls there are seem empty and it becomes clear that traders are afraid to come to Beamtune, and the local people are buying all they can to stock up for an unknown period until the disease passes. There is a sense of panic in the air. After all, Clanfield is only two or three miles further on from Beamtune.

The three of them ride up to the castle gates and Sir Richard is waiting for them. "Good day, my Lord Burford, Henry, Stephen. I hope you are well. You are very well come despite the imminent problems."

"We are well, Sir Richard," replies Lord Burford, "but even if we are well come, we cannot stay as we must return to our family as soon as possible and prepare the town for the arrival of the plague."

"I understand, My Lord, but can you not just stop for a drink?"

"We can, sir, and you can tell me about the progress of the disease."

The Burfords dismount and food and drink is produced as Sir Richard tells them what he knows. "A man showing the unquestionable signs of the plague five days ago is now boarded up in his home with his family. His door has been painted with a cross and food is being left by a window for them. He may well be dead by now. We do not know what has become of him or his family. The man works at the wharf in Radcot and is suspected of having caught the disease from someone who stopped on the river there. Whether that man went on downstream or took the road is not known. There is no sign of the disease in Faringdon yet, so it is unlikely it came from Southampton and Wight up the road. There is much panic abroad, but preparations are being made and Special Masses are being said in the churches. I have ordered the Clanfield Road to be blocked and no one is allowed into the town from the west."

After the food and drink has been consumed, the Burfords remount and as they are about to leave, one of Sir Richard's men runs up, shouting, "A woman has fainted in the market and cannot get up again!"

"Tell us more," says Sir Richard.

"Well, little more is known as the woman is lying in the road and no one will touch her."

"It could be the plague or she may just be ailing from the fear of what is to come," says Lord Burford.

"I shall send a woman to wash her in vinegar," says Sir

Richard as the Burfords turn their horses to leave, thanking Sir Richard for the loan of the horses and carts, the comestibles and the information.

They enter the town, which is now virtually deserted, only minutes after their arrival. As they pass the market square, the woman is lying on the ground moaning, with no one near her. The three of them give her a wide berth and turn north toward Northton. No one is leaving the town on the west road as this passes through Clanfield. Entry to the town is being blocked. Whether or not anyone has come from Clanfield through Alvescot and Northton, they do not know.

Soon they are galloping through Northton and up the hill towards Swinbrook. On top of the hill they stop at the Oxford Road and look back down the valley towards Beamtune. They can see the roads going north, south, east and west, but no one seems to be going west. The road they are on is full of traffic, all going one way.

They continue down the hill and into Swinbrook where Lord Burford stops at the inn on the bridge. As he enters, the landlord touches his forelock and says, "My Lord, it is good to see you back."

"Thank you, and please send someone into the town to announce my return."

"I will do so, sir."

Lord Burford leaves and remounts for the short ride to the back gate of Burford House, which they find is already guarded to protect the house and those within from any refugee seeking sanctuary from the plague. One of the men at the gates says, "You are well come, sir, we all await your instructions as to how to face the threat."

When they enter the yard, the back door bursts open as the

cook and kitchen staff flood out to the arrival of their Lord. Some fall to their knees and give thanks to the Lord Christ for his return. As Lord Burford enters the back of the house with Henry and Stephen, his wife, Mary, enters the kitchen along with his three daughters, Anne, Marion and Joan. Many expressions of love and relief are shown. Now that the Lord has returned, all will be well.

CHAPTER SEVEN

BACK HOME

There is no real bump this time, as I have landed almost perfectly on the settee, back at home. Immediately I look at the clock on the DVD. It reads 10:57. I look at my watch and it says the same. I have been away for two hours and 17 minutes. This seems a reasonable length of time to have walked to Brize Norton, had a chat with the priest and hurried back again. I've discovered that the passage of time in the other place is the same as the passage of time here.

Once more there is a moment when I wonder whether this has really happened, but really I have little doubt that it has. Yes, I have been to a different time. Not a different place, that's clear, but the same place in a different time. The only real question is how this has happened. Even this is a rather pointless question, as I doubt if I will ever know the answer and am sure that if I took my laptop to a computer expert and explained what had happened, he would be more likely to think I was mad than to explain anything. Not only is it confusing as to why this has happened, but why it always takes me to the same place and time? Why the Middle Ages? Why at the beginning of the great plague? Is there any reason for this or is it sheer chance? I don't know and cannot decide whether it is a good or a bad thing. Is it a great adventure for a young man or is it a dangerous game to play? Will I ever go back there again? I can't decide now, so I'll simply listen to some cricket and get on with my day.

It is day two of the test and although it is a lovely sunny day in Carterton, it soon becomes clear that overnight rain in London has delayed the start of play at Lords. What to do now? Get something to eat? Beans on toast? Why not? It's quick, easy and tasty! It does not take long to prepare and ten minutes later I am sitting at the kitchen table eating. When I've finished, my thoughts turn to Serene.

I dial her landline as I know her mobile isn't working and when her sister answers I ask to speak to Serene. She comes on the line and I am pleased to hear some excitement in her voice. After the social niceties I ask, "What are you doing this afternoon?"

"Well, nothing I can't change."

"So would you like to go punting on the Cherwell?"

"Oh yes, you're a member of the school rowing team, aren't you?"

"Yes, but this is punting – no oars."

"Oh well, it's all the same to me. Can you pick me up?"

"Yes, I'll be there at 12:30."

"That sounds good."

"Bye, then."

"Bye."

At the agreed time, I arrive at Serene's house and she comes out to meet me. I'm pleased to see she must have been waiting and I know it must have been partly to avoid me meeting her family again. There's nothing wrong with her family, but I really don't want to engage in social niceties. She looks gorgeous in a tight blue top, red shorts and sandals. Soon we are speeding along the A40 towards Oxford and I switch on the radio to see if play has started at Lords.

"Oh, I'd forgotten you were big on cricket. Will we have to listen to it all afternoon?"

"I probably will, but I have an ear radio for when we're in the boat but it doesn't work in the car."

"I don't mind cricket, but I couldn't listen to it all day."

Play has started and it is now 225 for 4.

We arrive at the Cherwell boathouse at quarter past one and, having paid to hire a boat, we are in it and push off before half past. I've paid for a three-hour hire, so we have plenty of time as I push off upstream. Serene has never been in a punt or a boat before, but she clearly likes the experience as we punt upstream in the glorious sunlight. Soon she wants to have a go at punting so I hand her the pole with a few simple instructions as to how to do it. As expected, she has no idea of what to do and hardly reaches the river bed with the pole. The punt moves two feet forward at a time as she gets little leverage. After a while, she gets the hang of pushing but she has no ability to steer the thing. Soon the inevitable happens: we crash into the river bank under an overhanging tree. This is no real problem and a bit of fun, so I get us back on track and tell Serene to have another go. Despite the difficulties she is not put off at all and takes the pole once more for another go. She's just getting the knack of it when she pushes the pole into the soft river bed and can't get it out again. The pole stays where it is as the punt moves on, leaving us up a creek without a pole. We put our hands and arms in the water to slow our progress and then have to hand paddle back to get the pole. Eventually we reach it and pull it out of the mud to continue our progress upstream.

It's my turn to punt for a while and on we go as Serene happily chats and observes, "We should have brought a picnic basket."

"Yes, we should have, but we had no time to prepare anything. Next time we shall have to plan things."

"Oh, there's going to be a next time, is there?"

I'm a little embarrassed but hope she's joking about her inabilities to punt. It seems she is and soon wants to have another go.

"Okay, but if the pole gets stuck in the water again, don't let go of it."

She is getting better and although we're going from side to side, we're making progress, avoiding other boats and not hitting the bank.

"It's stuck again!"

"Don't let go! Pull it. Hold on."

This she does, but it results in the amazing sight of Serene still holding onto the pole while the gap between the punt and the pole – with Serene clinging to it - widens. The pole is stuck at an angle and her weight slowly makes the heavy top end of the pole bend towards the river. As if in slow motion, Serene inches closer and closer to the water, and she eventually gives up the struggle against the law of gravity when her bum touches the water and she lets go. I stand and laugh heartily but then stop as I think she may be offended at my laughing at her plight. There's no need to worry because when she surfaces, she screams, "Augggh, it's cold in here!" If that's her greatest concern, there's no real problem. I don't know if I should wait for her to swim over or to do the big male thing and dive in. It isn't really my style, but soon I find myself in the water alongside Serene just because it all seems part of the fun. We swim towards the punt but, of course, can't get in without tipping it over, so we push it against the bank before we climb in. By now a couple of other punts are coming towards us to help and I call out to them that there's no problem, but someone retrieves the pole and passes it over as they pass our punt. Both of us are dripping water all over the punt and I'm glad I had decided to leave my ear radio in the car just in case I fell in. We laugh and fall into each other's arms. I remember that part of the reason I like Serene is because she's always up for a laugh and full of adventure. It's still very sunny and hot, so once we are out of the water we soon warm up.

By now we are more than two hours into our three hour hire, so I take the pole and punt us downstream. It's a lot easier going back, not just because I'm doing it, but because we're going with the flow of the river. Anyway, it's always quicker going back. Half an hour later we round the bend to see the boathouse and five minutes later the boatman holds out his hand and I throw him the rope which he grabs and ties around a post. He can see we've both been in and seems to think this a little entertaining, but he doesn't seem to mind that we've made the boat wet. After all, what can you expect if you let members of the public use your punt?!

Soon we're in the Mini and heading back to Carterton. Without thinking I drive straight to my house and then realise I'm being a little presumptuous, but Serene doesn't seem to mind as we walk in through the unlocked back door. Together we prepare some food. She fries some eggs and sausages as I make my own concoction of instant mashed potato, baked beans, and a large lump of butter seasoned with salt and pepper. Sitting at the table, Serene compliments me on my concoction and I praise her for not breaking the egg yolks.

Not long thereafter we're sitting on the settee with my laptop on a little stool next to it. I look at it and think about how I could raise the subject of my adventures, but the kisses and cuddles soon start so I can't be bothered. About an hour later it's time to take Serene home as her parents have not seen her since they left for work this morning and it's now after seven. We pull up outside her house and she takes off her seat belt saying, "No kisses, as it's daylight and they know nothing other than that we're friends."

I understand and say, "Okay, when will I see you again?"

"Well, we have family coming around this weekend so it will have to be next week. Call me on Monday."

"Okay, bye." Next week seems so far away, but I understand she has a life to live too and doesn't have the 'luxury' of her family being away for ten weeks.

As she gets out, I summon up my courage and say, "When I do see you, I have something very important to tell you, so can you remind me if I forget to tell you?" "Okay." She smiles and closes the door. I haven't told her but at least I've put myself in the position of having to tell her when we next meet.

CHAPTER EIGHT

PREPARATIONS

Henry awakes to the sound of a kerfuffle in the courtyard below his window. Jumping out of bed and looking out he can see Scabbard organising other members of the household and people from the town. He returned during the night with the luggage from London and Windsor and is already helping to prepare the town for its defence against the plague.

Henry dresses quickly and hurries down to find the house a buzz of activity. Word of his rising has already reached the kitchen and soon breakfast arrives, as Henry's three sisters run around fussing after their brother. They had not seen him for many weeks before his return last night after he joined his father's party as it passed through Oxford on its way to Windsor. Henry has spent the last two years studying at Balliol College and is now home for the summer. Lord Burford and his two sons had intended to spend a week in the royal household but news of the plague's progress has forced a change in plan.

During the meal, Lady Burford appears and hugs her son. She has been busy organising the kitchen household, whilst Lord Burford has given his orders to Scabbard, who is now outside ensuring the town knows what is required. The Lord is now elsewhere in the house writing letters to be sent to the surrounding farms and villages. Henry's father has been up for a long time and it seems the only one not up and working is his brother, Stephen.

Having eaten, Henry seeks his father.

"Ah, good morning, son. Did you sleep well?"

"Yes, Father, I am well refreshed and ready to play my part."

"Good, your learning at Oxford will do us well in the times ahead. I am nearly finished here, then we can both go to the town to ensure all is in place."

"Yes, Father, I shall order some horses to be prepared."

"Thank you, Henry. I will be with you soon."

As the sun approaches its zenith, father and son are trotting out of the courtyard and through the gate to find about 10 or 12 people from outside the town trying to get into the town but being blocked by Lord Burford's men. The Lord has given orders that no one is to be allowed in, except under exceptional circumstances and with the Lord's expressed permission. However, many have brought supplies of food, clothing, firewood and, especially, vinegar, all having been bought on Lord Burford's orders. The owners of these goods are sent back to their villages and farms to do their best to survive the pestilence. This morning, Lord Burford has given permission for only two people to be allowed in. They are two women, both of whom have nursing and midwifery experience. Their skills may be useful in helping the nuns with the sick in the times to come.

As the two travel the short distance down the hill to the bridge, the throng parts and hands are extended to their Lord. The guards on the north bank of the Windrush river turn their pikes as the two Burfords cross the bridge into the town of Burford. As their Lord passes the people touch their forelocks in deference. Even though this is a requirement of the lower orders, there is still genuine affection for their Lord. After all, he could be much worse. Henry is to inherit his father's title and it is somewhat fortuitous that as he reached the age of maturity, he is able to help his father, and the town, in this hour of need.

As they enter the town, Lord Burford can see the carcasses of dead dogs and cats being cast into the river upstream and he calls to a man. "You, my man, remind those people I gave orders for the animal carcasses to be taken to the top of the hill and burnt outside the town."

The two Burfords have discussed the arrangements for preparing for the plague and young Henry's learning about medical philosophy has advised that dead animals should be burnt. The Lord turns to his son and says, "Yes, I know you said the bodies of the dead should be burnt too, but these good people have done nothing wrong. Should their lives be cut short it would add to their suffering, and that of their families, if they were to be prevented from entering the Kingdom of Heaven because their bodies had been burnt. That is a punishment reserved for traitors and heretics."

On the left is the town church of St. John the Baptist, part of the diocese of Gloucester. A little further on, and set back from the high street, is the Abbey attached to the church. The nuns will be busy during the next few weeks and supplies are pouring in to assist in God's work. The street is full of traders and there is a buzz of activity, but no sense of summer excitement. Everybody is preparing for what will amount to a siege.

As father and son move slowly through the throng, their presence is acknowledged by the people of the manor. "Good day, My Lord."

"Good day, Robin. I trust you and your family are well?"

"Yes, My Lord, they are all well and my wife, Rebecca, is helping in the Abbey."

"Ah, I thought she would be. She is a good woman, your wife." Lord Burford squeezes his knees and his horse moves forward further up the hill, followed by Henry.

Half way up they turn right into Sheep Street and immediately are met by a man running towards them. "My Lord, My Lord!", he shouts.

"Yes, John, what is all the excitement?"

"I was coming to find you, sir. There are two men at the barrier wanting to come into the town. They are both from Northleach and say if they were allowed in, they could be of value to you and the town of Burford. One is the church priest and one is a barber surgeon."

"Oh yes, I have heard of the barber surgeon of Northleach." The Lord paused for a while as he thought. "We have no barber surgeon in Burford and he would be of more use here than in a small town such as Northleach. I will allow him in, but, as for the priest, we have plenty of God's servants here and the people of Northleach will need their own priest. Tell him he… No, I will tell him myself."

The Burfords walk their horses along Sheep Street to where the road is blocked and supplies are being purchased from all sorts of traders. Lord Burford has made arrangements for the purchase of items deemed vital for the coming siege and his Chancellor is overseeing the purchase, distribution and storage. As the Burfords approach the road block, Sir John, the Chancellor, is dealing with a purchase and does not see the approaching Lord and his son. "Sir John, how goes the day?" enquires Lord Burford.

Sir John rises from his seat at the table and spins around to greet his Lord, having not seen him since before he went off to get his sons from Oxford and London.

"Good day, My Lord.", says Sir John with a bow. "The day goes well and we have boosted the town's stores. But there are two men who have requested of you to be allowed into the town."

"Yes, I have heard," Lord Burford says and looks at the crowd where a priest stands out amongst the general peasantry. Next to the priest is a well-dressed man who Lord Burford assumes is the barber surgeon. He looks at the two men surrounded by peasants, all of whom are hoping they will be allowed into the town where they pray they will be better able to survive the coming plague. They cannot possibly all come in and it must be seen by all the people, especially those who are sent back to their own towns and villages, that those who are allowed in, are allowed in for very good reasons and not because of who they are.

Lord Burford beckons to the priest and he approaches obsequiously.

"Father, I hear you wish to come and minister to the people of Burford?"

"Yes, my Lord, I can give the people comfort and pray for them."

"That is a very kind offer, but we have many of God's servants here and the people of Northleach need you more than we do."

The priest opens his mouth to further plead his case but knows by the fact that Lord Burford's eyes have moved on that it is not open to negotiation. Lord Burford's eyes are now on the man he assumes is the barber surgeon.

"You, sir. You are a barber surgeon?"

"Yes, sir, I am and with many years of practice."

"You can cut out buboes?"

"Yes, sir, and I have brought my knives." He holds up a medium-size case he has in one hand. In his other hand is a larger case, presumably with his luggage in.

"You have come prepared. Go to The Abbess and tell her I have sent you." The guards part to allow him in, whilst the priest stands looking forlorn.

"Sir John, do you know where Scabbard is?"

"I believe he is at the barrier on the Gloucester Road, sir."

The Lord and Henry turn their horses and move back along Sheep Street. Lord Burford moves closer to his son and whispers, "The priest is not needed here and word will go around the county that no one gets into Burford without a vital skill for the town. It will help maintain law and order to see fairness enacted in Burford. There may be riots of desperation ahead and turning away the priest will ensure no one can claim preference is given to anyone."

At the end of Sheep Street there is a caravan of hay wains moving down the road to be stored in the Lord's barns. Once it has passed, father and son trot up the hill towards the junction with the Oxford Road and the Gloucester Road. They can see the smoke rising from the pyre on top of the hill and to the east. As planned, the smoke is blowing away from the town across the Windrush valley. Scabbard hears the horses and stands in the road as the Burfords approach. There is much noise on the other side of the barrier as Lord Burford says, "Good day, Scabbard. What is happening here?"

"Good day, sir. The people are objecting to being turned away and a man, his wife and seven children are saying they have no home and nothing to eat."

Lord Burford looks at the family and asks in a loud voice, "What has happened to your home?"

"Our home is on the farm at Sherbourne and the landowner has said there will be no planting this winter, so there is no need for me and my family." Lord Burford shows no emotion and looks at the rest of the crowd. "You must all go back to your villages and your homes. There is no room for you here and you will be no worse off in your own homes and villages. Anybody who remains here in five minutes' time will be arrested. Go back to your homes!"

He then turns his horse to indicate the matter is settled as the crowd mumble their displeasure.

"Scabbard," calls Lord Burford. "Give the family some food and some money and send them back to Sherbourne with a letter from me to the farmer telling him I will pay their rent over winter."

Back down the hill and at the corner of Witney Road they pause and survey the activities around them. Little is happening at the junction of the roads so they trot their horses to the end of the road where there is another barrier blocking those wishing to enter from there. Everything is quiet here, with few wanting access to the town. Witney is to the east and away from the progress of the pestilence, so few people are likely to want to move towards the problem. Having praised the guards for their vigilance, the Lord and his son trot back along Witney Road and back into the High Street.

Slowly they ride down the hill to the bridge, where the crowd on the other side has grown. Once more the Lord addresses the people telling them they must return to their villages and homes as there is no room for them in Burford and they will be no less safe in their own homes. Anyone remaining after five minutes will be arrested. The Burfords cross the bridge and the crowd parts in weary resignation. Then they go up the hill and into Burford House once more where Anne, Marion, Joan and Stephen greet their father and brother.

That night the whole household – family and servants – prepare to go to the church of St. John the Baptist to ask the Lord for deliverance from the pestilence. In the beautiful evening sunlight the household make their way out of the courtyard towards Burford, all on foot in order of social importance. At the front is the Burford family and behind comes the household with the men in the front, the senior female house staff and the Angles, Saxons and Welsh in the rear.

Down the hill and over the bridge goes the Burford party and as they approach St John the Baptist's, the whole of Burford is waiting for them to enter first. The crowd parts to allow passage and the Burfords take up their rightful place at the front of the church. Others take their seats in their social order with the Welsh at the very back. There are only two of them apart from one Welsh servant girl who is part of the Burford household.

The priest begins by welcoming the Burfords back to the town and thanking God for their return. He then goes through the Mass as if the congregation are not there. Having completed the ritual, the priest asks for God to save the town and its pious people from the sickness and commands the people to increase their prayers to the one true God.

Once the ritual is over, the Burfords leave the church whilst all the others wait for them to pass. Once outside they make their way towards the bridge, but as Lord Burford and Lady Mary step onto the bridge, there is a commotion behind them. A man is pushing through the throng towards the Burfords, shouting, "Lord Burford, Lord Burford!"

Lord Burford stops and shouts, "Allow him through!"

The man pushes his way to the bridge and immediately blurts out, "One of the nuns is ill and showing every sign of the sickness, my Lord."

CHAPTER NINE

MUNDANE LIFE!

The next few days pass slowly and I fill my time with usual summer things such as sunbathing in the garden and listening to the end of the test match. This has been a tight match with Australia needing 367 in the last innings but only 81 overs to do it in. England has failed to get all ten wickets and Australia has failed to get the 367 runs. So, a draw. Now all I need to restore normality is a couple of nights out with my friends, but first a phone call to Serene to arrange a night out with her early in the new week.

The phone begins to ring at the other end and I hope Serene will answer.

"Hello, Edmund. How are you?"

"I'm fine, Serene, how did your weekend go?"

"Oh, you know, just family stuff. What have you been doing?"

"Not a lot really. My days are a bit boring to be honest. So, when are you free, Serene?

"Okay, well not tonight, but how about tomorrow night?"

"Alright, can we go to the cinema if you don't mind?"

"Well, what do you want to see?"

"There's an old Harry Potter film I missed the first time around, if you haven't seen it?"

"Well, I'll be honest, Edmund, and tell you I've seen them all, but I'm more than happy to see a Harry Potter film again."

"Alright, it starts early, at 7:15, so let's go there first and then move on to Triumph's for a few drinks and to see the crowd."

"Yes, that's good. Can you pick me up at about 6:30?"

"Sure, see you at half six then. Bye, Serene."

"Bye, Edmund."

I'm missing my family and when Serene wasn't around for the weekend, I did think about her a lot. Now that she's available again and we've made a date, I'm really looking forward to seeing her. I spend the night watching television and thinking about how I'm going to handle the subject of my time travelling with Serene, as I told her to remind me if I don't mention it. How can I possibly tell her the full story? Should I just let it drop? I can't really do that as I've already raised the subject of something with Serene, but I could talk about something less unbelievable. Anyway, we shall see what happens.

The next day, I cut the grass as I promised my parents I would do. It gives me a bit of exercise, helps me top up my suntan and fills a few hours. When I've finished, I'm hot and sweaty so it's into the shower to get ready for Serene. At half past six I'm outside Serene's house waiting for her to come out. I sit and wait but no Serene. Is she playing games or just being a woman? I'm not sure, but after five or six minutes she appears and apologises for keeping me waiting. What had seemed vitally important ten seconds earlier doesn't seem at all important now. I give her a kiss and off we speed.

A quarter of an hour later we are parked at the cinema and walking towards the desk. To my surprise, Serene says, "This one's on me."

I don't argue as she offers her money to the cashier and I say, "Thank you." We walk into the cinema and settle down. It is almost empty, probably because everyone else saw the film a long time ago. We could have a good kiss, cuddle and fondle, but I really want to watch the film. When it has finished, I'm glad I've seen it as it seems to complete my Harry Potter education. I say to Serene, "You must have been bored."

"No, not at all. Just because I've seen it before didn't make any difference. I still enjoyed it. After all, I had read the book before I saw it the first time, so I knew what was going to happen. You'd read the book before too, so did you enjoy it?"

"Yes, I did, and thank you again for taking me. Let's go to Triumph's."

There has been no mention of what I want to talk to her about and I can't decide if that is pleasing or displeasing. It means I don't have to explain the inexplicable and, for some reason I cannot even explain to myself, I don't understand why I feel the need to tell her about what has happened. Why, I just don't know as I'm not even sure myself the experience really happened and I have decided never to do it again. Or will I? As the time since I last travelled – as I have come to think of it – passes, I find myself feeling less appreciative of a lucky escape and more curious about what else is out there. I know it's a silly thing to even think about, but what's the point of being an indestructible youth if I don't take risks?

In Triumph's we meet up with a few friends, one of whom has an older sister, which makes it easier to get a drink. Not that that is any use to me as I have to drive home. I'm beginning to realise there's a downside to being able to drive. I see now why groups have one designated driver and take it in turns, as it's not a lot of fun being the only sober one. It's also pretty boring having to deal with those who have drunk quite a lot and are getting very verbose, talking nonsense and thinking it's all very profound, intuitive and insightful.

Jade walks in and this is the first time I've seen her since I tried my luck at my birthday party. I look at her and she does look very tasty, but since then things have developed with me and Serene. Will she remember I tried to chat her up and will it make any difference to our long term school friendship now that I'm with Serene? Does she even know Serene and I are an item? Are Serene and I an item?

Jade walks up to me and with no sense of embarrassment says, "Hello, Edmund."

I'm relieved and reply, "Hello, Jade."

"Hello, everybody!" she shouts above the music and chatter. "This is my friend, Ewa. Ewa's Polish, so if any of you need any cleaning doing whilst she's in town, just shout!" This is followed by a mixture of raucous laughter and embarrassed silence. Ewa just stands there looking blank.

As the night passes, I wander around and find myself talking to a group of men who are dressed, not very convincingly, in women's clothing. As we're chatting I remark, "I assume you're all off to a fancy dress party?" They all fall about laughing and one says, "No, we were all meant to be going to Afghanistan today, but our flight's been delayed. However, all our kits and clothes are on the aeroplane, so we had to borrow clothes from any woman we could find on the base."

"Oh well, at least you're not wasting your time sitting on the base doing nothing," I respond. "So, you're all RAF blokes then?"

"No, none of us are RAF. We're all Royal Marines. We're just here to fly out. We've never been to Brize Norton before and we were told Witney's where it all happens around here."

"I suppose it is, as the only other places around here are all villages."

"Yeah, most of you talk like country bumpkins"

"Do we?"

"Yeah, lots of unnecessary 'Os' are thrown into words. It sounds like, "Oi loike to go for a roide on moi boike'." He and his friends think this is very funny and I wander off.

It's getting late and I know Serene can't be home too late, but I was hoping to take her back to my place before I have to get her home. However, she's having fun and drinking and although she's not as drunk as some others, she shows no sign of wanting to leave. Is she just having fun with our mutual friends or is she getting bored with me? I have no idea and had I been alone I would have left but, of course, I have to take Serene home. Time is now dragging and I make a note to myself not to go out with people drinking if I can't. How much longer will it be till she's ready to leave and will it mean I won't be able to take Serene back to my place first?

I wander around chatting to anybody and notice there's something happening outside. It seems the Marines have been involved in a fracas. I push my way outside along with most of the club. It seems a few locals tried to pick a fight with the Marines. Whether this is because they were all dressed in women's clothing or because they were big blokes who looked capable of looking after themselves is not clear. Maybe it was a bit of both. Anyway, the bouncers have broken things up and now a couple of police officers have arrived. After a while, the police leave with all the Marines. I don't think they were arresting them, but just escorting them to a taxi to take them back to Brize Norton. I wouldn't have minded that myself, as the officers who were 'taking the situation in hand' were a couple of fit women.

By now it's nearly chucking out time and people are starting to drift away. As Serene and I are leaving, the inevitable happens and I'm assailed by a chorus of, "Give us a lift, Edmund!" What can I say? Three people in the back seat of a Mini is quite a squeeze, but Serene can sit next to me. The bad news is that they all get dropped off in order and that means Serene is dropped off before the last one and I'm left to go home alone. Rather depressed I get home and go straight to bed thinking there must be a better way to spend the summer. And what might that be?

I wake up the next morning feeling the same way and mulling over once more whether I should 'travel' again. The reasons for doing so – excitement, education, fate – seem to be heavier than the reasons against it, which is the mere problem of never returning. As I'm cogitating the pros and cons, my mobile rings.

"Hello?"

"Hello, Edmund, how are you?"

"Oh, I'm fine Serene. How about you?"

"Well, I do have to admit I have a bit of a hangover".

"Ha ha! I haven't got one."

"No, you wouldn't, would you, Edmund?"

"No."

"But, that's why I'm calling, really. To say sorry for last night."

"Why?"

"Well, I did get a little drunk and I think I ignored you after we'd seen Harry Potter."

"Oh, that's alright. I was happy to see you enjoying yourself." What a liar I am.

"Anyway, Edmund, you said you needed to tell me something and I was to remind you."

Oh, my God! This is crunch time. What am I to say? I have virtually decided to travel again and think I need to tell at least someone in case I never return. Perhaps telling her on the phone will be easier than face to face. I take a deep breath.

"I, er, well, I was on my laptop the other day and as I typed in the URL 'bbc.co.uk/cricket', I started to fly off to some other place in a cloud."

I hear a little laugh at the other end. I'm aware of how silly this sounds and don't mind making a joke of it as I'm sure she will remember it if I don't return. "When the cloud cleared, I was in another place and didn't know what to do. Eventually I clicked 'undo' and found myself back at home."

"Riiight," says Serene.

"Then, later, I thought I'd try again and the same thing happened. This time when I got to the other place I started walking around and went towards a church in the distance. On the way I met a very smelly man who was tending to sheep. I tried talking to him but could hardly understand what he was saying. The church looked very like the one in Brize Norton. You know, St Britius?"

"Yes, I know it."

"Well, the priest came out of the church and invited me in. We chatted and I realised I was in St Britius, but it was the middle of the 14th century and the Black Death was about to arrive."

"Yes, Edmund, do you think you may have been watching too much Harry Potter?" "Well, maybe, but I am going back and maybe for some time, so if you don't see me for a while, you'll know why."

"Okay, Edmund, give me a call when you get back from 'the other place'," she says with exaggerated sincerity.

"Will do. Bye, Serene."

"Bye, Edmund."

I knew she wouldn't believe me, but at least if I don't get back she'll have some idea of why and won't think I'm just dumping her. Her call has also made me feel good for knowing that she hasn't lost interest in me. I now feel a new confidence that I can go travelling again without everybody thinking I have just disappeared.

I spend the rest of the day preparing what to take, thinking of what I might need and making sure it includes as little stuff from the 21st century as possible. I'll take a brown backpack made of artificial fibres which I can say is cotton. I know the middle of the 14th century is a strong, rich wool-based society but I think they knew of Indian cotton. My clothes will all be something that looks like wool or cotton, but I'll avoid bright colours which they probably didn't have then. Should I, or should I not, wear a watch? As mine is an analogue watch, I've decided I can get away with it. I think the Swiss were making mechanical clocks at the time so I can say it's just a little one. However, I finally decide this would be an unnecessary problem should the question of 'what is that?' ever come up so I'll leave it behind. After all, everybody in the 14th century survived without one, so I can too.

The biggest problem will be why I don't have any transport, like a horse. I'll have to say I had a horse but it ran off when it was frightened. As for my funny English, I can say I come from a land to the east and my English is not too good. I can keep my real name as Edmund was a name used at the time, I believe. It's just as well my parents didn't name me Wayne or Damien. Decovny will fit in too as I am told it is a name derived from my father's Russian ancestors. A thousand thoughts run through my head and I'm pretty sure I could come up with an answer if I have to. Serene didn't believe me, but I hope anyone in the 14th century will find me more convincing. I go to bed that night ready, ordinance wise and psychologically, for the next day.

As for food, I went to the supermarket yesterday and bought some German black bread as I'm sure they did not have processed, white bread in the 14th century. I think that was a 20th century invention from Chorley Wood. I used this black bread to make sandwiches and into them I wanted to put my favourite, peanut butter, but thought I'd better stick with jam as they would have had fruit and some sort of sweet preservative then. Along with the sandwiches I got some plums, apples and pears. There were some lovely bananas in the kitchen but I thought I'd better avoid them. Too exotic! As for liquid, I had got away with the plastic bottle last time when talking to the priest, so I put some apple cordial into it. If I share it with someone, I can explain away the taste of apples. I could even tell them it was weak cider!

The next morning, I wake up when the alarm goes off at 6. It has already been light for at least two hours, so the sun is full in the eastern sky. I have a good breakfast of cereal and toast, rather than one or the other, and finish it off with the banana I thought I'd better not take with me. Then I go to clean my teeth. As I look in the mirror, I see a new, confident teenager who is determined to take whatever chances life has to offer. I'm ready for the next stage of the adventure.

Before I set off, I wonder if the weather is the same here as in the other place, just like the time and other things, so I open the door and look at the sky. There are a couple of clouds but not much else. I put my backpack on, which is not comfortable whilst sitting on the sofa, and put the laptop on my lap. The blue whirligig is sticking out of the backpack. Opening up the laptop, I log on. I type in the usual URL of 'bbc.co.uk/cricket'. As expected, the mist gathers and the room swirls. Twenty seconds later the mist clears and I can see myself in the field once more surrounded by sheep who don't seem at all perturbed by my sudden arrival. At this, I wonder if I have just arrived or if I have merely moved into another time to take my place in a body that was just sitting there waiting. Who knows? I certainly don't.

I look around and there's nobody in sight, so I stand up and look towards the bush I hid the laptop in last time. There it is, so I pull the whirligig out of the backpack and stick it in the place I've just got up from. Then I remember I looked at the sky before leaving, so I do the same. There are no distinguishable clouds, just a layer of overnight cumuli stratus. So, the weather is not the same in this place even if the time is. Putting the laptop inside its case and walking towards the bush to hide it, I reflect on how differently I feel this time as opposed to my last trip. Now I'm confident and secure. I'm not necessarily secure in my safe return but secure in that I know what I'm doing and that I will make things happen rather than let things just happen to me.

I now know where I am in this other place and have a choice between two towns: Witney or Burford. Witney is seven miles away and Burford five . A no brainer really, so, looking at the sun I head north, as far as I can tell, towards Burford.

CHAPTER TEN

THE PESTILENCE ARRIVES

Immediately, and without comment, the Burfords turn towards the Abbey. Then Lord Burford stops and says to his wife and younger children, "No, Henry and I shall go. You must not put yourselves at risk."

His wife, Anne, wants to protest, but would never argue with her husband in the presence of the common people. As they make their way towards the Abbey, much of the population of Burford hurriedly disperses, thinking their homes will provide some security from the sickness, crossing themselves as they go.

The Burfords arrive at the door and the Abbess greets them. Young Henry has been studying apothecary and the medical philosophers at Oxford, and now is the time to put his knowledge into action. His studies have been an academic exercise with no intention whatsoever of becoming a physician by trade. Trade is not for one of the Burfords. However, it is important for the Lord of the Manor to show concern and take a lead in looking after the sick. The nuns and others need to be set a good example and young Henry's knowledge will be invaluable. Irrespective of the need for a public show, the Burfords do have genuine concern for the people of the manor.

The Burfords approach the door and it is opened for them before they reach it. They enter, ignoring the fawning of the sister who opened the door, and simply ask, "Where is the sick sister?"

"This way, sir." The sister leads the way through the Abbey.

Henry strides into the nun's sickroom followed by his father. On the bed is a youngish woman in nun's habit, Sister Cecilia, making a continuous, low moaning noise. Henry knows her, as he does all of the nuns and most of the town, and as he approaches her, he can see she is dripping with sweat and immediately diagnoses, "A yellow bile problem!"

He lifts her arm and can see buboes developing. Along with this telltale sight is the confirming stench associated with the Black Death; the smell of rotting flesh. Henry puts down her arm and walks towards the door to take a deep breath of fresh air.

At this point, the Abbess arrives and curtsies deeply to the Burfords. Lord Burford nods but young Henry does not look away from Sister Cecilia, saying, "This is a summer ailment and must be treated with purging and blood-letting."

The Abbess informs him, "She already has a bad case of diarrhoea, sir."

"Nevertheless, we must void the body of the imbalanced humour. Give her hellebore."

"Give her what, sir?"

"Hellebore, but if you have none, then salt water or mustard will suffice."

"How do you know this?" asks Lord Burford.

"This is the accepted regimen prescribed by the Islamic philosopher Avicenna."

Henry then turns to the Abbess and advises, "If there is no improvement by the morning, open a vein. The humour must be allowed to leave the body and return it to balance."

"Yes, sir." The Abbess nods deferentially.

Lord Burford instructs the Abbess to say special prayers for the nun, to which she replies, "The sisters are already in the chapel asking our Lady for intercession in our sister's ailment."

"Take her clothing and all her belongings and burn them before dowsing the room in much vinegar," Henry advises further.

"Sir, other than her clothing, she has no belongings."

"No, but you must also burn anything you think she may have used in the last few days."

"Yes, sir."

"And put flowers all around the Abbey to stave off the smell of the sickness and prevent it from being passed to the other nuns through the air."

"Certainly, sir."

The Burfords walk towards the door and into the fresh night air. Outside is a small gathering of people at some distance from the Abbey and Lord Burford walks towards them saying, "Go to your homes. There is nothing to be done here and my son and heir, Henry, has expressed his medical opinion informed by years of study at Oxford. In the morning you must all gather flowers and put them about your homes so that you do not catch the sickness from the foul odours. There is nothing more to be done other than to pray for all our deliverance. We are all in the hands of the good Lord and our Lady."

With this the people slowly move off and the two Burfords walk briskly towards the bridge, up the hill and into the manor house.

Once they are inside, the house cook is told to serve dinner. The rest of the house have been waiting for the return of Lord Burford and Henry and soon the whole family is seated and tucking into their food. Over the meal, the talk is of nothing other than the sickness. Henry talks of the four humours and Avicenna, Hippocrates and Socrates. With all this knowledge, the family and the common people of Burford are lucky to have the benefit of Henry's education.

"How did the sickness arrive?" asks Henry's mother.

"Maybe in some supplies brought in or contact with someone from outside the town."

"I doubt that anyone with the sickness would have entered the town," opines Lord Burford. "Even if they had, they would still be here and probably sick as well."

"Yes, but someone who came back in may have been with someone who had the sickness."

"But no one else is sick," adds Stephen.

Not yet, but some people may show the sickness quicker than others, thinks Henry, and their sickness may not yet be showing, or they may be sick at home and their families are keeping quiet out of fear of being locked in with them.

After the meal, they all retire to bed quickly but there is a new sombre atmosphere in the house. The much feared sickness has arrived. No one is sure how it arrived, but all the attempts to keep Burford separate from the rest of the world have failed. With Henry's help, the town may be able to fight the sickness, but no one is really sure what to do. Everybody will have to wait for the sickness to take its course. How long that will take, no one knows.

Early the next morning, Henry is up and soon talking to his father about what is needed. Lord Burford calls Scabbard to join the conference and father and son instruct him on what is necessary, but first Lord Burford asks, "Scabbard, what's the news on Sister Cecilia?"

"Sir, the news is that she is no better but still alive."

"We thank the Lord Christ for sparing her through the night," observes the Lord.

Henry then instructs Scabbard, "You must give instructions to gather flowers and put them about the house. All those flowers that are not put about the house must be made into posies for the family to carry at all times. Any loose petals should be crushed and made into a perfume to spread on clothes to ward off the miasma. The household will need these when going out and all those attending the sick must be told to do the same."

"Yes, sir, I shall ensure all is done this morning."

"We must also inform the outside world that the sickness has arrived in Burford," says Lord Burford. "Send two men in each group to go north, south, east and west to inform and to gather information on what is happening."

"Certainly, sir, I shall ensure all is done immediately."

Scabbard gives a shallow bow and turns to leave.

Once outside, Scabbard calls men and passes on the instructions of the two Burfords. Edgar and Knut are instructed to ride to Alvescot, Clanfield, Bourton, Beamtune and Norton to inform and gather information of the disease's progress. Up the hill they ride towards the Gloucester Road. The entrance to the town is still guarded to prevent entry and Edgar informs the guards of Lord Burford's instructions and they are allowed out. The earlier attempts by those of the surrounding villages to gain entry to Burford seem to have dissipated. Probably word has gone around the county that Burford will not provide a place of refuge for anyone except its permanent residents.

The barrier is opened for Edgar and Knut to pass and the two men ride briskly towards Alvescot. As they enter the hamlet, there is no sign of anyone, so the two stop and dismount. A voice emerges from the shadows asking, "What do you want?"

Edgar replies, "We have come from Lord Burford to ask if the village needs anything and to inform you that the sickness has reached Burford, but we two are not sick."

"Sick or not, stay away from us," comes the gruff response.

"Are all well in the village?" asks Knut.

"I know of no sickness but all stay in their homes and some may be hiding the sickness to avoid being locked into their homes."

"Is there anything you need?" asks Knut.

"Nothing you can provide, thank you. Now only the good Lord Christ can help us."

With this, the two emissaries get back on their horses and head towards Clanfield – the first settlement in Oxfordshire to be struck by the disease. As they approach the village, men of Clanfield see them coming and begin to wave the two riders away. The men reign in their horses some distance from the village and Knut shouts, "We come with news from Burford on the instruction of the Lord. It seems likely the sickness has come to Burford as one of the nuns is showing signs of the ailment."

One villager shouts back, "We are sorry to hear your news."

Knut then asks, "What of the sickness in Clanfield?"

"There are now three houses closed up and all the village is in much despair."

Edgar shouts, "Have you all you need in the village?"

"No, sir, we have not. Our food stocks will not last long and we ask you to inform Lord Burford of this so that he might help us."

Edgar replies, "When we return, Lord Burford will be informed and we are sure he will send what he can for the people of Clanfield."

"Thank you kind, sirs. Please tell the Lord of our loyalty and fare you well."

The two men urge their horses towards Bourton and as they approach, they can see a barrier across the road but no guards. Are all the people dead? As they draw closer, men come running out waving staffs and pikes at the two riders. They stop their horses and shout they have come from Lord Burford to gather information on the sickness and to inform them that it has reached Burford. One of the Bourton men shouts, "All of Bourton is sickness free and if you try to enter, we will have to kill you. We hope you, and Lord Burford, will understand."

"Yes, we do," Knut shouts back. "Our Lord has asked us to ask you if there is anything the people of Bourton need."

After a silence the response comes. "We could do with some ale as there is little to drink here and the stream is inadequate for our needs."

"We shall inform the Lord and he may be able to send some barrels. We wish you well and hope the sickness never descends upon the good people of Bourton."

The two riders turn back to the Clanfield-Beamtune Road and onto Sir Richard's town. Edgar says, "Bourton is lucky that it is not on the road to Beamtune and so few people pass through the village."

"Yes, and I have heard the people of Bourton are very godly," adds Knut.

As the two come close to Beamtune, once more they are met by waving guards who warn them to stay away. Knut shouts the same as before and the reply comes that many have fallen sick in Beamtune, but that Sir Richard is content the town has all it needs in the short term and Lord Burford is to be thanked for his concern. Edgar shouts back, "May the Lord be with you all,"

Then he begins to ride around the back of the church towards Northton. Apart from the church, there are few buildings in Northton so it is little surprise that no one stops them from entering the village.

It is silent as they approach and no one is to be seen. Edgar and Knut dismount and tie their horses to a tree before walking through the graveyard towards the church door.

As they approach the door, Knut calls, "Is anybody here?"

There is no response. They open the door and walk in cautiously to find the church empty. No one is praying and the priest is nowhere to be found. Where are the few inhabitants of the village? Where is the priest? Have they all died? Have they all fled? Even the priest? There are no answers to be found here, so the two men remount their horses and head towards Alvescot once more.

They come to the cross of the Bourton and Burford roads and turn north to head home. Soon they see a lone figure walking north and Knut says to Edgar, "We had better see who he is and where he is going" As they approach the figure he stops and turns towards the approaching riders. He is a young man of unusual appearance who looks as if he does not belong here. "Who are you, sir?" calls Knut from a safe distance.

"I am Edmund Decovny," comes the reply.

"Edmund de Covny, do you have the sickness?"

"No, I do not."

"Where is your horse?"

"Something frightened her and she ran off."

"Then you had better get on the back of my horse and come with us to Lord Burford."

Immediately, Edmund realises that this is not really a request and does as he has been bidden but finds it very difficult to get on a horse without any stirrups. Knut helps him up saying, "I am Knut and this is Edgar and we are Lord Burford's men", and before Edmund knows what is happening they are speeding towards Burford.

CHAPTER ELEVEN

HENRY AND EDMUND

As we gallop across the field, I think to myself that I had prepared an explanation for my lack of horse but never thought I would be using it so quickly. No sooner had I hidden my laptop under the bush than I found myself effectively a prisoner. Already I'm regretting my foolhardy decision to travel again.

Soon our two horses and three men are going down into the Shilton dip and on our left, to the west, I can see a few hovels near the stream. Up in front is what will later become the A40. Straight ahead I can see men gathered looking towards us, and the three of us are heading in their direction.

When we approach, Edgar is in front of Knut and I can just about hear Edgar speaking to the assembled men as he reins his horse in. "We have found a stranger by the name of Edmund de Covny whom we must take to Lord Burford. He says he is free of the sickness and looks in good health."

By now Knut and I are by Edgar's side as I hear the man who seems to be in charge say,

"Alright, if you are sure, you may bring him into the town, but you are answerable to Lord Burford, not me!"

The barrier is raised and the three of us pass through. I'm

aware that all eyes are on me as we pass and proceed towards the town. There is no hotel on the corner at the top of the hill, but soon there are houses on either side of the road which are almost recognisable as those still standing in the 21st century. The three of us move quite slowly as the streets are full of people; almost as many as on a summer's day in my own time. To my left, I can see a turning which I assume will later become Sheep Street. Further down there's no pelican crossing and no supermarket, but the noise is becoming louder and louder. By now there are cobble stones underfoot and the noise of the horses' hooves echoes against the buildings on either side. This noise is added to by the noise of other horses' hooves, the wheels of carts on the cobbles and the shouts of people above this cacophony on what seems to be market day. There are vendors on either side selling all kinds of goods, mainly comestibles, and the whole town stinks of all sorts of unpleasant odours, the most prominent of which is horse manure. I look down and can see it is everywhere, so much so that the horses are almost wading through it. It seems that it has not occurred to anyone to clean it up! As a consequence, there are millions of flies around and by now many are beginning to feast on me. In front, and to my right, I can see the St John the Baptist church, but from what I can remember of the church this one is a little smaller, as though bits were missing. Either it is not the same church or bits have been added on after the time I'm in now.

Once again I become aware that people are looking at me and I don't know if this is because I'm a stranger to the town or because I look strange. Either way, I'm on my way to see Lord Burford, whoever that is, and this seems as though it will determine my future. A mere ten minutes ago I was a free man in the Carterton of the 21st century and now I am effectively a prisoner in the 14th century. What am I to do? There's nothing I can do except rehearse my story about how I came to be wandering in the Cotswolds and create my new background. Anything I tell my captors will sound more convincing than the truth.

The three of us proceed towards the bridge over the Windrush river, but instead of the beautiful 'old' stone bridge, there is a wooden structure that amounts to little more than a few planks laid on a couple of stone pillars on either side of the river, with the water lapping around the pillars. As the horses mount the bridge, I have the chance to experience a new way of crossing a river I have crossed many times before. This crossing is much slower and I have the opportunity to look up and down stream as we pass. But where are we going? By the 21st century there is nothing on the other side of the bridge, so where are we going to in the 14th century? As in my time, the road forks on the other side of the river and there's a choice of going towards Chipping Norton or towards Stowe. The two horses take the right fork towards Chippy and, set back from the road, is a large house with a driveway coming down towards what will later be the A361. A few moments pass and the horses turn right into the driveway of the large house.

Is this where Lord Burford lives? Is this an ancient building long since demolished so that there is no trace of it in the 21st century? Is this all still a dream? Then a new thought enters my head: Is it because the computer has induced some sort of hypnotic state that makes me think this is all real? The idea of closing my eyes and screaming, 'This is not happening!' occurs to me, but I think better of it. Whether or not this is all real, I will have to deal with it as if it were real.

As Edgar and Knut walk the horses down the driveway, with me still on the horse, a man comes towards us.

"Knut, who is this you have with you?" asks the man.

"He calls himself Edmund de Covny, Scabbard, and he says he does not have the sickness." Scabbard, I think to myself. I must remember that! "He certainly looks well and he says he lost his horse when she was frightened, so we thought Lord Burford would want to help a Norman wandering in the fields".

"You have done well, Knut and Edgar. Lord Burford would want this man to be brought to him."

Suddenly I realise that it is not just my 'old fashioned' first name that fits in well in the 14th century but that my surname is being misinterpreted as de Covny and not Decovny as it should be spelled. My name isn't French or Norman. In fact, as far as I can remember, my family name has Russian-Jewish origins. My mind races back to my history lessons. Weren't the Jews driven out of England in 1290 by Edward I, less than a hundred years before the time I'm in now, accused of bringing disease, the evidence for which was that the Jews didn't get diseases nearly so much? Of course! It's perfectly logical. It couldn't have anything to do with the kosher dietary requirements which meant their lives were so much cleaner than the rest of the people. Yes, July 18th 1290, I think, and it was very convenient that all the debts The King had with the Jews would be written off with their expulsion. Not until the 1650s did Oliver Cromwell allow the Jews back into England, and then for financial reasons, and because the Puritans believed The Kingdom of Heaven could only come when Jews converted to Christianity and that could only happen if they had contact with Christians. My research to prepare for this travel had informed me that the 'present' King is Edward III, so Edward I must have been his grandfather. It's probably best to play along with the Norman ancestry assumption, rather than to tell them I have

Jewish ancestry. Anyway, my father has never felt Jewish any more than my mother has felt Christian. I don't suppose telling my new captors that being Jewish is through the mother's line because, as Jewish women are not sexual beings, they couldn't possibly get pregnant with anybody other than their Jewish husbands. There were no genetic tests in those days. Yes, it's best to play along with being Norman. But how to behave in the presence of my 'betters'? The only thing to do is to follow the cues from others.

Knut half turns and looks at me, which I take to be an instruction to dismount. Although I can just about ride, I am certainly not a horseman and holding on with my legs has left my thigh muscles a little aching. Scabbard has already disappeared into Burford house and as I am stretching my aching muscles, a man appears at the door and Edgar and Knut suddenly acquire slightly weak knees and a stooped posture.

"Sir, this is Edmund de Covny," says Knut.

"I have heard, Knut. Thank you both."

As Lord Burford turns to me, a young man arrives at his side. "Come along in, de Covny. I am Lord Burford and this is my son, Henry."

No hand is offered, so I do not offer mine. Lord Burford and Henry step aside as I enter.

"I hear you have lost your horse, de Covny."

"Yes, she ran off when something frightened her and I was unable to catch her again."

"When was this?"

"Oh, er, not long before Edgar and Knut found me."

"I will send Edgar and Knut out again to look for her. Henry, take Edmund to the kitchen and get him some food."

"Certainly, Father."

Oh dear! Now they are going to look for a horse that won't be there. What a tangled web we weave when first we practise to deceive.

"Follow me please, Edmund," Henry says as he walks through to another part of the house.

He called me Edmund, so I assume I can call him Henry. As the son of the Lord, he must be the heir to the title and the estate of Lord Burford, I assume.

I follow Henry through to the kitchen where he asks the genuflecting cook to prepare a meal for me. Henry then walks through to another room, where I follow, and he indicates that I should sit down.

"So, tell me how you came to be wandering, horseless outside the town?"

"As you know, my horse was frightened away...."

Henry cuts me short and clarifies by saying, "What I meant was how you came to be there at all. Where are you from and what was the purpose of your journey?"

I've prepared for this and now is the time to relay the story I have created. Certain parts will have to be spontaneous as I now know I'm meant to be Norman.

"My family currently live in Saxony where I grew up and I was on my first travel to England. It has taken me many weeks to get here and then I lost my horse."

"Oh, I see, that goes to explain your strange accent. You speak French?"

Oh God! He'll expect me to speak French if I'm an educated Norman. What now? I do speak French but it's modern French. I summon up a few words in French telling him I also speak French with a strange accent. Henry seems to understand, so I assume French has developed less in the last 700 years than

English has. I quickly revert to my best Chaucerian English and hope I have got away with it.

Changing the subject, I say, "But tell me about you and your life."

"As you can see, I live here and I am studying at Balliol College, Oxford. It was founded in 1263 by John de Balliol, the wealthy Scottish Lord."

"Oh yes, what are you studying?" I enquire.

"Greek, Latin and medicine."

"Medicine! So you know a bit about the current epidemic?"

"The what? E-pi-de-mic! That's a good word for it. It arises suddenly and is everywhere. You mean the sickness?"

"Yes, the sickness. Tell me what you are doing to fight it." I ask, hoping to keep the subject of the conversation off me.

A teenage girl appears with a large plate on a tray and puts it in front of me. "Thank you, Megan," says Henry.

"Yes, thank you Megan. It's very kind of you," I add, whilst looking at the girl who I think would be very attractive if she washed her hair and had some decent clothes. This is clearly difficult in the 14th century, especially if she is poor.

Megan curtsies and gives me a flirtatious look as she leaves the room.

"A pretty girl.", I observe, to myself really, but out loud.

"Yes, she is Welsh, of course, but she is of no danger. Her family were all killed in an uprising," Henry mentions casually.

"So, how did she get here?"

"She was brought back by a Burford man in the King's army and my father gave her work in the house. This was about five years ago."

By now, I'm staring at my plate as I have never seen so much meat in my life. It's not been long since I had breakfast, but I know I have to eat as much as possible as I am supposed to have been found wandering. My backpack, with some food in it, was taken from me as I dismounted and I have no idea where it is now.

"So, as you were saying, about the sickness?" I ask.

"We have ordered the killing of all the cats and dogs as a start…"

I lose all restraint and blurt out, "Oh no, that's the worst thing you can do!"

Henry looks bemused and says, "But they spread the sickness."

"No. they don't. The fleas on the black rat spread the sickness."

"Eh, rats?" enquires Henry, somewhat surprised.

"Yes, rats. That's why you must not kill the cats and dogs because they kill the rats."

Henry looks very confused. "What makes you think that?"

I've given some thought to this question as part of my travel preparations. "Where I come from, the sickness, or the Black Death as we call it, has already passed through and we have learnt many things. There are three sorts of this plague and you have what is known as bubonic plague."

"Oh yes, bubonic – it produces buboes," interjects Henry.

"Do you know this from your knowledge of Latin or from your medical training?" I ask.

"Training?" questions Henry.

"Yes, um, learning," I clarify.

"Oh, a bit of both."

"There is so much I could tell you to help if you will only listen and trust me," I plead as I lean forward.

Suddenly I realise how desperate I sound and that I'm no

longer the cool foreign traveller. Henry sits open mouthed as I regain my self-control.

"The most important thing for everyone to do is to clean the place and keep it clean," I continue, regaining control of the conversation.

"We are all clean in this household, even the surfs," Henry replies rather indignantly.

"I didn't mean any disrespect, Henry, but you don't understand bacteria."

"Bacteria?" questions Henry.

"Yes, it is a Latin word."

"I can hear that, but what does it mean?"

"They are very little creatures, far too small to see, and they live inside our bodies and make us ill."

Henry seems to be trying to suppress a little smile and asks, "What, like worms?"

"Yes, yes, exactly like worms, but much, much smaller."

"How can something so small make people ill and kill them?"

"Because there are millions and millions of them and our bodies need to develop white blood cells to fight them and this makes us ill," I try to explain as simply as possible.

"White blood cells?" questions Henry once more.

"Yes, they run through our bodies in our blood and fight bacteria. Once we have them, they can fight off the sickness, but only if it does not kill us before we grow these white blood cells."

Henry looks very confused now, but is no longer laughing. I wait a while for this to sink in. Finally Henry says, "So, if we get ill and don't die, we can survive any illness?"

"Er, no, it's not quite that simple. There are all sorts of bacteria that cause all sorts of different sicknesses. Our bodies need to develop different defences for all the different illnesses."

There is more silence as Henry thinks. "So, if anyone survives the sickness once, they won't get it again?"

"It certainly makes it far less likely," I respond after a brief pause.

More silence follows until Henry says, "I have heard this about the pox."

I'm not sure if Henry means chicken pox, small pox or syphilis but it doesn't really matter and I exclaim, "Yes, yes! That is right. When a child gets the pox, he never gets it again."

More silence ensues and it lasts much longer this time as I try to remain quiet. I remember what my father used to say when he was selling something to a pharmacy customer, "You have two ears and one mouth, so say half as much as the other person if you are trying to sell something." I'm trying to sell my ideas, so I'm doing my best to keep quiet.

Eventually Henry expresses his next thought. "But people are always getting ill with a runny nose."

"Oh yes, this is true but when we get a cold, or a runny nose, it is never the same bacteria as the last cold." As I'm saying this, I realise a cold is a virus and not bacteria, but I don't think this is the best time to discuss the difference between a virus and a bacterium even if I were sure of the difference myself.

"So, what are the bacteria that are causing this sickness?" asks Henry as he begins to put things in order in his head

I know the answer to this one as I found its name in my research before travelling. "This bacterium is called *Yersinia pestis*."

More silence follows and I cannot resist adding, "And it is the worst bacterium in human history."

"Is this like the runny nose bacterium?" enquires Henry.

"No, it is always the same. Well, it changes very slowly, anyway."

"Changes?" asks Henry, feeling confused once more.

"Yes, the runny nose bacterium changes very quickly, so the cold you got last month is not the same bacterium that gave you a cold this month, but *Yersinia pestis* remains the same, virtually."

Henry's face lights up like a light and he asks, "If the sickness has been around for ever, why do people still get it?"

"That's a very good question! It is because children who have not been immunised, will get it, which is why it recurs roughly every generation."

"Immunised?" enquires Henry, looking confused again.

"It means that because they have been exposed to the virus once, they are immune to it the next time."

"Have you been immunised, Edmund?"

I think quickly and then answer, "When the sickness passed through Saxony, I may have caught a little bit of the sickness or I may just be lucky, but immunisation is not the only thing that will help avoid the sickness."

"Oh dear, this is getting too much!" exclaims Henry feeling exasperated.

Fearing that I might lose Henry's attention, I think it better to move on and say, "It is not so important to cure the sick but to avoid getting it in the first place."

Henry thinks once more and asks, "Is it too late for Sister Cecilia who already has the sickness?"

At hearing this, I shiver as I had not realised anyone in Burford actually had the Black Death. It's now my turn to be silent and eventually I say, "I do not know, but if you trust me, I will do my best to help you save her."

Henry smiles gently. Just then, there's a knock at the door.

"Come in," says Henry and the door opens to reveal Megan standing there with a frightened look on her face.

"Yes, what is it, Megan?"

"Scabbard has just come to tell Lord Burford that one of the sisters who was nursing Sister Cecilia has fallen ill as well."

CHAPTER TWELVE

THE COUNCIL

I sit outside waiting whilst Henry is talking to his father. Despite his initial scepticism, Henry does seem to think there's something to what I said about the sickness and he's now telling his father, who, of course, has the power to do something about it. But how will Lord Burford react? All these strange ideas that hold no logic in their world.

As I sit, trying to be patient, I hear footsteps coming towards me and around the corner comes Megan bearing a cup. I look up and catch Megan's eye as she says, "I have brought you some ale, sir." The thought flashes through my mind that it is strange to have beer this early in the morning, but then I remember that as there is no pure water, people drink beer because it's safer.

"Thank you, Megan, that's very kind of you." I take the cup and Megan remains standing there. "Er, what brings you to Burford?" I ask, trying to think of something to say. As the last word leaves my lips, I remember what Henry told me about her parents' death.

"Oh, my parents were killed in Wales and one of the soldiers from Burford brought me back here. Since then, the Lord has looked after me."

I feel embarrassed but try not to show it as I wonder if the 'the Lord' looking after her is meant to be Lord Burford or the Lord Jesus Christ?

"Oh, I see," I reply nervously and there is another uncomfortable silence.

Then Megan says, "I'm sure there are many things I could do to help around the town, but I am told to remain in the house where it is safer."

I look at her for a moment and say, "Sit down." and shuffle along the bench to make room for her.

She sits nervously at the far end of the bench as I begin to think of all the things she could help out with around the town.

"The most important thing in the short term is to clean up the town and get rid of anything that attracts rats, because rats are where the disease comes from."

"Rats? But rats are always with us! They sometimes attack babies but they don't bring sickness."

This is clearly going to be difficult to explain, even to Henry and his father, let alone to an uneducated young girl. Can she even read?

Inside the room, Henry has outlined Edmund's ideas to his father and, of course, Lord Burford seems very sceptical. However, young Henry has two powerful weapons on his side. First, he has been studying medicine at Oxford and second, he is Lord Burford's son and heir to the estate. On the other hand, not only does Lord Burford live in the Middle Ages – though, not in his mind of course – but he is also constrained by what is expected of him. He may be Lord of the Manor, but he is not free to think and do as he wishes. I'm aware of this and think to myself, Man is born free, but is everywhere in chains. That concept will not be around for another few hundred years!

As Henry comes to an end of what he has to say, his father sits silently, looking a little perplexed and concerned. Henry remains silent. He knows his father well and is aware that at times like this, it's best to leave him to think in silence.

Finally, Lord Burford breaks his silence and asks, "What if all your friend's ideas are wrong?"

Henry thinks carefully and replies, "I believe we would have little to lose as our present methods seem to be having little effect."

Silence follows once more until Lord Burford takes a deep breath and says, "We shall call a council of the town and see what reaction we get."

After what seems like hours, but is probably no more than 30 minutes, I hear movement in the room I'm seated outside. The door opens and Henry stands and looks at Megan and me. Megan jumps up immediately and gives a little curtsy.

I sense that she thought she was doing something wrong and feel the need to protect her, so I say, "I was just explaining to Megan about the rats."

Henry's eyes drop from Megan to me and he says, "Well, perhaps you would like to come in and explain more to my father."

I get up and Megan hurries away down the corridor.

As we enter the room, Lord Burford is standing and looking at us.

"Sit down, Edmund" he says.

"Thank you," I say, trying to avoid any name or title as I'm still not sure how to address the Lord of the Manor.

"Henry has explained your thoughts to me and there are a few questions I would like to ask."

"Okay."

"Eh?"

"I said that's alright. What can I tell you."

"First of all, what makes you think the rats bring the sickness?"

This is an easy question for me as I learnt about the Black Death in school as part of history lessons and also because I studied Chaucer and the period he lived in.

"It's very simple really. The sickness started in the far east, near China, and is carried by fleas that get onto the rats. The rats get onto ships which go from port to port, and when the rats get off, that town then has the sickness. Soon it spreads out from there. The ships then move on to other ports and the sickness becomes a pandemic…"

"Pand….?"

"Yes, pandemic. It means that it is everywhere."

"Oh, yes. Two Greek words put together."

I realise that Lord Burford can also speak Greek, or at least ancient Greek, and remember that all the Kings and Queens of the past had been schooled in the classics, so I assume any rich, educated person would also be. How strange that some can read and write in a dead, foreign language when the vast majority cannot even read and write their own language.

"So, more rats get onto other ships and are taken to more ports and so the sickness has spread west and eventually reached England."

Lord Burford's face lights up. This fits in entirely with what he knows: that ships always carry rats and that the disease has spread across Europe and eventually probably landed on the south coast and spread up to Oxfordshire and Burford.

I sense I'm making progress and carry on. "It is not really the rats that are a big problem, but the sickness they carry with the fleas. We cannot get rid of the fleas, but we may be able to get rid of a lot of the rats."

"Henry tells me you suggest cats and dogs."

"Yes, the cats and dogs will kill some rats and frighten off others, but we also need to stop encouraging the rats to come into our houses."

" How?"

"The rats can only live if we feed them by leaving around things they can eat."

"But all the granaries are on raised platforms to keep the rats out," Lord Burford explains in a rather perplexed voice.

I remember that they used to put the granaries on top of little stone 'mushrooms' so that the rats couldn't get at the grain. "That is true, but whenever food is thrown into the street, the rats come and eat it. Rats cannot survive in such large numbers without help from humans who feed them."

"I think I understand."

"It's not just food, though. It's also the mess left by horses that encourages the rats. We must try to clear that up too."

I'm not clear what term I should use for horse 'mess'. Should I call it manure, shit, or what? Mess seems to do the trick, though.

"That could be a pretty big job," Lord Burford states the obvious.

"Well, whatever we can do will help. It is also very important to keep everything around us clean and to keep on washing our hands."

"Why?"

"Because any bacteria on our hands make us ill and we pass that illness on when we touch others."

"Henry has told me you speak of 'bacteria'. What exactly is it?"

"They are tiny organisms that…"

"Organisms?"

"They are little animals that get into our bodies and make us ill."

"Oh, a bit like worms, you mean?"

"Yes, that is exactly right, like worms."

"But we have never seen these bacteria?"

"That's because they are far too small to see and there are millions of them in each body. The body makes little things to fight them but this takes time and we may die before they have fought off the bacteria."

There is a long pause and Lord Burford asks, "How long does this take?"

"A few days, usually, but often the bacteria win the battle before they are killed."

Another silence ensues, and then he asks, "That is why, if a sick person survives a few days, they may well recover?"

"Yes, you are right, sir. Bacteria are everywhere, so we need to wash them off our hands and anything else we touch very frequently. It is also important to wash our food before we prepare it and to wash all things associated with food preparation."

"Mmm, it seems a little excessive to me."

"I assure you, it is completely necessary, sir."

I've now used the term 'sir' twice and it doesn't seem to be the wrong thing to say. At this point, Henry makes a rare interjection. "I have given a lot of thought to this concept of 'bacteria' and it does seem to make a lot of sense to me, Father."

Lord Burford's face becomes less sceptical. It is increasingly clear that he puts a lot of store in his son's thoughts, but whether this is because of what he says or because he is his son, I can't be sure. It's probably a bit of both.

I can see I'm making progress with Lord Burford and leave him to think for a while. I remember once more what my father told me: if I ever want to sell an idea, I should remember that I have two ears and one mouth, so I should listen twice as much as I speak. Finally, Lord Burford speaks. "I think there is much merit in what you say and Henry has pointed out that our current methods seem to have little effect, so we may as well try something else."

I take a deep breath and Lord Burford proceeds. "I will convene a council this afternoon and we will discuss the matter."

An hour later, Henry and I sit as Megan serves us food before the council meeting that is to be held this afternoon. We two young men chat easily as if we've known each other for years. Henry asks more questions and I do my best to explain without giving away the truth of how I know all this, and where and what century I really come from. I keep reminding myself that no matter what Henry, his father, or anyone else thinks of my strangeness, nothing could come anywhere close to the truth. As we eat, Megan is in and out at every opportunity, always giving me a big smile, so much so that I begin to observe whether she gives the same to Henry. I can see that she's polite and deferential towards him, but she doesn't give him the big smiles. Is she flirting with me? How should I react? Although she's pretty, she is so dirty and her hair is matted. How is a high-class Norman lad meant to behave towards a low-class Welsh girl? Also, is Henry catching on to it?

After three courses the meal seems to be over. All the courses had meat, meat and more meat. What I really want now is a nice piece of cheesecake, but that doesn't seem very likely. Even an apple would be nice! Soon we are both downstairs waiting for Lord Burford. The big door leading outside opens and Scabbard appears. His eyes scan the entrance hall and then he says, "Oh, I just came to tell His Lordship we are all ready for the council." Just then, Lord Burford appears and Scabbard repeats, "We are all ready for the council, sir."

"Thank you, Scabbard, we are leaving now."

The party walks out of Burford House, down the road, across the river and into the church. Upon entering, all those waiting stand up and give a little bow. The church of St John the Baptist is always on the Decovny family tourist route for any visitor, so, even if it wasn't during a service, I've been in it a few times. When the Burford party approaches, others entering hold back. All who enter dip their fingers into the Holy water and cross themselves, and I find myself following, without thinking what I'm doing. I look at the murky mess left behind and think of all the bacteria in there that could enter someone's body through a cut or when one's fingers came in contact with one's mouth.

As I enter, I'm conscious that the church is smaller than I remember. At the front there is room for a large table around which a number of dignitaries are seated. They rise as their Lord enters and he waves his hand to indicate they should resume their seats as he sits.

I wonder if this council is like a King's council where they do what they're told or whether it's like a Carterton town council where things are debated and free conclusions reached. As soon as Lord Burford begins to speak it becomes clear that he is in charge. He indicates that before the meeting discusses what to do, Edgar and Knut are to give an introductory outline of what they have found in the surrounding villages. The two men stand up and nervously begin to tell of what they have discovered in Alvescot, Clanfield, Bourton and Beamtune. It's obvious they are not used to speaking publicly, let alone before such a grand council, but they convey their findings clearly and as their story grinds to a halt with the words from Knut,

"And that's all I have to report, sir.", Lord Burford indicates that they can sit. This they do, both with an audible sigh of relief.

Soon the Lord introduces me as a traveller from the east of Europe where the sickness has already passed through and a lot has been learnt. The council deferentially sits in virtual silence but there are a few intakes of breath as Lord Burford explains about the rats and their fleas. When he asks for messages to be sent out to all surrounding villages for any dogs and cats to be brought into the town, there is much shuffling and murmuring as the priest indicates he wishes to speak. He is the only council member brave enough to open his mouth and shows that although Lord Burford is in charge, he does not have total control. The priest asks, "My Lord, did Pope Gregory IV not declare the association between Satan, witches and cats a century ago?"

"Indeed, he did, Father, but God has put all animals on this Earth for our benefit and so cats must be here for a reason. Perhaps we have so far not realised God's purpose for cats."

"Yes, Your Lordship, I am sure that cats do have their uses for God, but I am also sure that if God wanted us to, er, welcome cats into our community, he would have told us so."

"I am sure that he would have done so but we may have missed his purpose. Perhaps cats have become the Devil's agents only because we have not set them to God's purpose before?"

The priest is silenced and I realise Lord Burford has given this a lot of thought and is ready for any objections. It also becomes clear that the whole exercise will not be as easy as I had hoped. The people of 14th century Burford are not going to welcome my greater 21st century knowledge with open arms and overwhelming thanks.

Lord Burford moves on to talk about the need to clean the streets and remove anything that might attract rats. A site will be established just outside the town for dry rubbish and any waste food is to be cast into the river. I nearly fall off my seat at hearing this, but realise that with no municipal dustmen, there is little alternative. I decide that I will later ask Lord Burford to set up the site down river from the town, away from where fresh water will be drawn from the river for washing and drinking. Let the people of Witney get cholera! As for the two nuns who have already contracted the disease, they are to be nursed by the same volunteering nuns and all others are to be kept away from them.

I listen carefully to check whether the Lord has left anything out and am relieved when he starts to talk about the frequent washing of hands, cleaning of all work surfaces, especially in the kitchen, and washing of all food before it is prepared. Once more the priest indicates his desire to speak and this time he looks even more disapproving than he had over the cats. Lord Burford nods to the priest to speak. "This sounds very Semitic to me." He seems to spit out the word 'Semitic'.

"The Jews do many things the same way in which we do them, or in similar ways, and they also do some things that we may not always do" says Lord Burford. It is not their actions that render them unacceptable to God, but their rejection of Christ. We all here accept the truth of the Lord Jesus Christ and that the only way to Heaven is through Christ and his One Holy Church."

The priest gives a benign smile, lowers his head and says, "My Lord."

Once more I realise how much thought the Lord has given this matter and how cleverly he has silenced his most powerful objector.

As the meeting is coming to a close, Lord Burford tells the council that his instructions are to be carried out and that most of the detail will be overseen by young Henry, Edmund de Covny and Scabbard. He finishes with, "Thank you, gentlemen. I am sure…"

At this point, I suddenly interrupt with, "Oh, and get rid of that water in the church entry or keep changing it."

At this, the priest jumps up and exclaims, "This really is too much, My Lord! He speaks as if Holy water is just… well, er, just water!"

"Of course Holy water is pure and will always remain pure. I am sure de Covny was not referring to the water in the font, were you de Covny?"

"No, My Lord, I meant it was, er, er…"

"Good. Just a misunderstanding. We shall start first thing tomorrow morning, but you are all to start spreading my instructions immediately."

The Lord's face is stone cold and as white as a sheet as he walks towards the door. The council members bow and Henry follows his father out with me close behind him. My mind is racing and the only consolation I can find is that I have at least mindlessly followed the others in dipping my finger and crossing myself. How much worse things would be if I had been seen not doing what all good Christians do, and if I'd never seen how those in the Catholic Church of the 21st century, who still habitually maintain the crossing ritual, were conditioned and compelled to mindlessly follow this ritual. The consequences of not doing so would mean social exclusion at the very least. In the 14th century it will probably mean being burnt at the stake.

The walk back to Burford House is in silence. Once back inside, Lord Burford disappears and Henry nods his head to show that I am to follow him. We go into a room and Henry closes the door. Then he turns towards me. "What did you think you were doing?"

"I'm sorry. I should have chosen my words more carefully."

"Chosen them more carefully? What made you say such a thing at all?"

I keep my mouth shut.

"Apart from what you said, you should not have spoken at all without permission from the Lord."

"Yes, I know, Henry. I don't know what came over me."

"My father is trying his best to help you and what do you do?"

I remain silent.

"My father may be Lord of the Manor, but he can't be seen challenging the teachings of the church. You could have done irreparable harm to what…"

At this point, there's a knock at the door and Henry bites his tongue before saying, "Come in."

The door opens and Scabbard stands there with an expressionless face. "Lord Burford commands to see Edmund de Covny."

I freeze as Henry remains silent and averts his gaze.

After a few seconds, I find the strength to walk towards the door and follow Scabbard out and along the corridor. My mind is racing. What will Lord Burford say? What will he do? For the first time since I was 'captured', I wish I had stayed at home. A few minutes ago I felt like a great prophet and now I feel like Judas.

The walk through the house seems like a long walk to the gallows. Eventually we come to a door and Scabbard knocks. "Come," says the voice of Lord Burford through the door.

Scabbard opens the door and indicates that I should go in. As I do, Scabbard closes the door behind me.

"I am sorry, Lord Bur…""Sit down, Edmund," Lord Burford cuts me off forcefully.

There is a long silence and then he says, "My son and heir is very taken with your thoughts and I can see much merit in them but you must see that some may find them strange and frightening. Others may even find them threatening."

"Yes, sir."

"You must know that your ideas have no power without my endorsement. You must learn to say nothing without first expressing it to me or Henry."

"Yes, My Lord. I cannot sufficiently express my remorse for my foolhardy behaviour."

There is another silence. Then he says, "As you come from a far off land, you may have different customs but you must remember where you are. Go now. Have a good evening with Henry and we shall start early in the morning."

"Yes, My Lord. Thank you."

CHAPTER THIRTEEN

THE MUSIC ROOM

As I walk back to where I left Henry, the full enormity of my situation is beginning to dawn on me. No longer am I on a little adventure from which it's easy to return. I'm now caught in a time from which I cannot return easily. I'm so far from my laptop and I can hardly just walk out of the town. Even if I could try to explain my situation to the people who now know me in the 14th century, there are guards at all the exits from the town who would prevent my exit. They may be there to stop people coming in but how would I be able to get past them without having to explain why I wanted to leave and where I was going?

There is the sound of a flute which gets louder as I approach the room where I left Henry. On reaching the room I knock and hear Henry's voice say, "Come."

Opening the door with some trepidation, I'm greeted with a broad smile from Henry who ushers me in and gestures to a seat. As I sit down I notice the flute in Henry's hand. He holds it up and asks, "Do you play?"

"Er, well, not really, but I can play a little on the keyboard, usually with only one hand."

"Keyboard?"

Realising that I have used another anachronism, I decide to adopt another approach and create the impression that I would expect Henry to know what a keyboard is.

"Yes, you know, where you press a note on a board and it causes a little hammer to hit different strings that ring on different notes."

"Oh, you mean like the new form of dulcimer?"

"Yes, sort of, but the hammer is moved by a mechanism that is operated when the note is pressed."

"I see! Come with me," says Henry as he jumps up and heads for the door.

I follow Henry through the house to parts I have not been to before. As we walk, I realise there has been no mention of what Henry's father had to say about what I said in the church. Why is this? Is he too embarrassed to raise the subject? Did Lord Burford tell his son that he was going to give me a bollocking and that would be all? But when would he have said this? He's had no time alone with his father. Is it that he knows his father so well and knows that he would merely express his opinion and leave it at that? Is Lord Burford's forgiveness just because I, Edmund, am now Henry's new friend? Is it just because Henry was impressed with what I had to say, and because Henry is medically educated that his father, too, thought there must be merit in what I have to say?

We make our way through the house, a long labyrinth of corridors and doors, until we reach a 'staircase', except that it isn't a proper staircase, but really just a ladder up to the next floor. Henry bounds up it and I follow as we pass along another corridor. Eventually Henry turns into what is obviously a music room. I've been in music rooms at school but have never seen one in someone's house. All around us are musical instruments, some of which I recognise, others that I have no concept at all of what they might be or what sound they might make.

Henry moves across the room to one instrument saying, "Here you are, a dulcimer. I think this is what you mean by a keyboard!"

Moving towards the instrument and looking at it, I say, "Yes, but a keyboard is more complicated."

Henry picks up a couple of sticks and begins to play but, of course, it is not a tune I know and not in a time signature I recognise.

"The dulcimer is usually played with a bow but this new form of dulcimer is becoming popular. Now you play," Henry says as he passes me the sticks.

What can I say or do? I've played a xylophone before and that wasn't too difficult, so I'll try, but what to play? Something traditional and not too modern; something nice and easy in C. I make a few random strokes with the hammers to find out where the notes are, before saying, "I have never played a dulcimer before but I will try." Then I begin to knock out 'Auld Lang Syne'.

Henry's face is a mixture of puzzlement and pleasure at his friend's musical production. "Is that a tune from your country?"

"Yes, we sing it each New Year."

"Why?"

"I don't know, it's just a tradition." Obviously that old tune is not old enough.

"Oh. Anything else?" enquires Henry.

I think for a few moments and then tentatively start to play 'Greensleeves', thinking that if it were not written by Henry VIII, it may be a little older and Henry Burford might just recognise it. He doesn't seem to but then he puts out his hands to take the hammers and moves around to the other side of the instrument and begins to play. Out comes 'Greensleeves', but as a very augmented version. I smile and exclaim, "Oh, you know this tune!"

"No, I just heard what you were playing." I then understand that Henry is a very good musician.

Realising that any further attempts at playing myself will merely add to my embarrassment, I listen to Henry playing various pieces and then, looking around the room at all the other instruments, I ask, "Would you tell me a little about all these other instruments? Some I don't recognise."

Henry looks pleased and turns to the nearest instrument, which has a round pear-shaped body, and begins to bow it. "This is a rebec."

"A rebec? We have something very similar called a violin but it makes a different sound."

Putting it down, Henry then picks up another instrument which seems to be a cross between a harp and a violin and begins to produce a strange sound. "This is called a psaltery but it's not very easy to play."

"So I see," I say, looking around at other instruments and my eyes light up as I see what looks like a recorder. Picking it up, I begin to play what I believe is an Irish jig that I don't know the name of. Henry picks up a flute and joins in as if he has been playing the tune all his life. Once more I'm very impressed. Then he picks up an extremely strange looking instrument which has many different strings and as many tuning pegs in different places.

"This is a nyckelharpa," Henry explains with a proud tone to his voice.

"Is it really?" I exclaim.

"Yes. It's a traditional Swedish instrument and extremely difficult to play. We haven't had it for long and father has commissioned a Swedish troubadour who lives in London to come and teach me how to play it."

Henry puts down the nyckelharpa very reverentially and says with a sigh, "So I won't try to play it now as I have little idea how to start."

At this point, there is a knock at the door and again Megan is there with some food. On entering, she looks at me and says, "Lord and Lady Burford send their apologies for not having a family meal tonight but they are both very busy."

"Oh, please tell them I am happy with this and I thank them for their hospitality." Once more, Megan is very chatty and full of big smiles for me. Henry sits almost silently and grins as he watches Megan and I flirt. I'm beginning to warm to her and see the beauty behind the grime. Even so, I do wince a bit when she reaches past me and I can smell her odour. I would like to chat her up but don't know how to behave towards a servant girl in medieval society, when I came from a society that doesn't really have servants any more. Even if I did know what to do, it would be impossible with Henry sitting in the corner smirking. Eventually Megan runs out of excuses to stay and leaves with a little curtsy.

As the evening progresses we munch through the food, mainly some sort of bread and cakes with cheese. I cut the cheese with a knife and rip the bread with my teeth and I become aware that Henry is giving me funny looks.

"What?" I ask.

Henry is obviously fully aware of what I mean as he immediately says,

"Why do you eat your food like that?"

"Like what?"

"Biting into it like an animal would," Henry explains with obvious distaste.

"Well, how else would I eat it?"

"Like a human being and not like a base animal."

I suddenly realise I have committed a totally unacceptable social 'no-no' and just look at Henry for guidance.

After a couple of seconds, he smiles and says, "Like this." He's holding up a piece of cheese between the thumb and forefinger of his left hand whilst he holds the bread with his other fingers against the base of his thumb. He then uses his knife to cut a piece of bread and then cut a piece of cheese before he pops it into his mouth.

I follow his example and Henry smiles, saying rather patronisingly, "Well done! I assume the other way is how the people of Saxony would eat?"

"Yes!" I exclaim, thankful for some excuse for my taboo behaviour.

"Well, here even the most lowly serf would not eat like an animal."

Oh my god, I think with a mixture of shame, bemusement and relief at the realisation it could have been so much worse had I eaten like that in front of the rest of the Burford family or the peasants and serfs of Burford.

I feel very embarrassed but soon the conversation moves on. As the meal comes to an end, Henry proceeds to play me more instruments I did not know such as a viol, clearly an early viola played on the lap or between the knees, and a set of bagpipes which apparently is usually only played by poor people, as it can be made from reed pipes and the bag from goatskin. After many good tunes from Henry and a few painful noises from me,

Henry picks up a strange looking object with a handle he begins to turn and produces a rasping sound. "What is that?" I ask in amazement.

"It's called a hurdy-gurdy."

"Oh, I have heard of a hurdy-gurdy but never seen one and definitely never heard one."

As Henry tries to teach me to play the instrument, it begins to get dark outside. I think it must now be about half past nine on a midsummer's night and another obvious observation occurs to me: there is no form of artificial light other than candles, and why use them during midsummer when it is only dark for six hours? It is just about enough time to sleep. Another obvious problem suddenly occurs to me: where am I to sleep? I have no idea where I will sleep and no idea how to broach the subject. I just hope Henry will tell me.

Soon the evening draws to a halt and Henry puts down the hurdy-gurdy. "I will show you to your room" he says.

"Oh, thank you, Henry."

I follow Henry upstairs once more and when we come to a door, he asks, "Do you want to go in there first?", pointing to a door.

Hesitantly, I push open the door to reveal what I assume is a privy, mainly by the smell. Oh thank God, I think, because although the day has been full of excitement and despite having had little to drink, I am now busting for a pee. Inside is a stone chair with a hole in it that seems to overhang the house to the outside. Having had a long wee I turn to the sink – what sink? So I walk out to where Henry is still waiting.

Once more I follow Henry until we come to a room with the door ajar. As we walk in, I see a room that is quite large for a guest room, with a big bed in the middle. This is obviously not a servant's room. Henry turns to leave, then stops and pauses before saying, "I know my father spoke to you, so that is finished with, but do you mind if I ask you one thing?"

"No, not at all," I reply, fearful of what is to come.

"From my knowledge of medicine you talk a lot of sense, but I cannot understand why you think Holy water could ever be harmful?"

"I, er, wasn't thinking straight whilst in the council meeting."

Henry nods in silence, turns once more and closes the door behind him.

It becomes clear to me that no matter how intelligent, 'educated' and open-minded Henry is, he is still a product of his society and time so he does actually believe Holy water is something other than ordinary water. Climbing into bed I can feel some of the feathers sticking through the bed and the pillows. However, it is quite comfortable and seems pretty clean. I lie awake for a while reflecting on the strangest day of my life and wondering if I will ever be able to return to the 21st century. That is the last conscious thought I have and the eventful day soon has its inevitable effect – sleep.

CHAPTER FOURTEEN

BREAKFAST

I'm woken by a loud knock and I automatically call out,

"Come in."

The door opens and Scabbard is standing there.

"I am sorry to wake you, sir, but it is morning and breakfast is prepared."

I look at Scabbard, in shock, not realising where I am or who this man is. A second later it all comes flooding back to me.

"Oh, thank you, Scabbard."

I notice a large bowl in Scabbard's hands and he places it next to the bed. Looking at it I can see there is water in it. He then drops a cloth next to the bowl, saying, "For you, sir."

Scabbard turns to leave and my head drops back onto the pillow. Yes, I'm awake and it hasn't all been a dream. I really am still in the 14th century, in a large house five miles and seven centuries from where I should have been sleeping.

Quickly I jump out of bed and find my clothes on the floor where I dropped them after the long day yesterday. As I have brought nothing to change into with me, there is no choice but to wear them again. This reminds me that I had not intended to be in this present position. A planned short exploration has turned into an adventure, the outcome of which is completely unknown. Had it been a good idea to travel again? We shall see! I have a quick wash in the water, which is warm at least, and put on my clothes.

I walk down the stairs to where Megan is waiting to show me into the breakfast room. "Good morning, Megan."

"Good morrow, sir. Did you sleep well?"

"Yes, very well, thank you."

"My Lord is waiting for you," she said as she opens the door.

"Ah, Edmund," says Lord Burford, indicating a chair to sit on.

"Good morning, sir."

"Good morrow", he responds.

"Good morrow, Edmund", Henry says with his beguiling broad smile

"Good morrow, Henry," I reply, picking up on the socially accepted terminology.

At this point, I notice Scabbard standing a little away from the table as if waiting to serve. "Good morrow, Scabbard."

"Good morrow, sir."

This is not the room we ate in before. It faces east so that the midsummer morning sun streams into the room. It is a real breakfast room.

Soon the door opens again and in walks Megan with a tray laden with food. She's followed by an old woman also carrying a tray.

"Ah, thank you, Megan and Rachael. Edmund, this is Rachael, the housekeeper," Lord Burford says.

"Good morrow, sir," Rachael says. Then she turns to me. "I am pleased to be of service to you." She finishes with a curtsy.

At least, that's what I think she said because her accent is even stronger than the Burfords'. Even Megan is easier to understand with her medieval Welsh accent.

"Thank you, Rachael," I reply with a nod, not really knowing what the social etiquette is towards a housekeeper in the 14th century

The two women leave the room and I can't help but think that Megan wasn't at all flirtatious in the presence of Lord Burford. Or maybe it was the presence of the housekeeper. Maybe both.

Following the lead of the Burfords, I get stuck into breakfast, this time being even more careful to watch for the eating etiquette of the 14th century. I wouldn't want them thinking I'm lower than the lowest serf! There are various sorts of bread, warm milk, probably fresh from the cow, what smells like fish and, of course, meat, meat and a little more meat. Don't these people ever eat any fruit or vegetables? Their turds must be like bricks! My father could make a fortune selling Senokot to them, and lots of haemorrhoid cream too. Mind you, having seen, and smelt, the privy last night, it is hardly surprising that the people of the 14th century try to defecate as little as possible.

It quickly becomes obvious that this is a working breakfast and soon Lord Burford asks, "Well, Edmund, where do you suggest we start today?"

"Okay, I have thought about this and it's probably best if we start with Burford House." I stop here to check their reaction because I'm aware that I'm suggesting that the place needs cleaning up.

"What would you do?" enquires the Lord.

"First of all we will go to the kitchen. Let me look around and see what's needed. Then perhaps we can do something with the privy."

There is a pause and Lord Burford looks at Edmund so I think I had better take the lead. "I have told you about little bacteria that make people ill and the present sickness is just one particular sort of bacteria that is more dangerous than others, but any sort of sickness will make the sufferer ill and, therefore, far more likely to succumb to the Black Death when it comes along. We will all be more resilient towards that sickness if we don't have any other sort of sickness. These little bacteria grow in all sorts of places and then get into our bodies where they make us ill and weak. Because we are weak the Black Death has a greater chance of killing us when it comes along. If we eliminate as many places as possible where bacteria can grow, then we will all be much healthier."

"I see, but if these bacteria are so small that we cannot see them, how do you know they are there?"

"Good question!" I have thought about this one and decided to tell him something close to the truth. "If you look through glass," I say as I look through the window glass that is not perfect, "sometimes things become distorted and sometimes what you are looking at becomes bigger." I pause for confirmation.

"Yeees."

"If the glass is made carefully then things can be made to look much bigger. If that glass is put at the one end of a tube and another glass is put at the other end of the tube, then it is possible to see things that are very, very small."

"I see."

"This tube is also very good for looking at the stars."

"I suppose it would be. What is this tube called?"

"For looking at small things, it is called a microscope. For looking at the stars, it is called a telescope."

"Ah, yes, Greek again. 'Small' for looking at little things and 'distance' to look at the stars."

I had given it little thought but become aware again that all educated people of this time, Lord Burford included, can also speak Greek. I suppose he would, being an educated Lord. Never mind the fact that he thinks water can have magical qualities if it's blessed, just as long as he can speak Greek!

"But tell me, do they have these tubes in Saxony?"

I realise I need to be careful and reply, "Yes, but not very many. They are difficult to make and very expensive."

"And was it invented by a Saxon?"

I feel a little gremlin get onto my shoulder and tell Lord Burford, "No, it was invented by an Italian called Galileo."

"Mmm, a clever man."

"Oh, not really; he thought the Earth went around the sun and not that the sun went around the Earth."

A little chuckle is heard from Henry and his father.

After a long silence, I move things on to say, "Then we shall go over to the Abbey to see if there is anything we can do for the sick nuns."

I know this will be very dangerous for my own health and that it would be better to stay away but I also know I have to try to do something. "This is a very risky thing to do, so I think I should be the only one to enter their sick room" I add.

Silence fills the room. Then Henry says, "Father, I would like to accompany Edmund in anything he has to do."

More silence ensues.

"Alright, but you must not do anything more than is absolutely necessary." Lord Burford seems to be caught between wanting to protect his son, needing him to be able to behave like a man and not just the Lord's son, and knowing the public image of the Burford family is important.

"Something that would be helpful is very fine muslin." Not

knowing if muslin is around in the 14th century I just hope for the best.

"Yes, we can arrange that, but what for?"

"The bacteria enter our bodies mainly through the mouth and nose, so if we can filter this out, it may help us to avoid catching the disease. We need to have it layer upon layer and made in such a way that it can be tied around the mouth and nose."

"Oh, and filled with flower petals against the stink," the Lord adds helpfully.

I have a picture in my head of the Black Death of 1665 with a man wearing a pointed face mask with petals in the nose piece.

"No, a ring of roses won't really help. The smell of flowers doesn't help other than to cover up the smell. The muslin is just to filter the bacteria."

"That sounds like a job for Megan, Scabbard", Lord Burford says looking towards Scabbard.

"Yes, sir, I shall instruct her."

Now I realise why Scabbard is here: to hear what is required and ensure instructions are carried out. I wondered why he sat there not eating, and felt a little rude eating in front of someone who was not, but I suppose a servant is used to that.

By now nearly all the food has been consumed and Lord Burford wipes his mouth with a cloth napkin. At this, Scabbard walks towards the door and disappears for a few moments before returning. I assume he has done this a thousand times before and knows the signals for the end of the meal. During the silence I ask,

"What is happening with the street cleaning?"

Lord Burford's eyes move towards Scabbard who says, "All is in hand, sir, and should already have started."

It becomes clear that Lord Burford started giving instructions last night when Henry and I were in the music room. They seem to work well together.

At this moment, the door opens and in walk the cook and Megan, who begin to clear the table. Soon the strange work in this strange time will start and I remember something I forgot to mention before. "Oh yes, Lord Burford, we need to dig a rubbish pit."

"A what?"

"A pit, or a hole, to put all the rubbish in."

"Oh, a hole for the garbage," interprets the Lord, translating my words to 14th century terminology.

"Yes, somewhere outside the town."

"Well, we usually burn most of it and a lot goes into the river."

"Burning is good, but dumping garbage into the river is not because it poisons the water we have to drink," I explain.

"We can get drinking water upstream and dump the garbage downstream."

I pause and ponder on this logic before saying, "That means we get the poison from upstream and poison other people downstream."

"There are few people upstream and Witney is outside our jurisdiction," the Lord says logically.

There is another pause whilst I think of a way to deal with this one. "The garbage will poison the water and the fish we eat from the water, so we all need to ensure that others don't get poisoned to ensure we don't get poisoned."

Lord Burford looks a little bemused and then shrugs and says, "Very well, if you think it's necessary, I will issue instructions that garbage is not to be dumped in the river under any circumstances."

During this exchange, the table has been cleared by Megan and the cook, and as they are leaving the room, Lord Burford says, "Megan, you are aware you will be assisting these men today?"

Megan turns and with her best little-girl-smile says, "Oh yes, My Lord. I know I am to do whatever they ask of me."

"Good girl." Megan and the cook depart with their laden trays.

Lord Burford's face now turns solemn as he says, "So, we're off to the church first where a Special Mass will be said for our work today."

I try my best to prevent my face from showing the horror I suddenly feel. What is a Special Mass? I will be expected to go, of course, and how should I behave? I must keep my mouth shut and act as if I take it all seriously! Finally, I stammer, "Oh, er, yes, of course, sir."

CHAPTER FIFTEEN

THE SPECIAL MASS

As we approach the church, along with the full Burford House entourage, my mind is processing how to deal with this new test. I've already messed things up big time over religion by not knowing what all medieval people would know and now I'm to face a bigger test. My heart is in my mouth as we enter the church where I recently nearly ruined it all.

The priest welcomes Lord Burford and it becomes clear this is not for the whole town but just for the Burford household. But what is a Special Mass? In fact, when is a Mass not special? My mind springs back to all my Religious Education lessons at school and how Catholics don't just go to church, but that they have to go to Mass, where it seems they get a special sort of magic they cannot get without going to Mass. In fact, it seems that if they don't get whatever it is they get from a Mass, they think they will go to Hell. I remember the class being in raptures of disbelief when this came up in Religious Education. What do they get from a Mass that they cannot get anywhere else? Surely this is just a sales technique to get people to go to church, by frightening them with the consequences of not going? It's just like those online con merchants who try to convince people that if they don't send thousands of pounds to an account they will miss out on the opportunity of millions. Surely even a medieval mind could see through that little gimmick?

The priest turns to the altar and begins speaking in what sounds like Latin, but it does not quite resemble the little Latin I know. I assume this is what they call 'Church Latin'. But why God would need a different sort of Latin, or any different sort of language from the one the congregation understands, I just cannot get my head around. Surely if they believe God is omniscient then he knows all languages, so why would medieval English not suffice?

I learnt about the Second Vatican Council, known as the Vatican II, which apparently allows people to talk to their God in their own language, but that was not till 1967 – over 600 years from where I am now. What confused me in the lesson was why people needed permission from an earthly being to do this?

As I watch the priest wave his arms about and talk with his back to the congregation, all the other bits of my Religious Education lessons come to mind, and when those around me start to chant, I easily mumble along with them at the right time. I remember that a Special Mass has to be paid for, which seems very strange behaviour for any sort of god. Then the Counter-Reformation comes back to me, which was apparently an answer to Luther and his followers who criticised the Roman Catholic Church for selling indulgencies and forgiveness. That will have to wait another few hundred years to happen as well, but at the moment they still charge to get God's favour.

Then the memory of going to a Midnight Mass a couple of years ago with a Catholic friend, Gerry, springs into my mind, and I remember being so disappointed that there was no sing-along. It was just a professional choir that people listened to. In front of me, pasted on the back of the next pew, there had been a plaque that read, 'Pray for the family of Timothy Leary' or whoever. I had asked Gerry why they should pray specifically for any particular person, or their families, and what praying does. Gerry had been very reluctant to talk about his beliefs and I assumed this was because he was embarrassed when he put his beliefs into words for someone who had not been conditioned into his belief system. Then I remembered seeing a book on a shelf in my house and wondered if it might answer some questions. There it was: a bright yellow book entitled The Complete Idiot's Guide to Catholicism. I had picked it out and over the next few weeks, with growing astonishment, waded through what all Catholics – no matter of personal choice – had to believe.

Apparently, if he did not go to Mass once a week and on Holy days, he would have a break in his relationship with God and then he would have to go to Hell. I did ask Gerry why God would send him to Hell just for not going through some ritual, but he seemed to have no idea. In fact, he knew very little about the doctrine of Catholicism and even less about why things were a certain way. As for the 'history', or the Bible, he knew virtually nothing. Even more surprisingly, it soon became clear he did not want to know. So why was he such a fervent Catholic? Gerry claimed he was not a fervent Catholic. So why did he always go to Mass once a week and on Holy days? He had no answer to this either. It seems he just did it because everyone around him and in his family did so, and no one ever said no!

When Gerry and I had left the church I asked him again about the plaque saying, "Pray for the family of Timothy Leary" and once more pursued him as to why people should pray for Timothy Leary and his family, rather than any other family, but once more he avoided giving an answer. He was good at this when it came to awkward questions. Then it occurred to me that the commandment to pray was there because the family of Timothy Leary had paid to have the plate put there. A 'contribution to the church' I think would be the term used by these victims of the con merchants to have the plate put there in the belief that if people prayed for them, they would get extra 'points' in Heaven and would have to spend less time in Purgatory: a concept for which there was no biblical reference at all, and had been completely made up as had the concept of a 'sacred heart'. It seemed they had special word for theses 'points in Heaven' - they called it 'Grace'. As Timothy Leary's family had paid for the plaque, what was the difference between that and paying to buy an indulgence in pre-Counter-Reformation times? Not a lot, really!

The book did not say so, but I remembered how in a Religious Education discussion, it had been observed that the Greeks and Romans believed that there was a family of gods floating in the sky and how, when the Romans took over the Christian sect, they had simply grafted Christianity onto these traditional beliefs. The father of the gods, Zeus, became God the father and his wife, Hera, became Mary the mother of God. The children of the gods had their roles filled by the son of God, Jesus. As for the lesser gods, it seemed that they were now referred to as The Saints. The commandment, 'Thou shall have but one God' could thus be compatible in their minds with worshipping the different variations of these gods. There was general consensus within the student group of this analysis but the Religious Education teacher, Miss Priest – yes, that really was her name – didn't seem to be very comfortable with it. In fairness, though, she was happy for us to discuss the matter and express any views we wanted. Something that would not likely to be tolerated in the 14th century. Come to think of it, would it be tolerated in a Catholic school in the 21st century? Looking around the church at the very beautiful stained-glass windows, the models of Mary and the crucified Jesus, not to mention the gold and royal standards, I remember that the 'Ten' Commandments were actually seventeen for the Protestant churches and in the original Hebrew, but only sixteen for the Catholic Church. They, very conveniently, left out 'Thou shall not worship graven images'. If you took graven images out of the Catholic faith, there wouldn't be much left!

At the time of studying Gerry's beliefs – but were they really his beliefs? – I had just looked into the subject because Gerry was my friend and as a matter of interest, but now I'm in a situation where this knowledge is vital. Although I've opened my big mouth before, I now realise the necessity of knowing how to play the game. Having had some insight into the Catholic faith in the 21st century, I have some idea of how much stronger, and less questioned, the same beliefs are nearly 700 years earlier. This is before the age of the Enlightenment, and before any scientific analysis of the temporal world, let alone the spiritual world. I doubt if anyone in this church, or in the whole of Burford, questions that their mumblings might not be listened to by anyone except those in the church. Whilst I can understand that people living before the Age of Enlightenment might believe such nonsense, having had personal experience of the workings of the medieval mind, I'm becoming increasingly bemused as to how anyone in the 21st century could possibly be taken in by such illogical beliefs. Every time this thought enters my head, I remind myself never to show any incredulity. I remember that the price to pay for heresy is to be burnt at the stake. I do not fancy myself as a latter day Ridley or Latimer. Latter day, or is it future day?

Suddenly the whole congregation begins reciting the Lord's prayer. I know this and can join in enthusiastically. I get to the bit about 'as we forgive them who trespass against us' and carry on with 'for thine…' but realise no one else is following me. Then I remember that the bit "For thine is the Kingdom, the power and the glory, forever and ever, amen", was added by Henry VIII who didn't think God's version – as Christians would see it – was good enough. Henry VIII added it but I cannot understand why the Church of England keeps it nearly 400 years later. So, Henry separated the English church from the Roman church but that was no reason for keeping in his addition centuries later. Either God was right or he needed to have his thoughts added to by mere mortals. Surely it makes a mockery of the word of God?

It is now clear that the service is over and everyone starts to leave the church. It seems there have been no obvious conflicts between my behaviour and what is expected of me. Even the 'for thine…' insertion seems to have gone unnoticed. I had got away with it! We all exit the church and make our way over the bridge, up the hill and into Burford House. I've passed another test and now the job of helping the people of Burford to avoid the worst of the Black Death can commence.

CHAPTER SIXTEEN

THE KITCHEN

There is no time to waste and as soon as we are back at Burford House, Scabbard joins us as Lord Burford bids farewell and leaves the task to Henry and me. The first visit will be to the house kitchen.

Scabbard opens the door and ushers us in. There, lined up, as if awaiting a royal visit, are all the kitchen staff and the rest of the house staff. Cook steps forward and gives a little curtsy.

"Good day, sirs."

"Good day, Cook," replies Henry.

"Good day, Cook," I follow, now that I'm clear on how to address her.

I look along the line and there is Megan, who seems to give me a knowing smile but it's probably just my imagination. Then my eyes move around the large kitchen; the largest room in the house. The first thought that strikes me is that it is covered in more grease than John Travolta! It is everywhere. Oh dear! How to explain this?

Not wanting to jump in straight away with what will probably be seen as criticism, I start to move around the kitchen. As I move past a smaller table at the edge of the room, there is a sudden 'whoosh' and I see what seems to be a black shadow move from a corner to under a large oven. I jump a little and exclaim, "What was that?"

"Oh, don't you worry about that, sir. Them ain't rats: them's just cockroaches," reassures Cook.

Pulling myself together I think, Oh well, that's alright, then. It's only a swarm of cockroaches. I shiver and then remember being told that some of the best hotels in London still had cockroaches in the second half of the 20th century.

Moving around the kitchen I notice the tables look clean, but how clean? Moving on to the pots and pans, I can see they've all been washed but they still seem to be covered in a thin film of grease. Well, with no Fairy Liquid, what else can be expected? They are obviously cleaning where they can but the floor is in a sorry state! It's covered in bits of food. What rat could resist this? What to do? How can this be explained without upsetting too many people too much? Remembering I have been given the authority of Lord Burford, I decide to explain things before I give instructions.

Turning to the still assembled domestic household, who are standing in unmoving silence, I move around the kitchen and begin to explain things.

"Rats only live where humans provide food and warmth for them" I say. "Before humans came onto the Earth, there were virtually no rats. They only thrive because we provide food and housing for them." I pause for a while for this to sink in. As I am about to proceed, I become aware that Scabbard wants to speak.

"Yes, Scabbard, what is it?"

"Well, surely before God put us on the Earth there was nothing else? He only put the rats and other creatures here for us after he had made us."

Oh dear, here we go again. This time, however, it seems no big deal. Thinking quickly I say, "He only created two of us at first, so as the population grew, we made life easier for the rats and their population grew as well."

"Oh, I see," said Scabbard, who seems satisfied.

Moving the conversation back to what is needed, I say, "So, what we need to do is to ensure there is as little food as possible available for them to eat. This means that no food at all must be allowed to fall onto the floor, or if it is, then it must be cleared up immediately. Any stored food must be kept out of reach of any rats that may be around."

As I pause, Cook says, "Er, excuse me, sir, but we already do that. All the flour pots and meat barrels are on these stands, sir." She points to a large barrel-shaped container on a raised platform.

"This is very good, Cook. I'm very pleased to see it. It just means no waste must ever be left behind, especially last thing at night."

Cook straightens herself up and beams with pride. I realise I will get furthest by complimenting her and the staff, so I add, "I think we're going to get on very well working together, Cook."

Cook beams more and I take the opportunity to add, "And I can see you make sure the tables are kept very clean too, so it is only important that you make sure they are cleaned every night with water, and once a week with vinegar, to clean any little insect that may get into the cracks."

"Yes, sir, certainly, sir. Anything I can do to help, sir," she says with another little curtsy.

"Another important thing is what you do with any leftovers from plates, peelings or even things like egg shells. All of these things must be buried, not left lying around, not put in a pile outside and not thrown into the river."

"Oh, why not the river, sir?" asks a man I had seen before but never spoken to.

Not knowing what his position is, I assume he's some sort of butler or the male equivalent of Cook. "I'm sorry, I do not know your name?"

"Oh, it's Peter, sir" replies the man with a little lowering of the head.

"Well, Peter, the rubbish, I mean the garbage, poisons the river and attracts rats to eat the garbage. This will poison the people who drink the water downstream."

Peter then goes on to point out the blindingly obvious in any rural community by saying,

"I think all our kitchen waste and any leftovers are fed to the pigs, sir."

Ah yes, of course they are. Now, how do I get out of this one?

I umm and err for a couple of seconds and then 'explain'

"Yes, I know that but there are always little bits left lying around, or not picked up, that the rats can feed on so we must all be extra vigilant to ensure nothing is left for the rats."

Peter gives a little smile and I add, "But that's a good point and thank you for pointing it out." Peter's smile then turns into grin from ear to ear.

There is silence and then I notice that Cook's body language means she wants to say something. "Yes, Cook?"

"Begging your pardon, sir, but why should we worry about people downstream?"

This seems to be a strange question, especially when considering these people are all obsessed with calling themselves Christians. I think for a couple of seconds and then decide to explain the blindingly obvious. "Cook, if we look after the people downstream, then we can expect the people upstream to do the same for us. We must make sure all the towns and villages are persuaded not to dump their garbage in the river either."

There is general sighing and shuffling at the enormity of this task. I can imagine them thinking that surely the river is always the natural place for everyone to dump their rubbish. It seems as if this is going to be a big stumbling block to my ideas, but then Scabbard raises his hand. "Excuse me, sir. I will send messages with the authority of Lord Burford to all settlements upstream. In fact, I shall go there myself tonight!" he exclaims triumphantly.

"Good man, Scabbard," I respond as I'm taken aback by my own presumptuous attitude of superiority, but then I realise that this is what is expected of me and what is necessary if I'm to get my point across. I'm also beginning to realise that Scabbard is more than just a servant. He is a very capable man who does what he assumes his Lord wants without having to be told each minor detail. I decide that in future I must confide in, and trust, Scabbard more. He could be nearly as good an ally as Henry Burford and he has the authority of Henry's father.

At being referred to as a 'good man', Scabbard gives a little nod and seems to be striving not to show too much pride at this flattery. I wonder if Scabbard's pride is just because it will please his Lord or if he genuinely takes pride in his own abilities. I'm getting a little tired of all the obsequious behaviour and genuflection. I remember being embarrassed when I accompanied my Catholic friend, Gerry, to his church and saw him genuflecting as he entered, and that was in the 21st century. It seemed like something from a bygone age: Medieval! Even in the Middle Ages I find it so degrading for any human being to feel the need to behave like that. Scabbard then goes on to say,

"I shall arrange for empty corn barrels and pots to be set up outside the kitchen to put things in before we bury them."

"Well done, Scabbard, good idea! It will be possible for some things to be burnt, so only the food waste and similar things need to be buried. Could you arrange that, Scabbard?"

"Thank you, sir, that will be easier. And, yes, I will arrange for the waste to be burnt; or at least that which we cannot feed to the pigs," says Scabbard with another smile of pride and his posture seems more upright than before. Pigs! Of course. I hadn't thought of pigs until Peter mentioned them but it's logical that any waste would be fed to the pigs in an agricultural society. Oh well, just another of my faux pas .

Silence falls and I look around the kitchen once more. I then turn to Cook and say, "So, I shall leave it up to you, Cook, and I'm sure you will ensure that anything that may attract rats will be removed."

"Oh yes, sir, you can rely on me, sir, yes, sir." she says, beaming with pride yet again.

Turning to Peter, I say, "And I'm sure you will ensure the rest of the house is kept rat free."

"Oh yes, sir, I certainly will and I'll make sure all the house staff know what needs to be done," he says, grinning and nodding.

Then his demeanour changes and he says, "If you wouldn't mind my being so bold, sir, may I offer to get together a group of the young men in the town and organise rat hunts all over the town?"

"Wonderful thinking, Peter; that will be very helpful!"

Peter looks as if all his Christmases have come at once.

"But rats breed so fast we couldn't possibly kill all of them, so what we need to do in the long term is to ensure there is nothing for the next generation of rats to eat. In doing so, they will either go elsewhere or starve to death. However, any rats we can kill now, will help this summer and that is why I want all cats and dogs to be brought into the town to help kill the rats."

The assembled staff receive this in polite silence, so I seize the opportunity to take this idea onwards. "Yes, the church is concerned that cats are the work of the Devil, but if we can use cats for God's work, then the Devil will be beaten."

Having said this almost spontaneously, as a paraphrase of what Lord Burford said to the priest, I'm unprepared for what follows. A whoop of joy erupts from all those gathered in the kitchen. Of course, these people believe in the reality of the Devil as much as they believe in the reality of God! Now I feel like Henry V rallying his soldiers before Agincourt. However, there is no point in telling the people assembled in the kitchen who Henry V would be!

At this point, I notice Megan is gesticulating that she has something to say, so I look at her and enquire, "Yes, Megan, what do you wish to say?"

"Well, sir, as you know, the Lord has requested me to help you and Sir Henry around the town in any way you want me to."

If you know that I know, then why tell me? I think to myself.

"So I hope you can trust me to do what you tell me to do."

It is obvious that she's proud of having been asked this and wants to advertise it to the rest of the staff rather than inform me. After all, being a Welsh serf probably makes her the lowest on the kitchen social scale and this gives her some kudos, so I play the game by saying, "Thank you very much for that, Megan. Sir Henry and I appreciate your vital contribution to the task in hand."

Megan looks like a five-year-old having 'Happy Birthday' sung to her and I'm pleased I've made her day – if not her year!

When I'm pretty sure that my work in the kitchen is done, I say, "We must move on now, but between keeping the house and kitchen free of food for rats to eat" (I am always careful to avoid the word 'clean' for fear of implying it is not clean now), "Peter's rat hunting parties and Megan helping Sir Henry and me, I'm sure we will do much to diminish the pestilence." At this, I turn to leave the kitchen, followed by Henry and Scabbard, but as

I do, that little gremlin appears on my shoulder once more and I cannot resist looking at Peter and asking,

"I don't suppose you can play the pipe can you, Peter?" I wiggle my fingers in front of my mouth to make it clear what I mean.

Peter looks a little confused and says, "Yes, I do, sir. Quite well, but why do you ask, sir?"

"Oh, never mind," I respond.

As I walk out of the kitchen I hear Henry saying behind me, "Don't let it trouble you, Peter. Sir Edmund has often said strange things to me that I cannot understand!

CHAPTER SEVENTEEN

THE ABBEY

Now it is time for the most dangerous part of the 'adventure' so far! It is on to the Abbey to see the sick nuns.

Megan has been commissioned to help with 'womanly duties' and the four of us walk out of the house, down the road, across the bridge and into the town: Henry and I in front, followed by Scabbard and then Megan bringing up the rear – in her 'rightful' place. We turn right towards the Abbey, at which point I stop and turn to the others..

"Ah hem! This will be an unhealthy place to enter, so there is no need to take unnecessary risks. Why don't the three of you stay outside?"

I'm then buried in a torrent of defiant rejection of the idea. Both Henry and Scabbard insist they must accompany me into the Abbey. There seem to be a number of reasons for this: The nuns have to take the risk, so why shouldn't they? The 'common people' need to be set an example, and if I have to enter, then they will accompany me. Megan remains silent but shakes her head when Henry asks if she wishes to stay outside. This is all very honourable, I think, but we need to agree to set certain limits.

"Very well, but none of you," I say, pointing at each one of them in turn, "should come further into the room than the door, and in the Abbey you are all to avoid touching anything before washing your hands and bare arms, and again on leaving and when you are back at Burford Hall. Then all of you must have a bath and have your clothes washed."

They all agree! Although this is justified by the risk of infection, I'm also calculating that I can have a bath for the first time since I arrived and have my clothes washed.

As we approach the Abbey door, I become aware that there are people gathering around to see us going into the Abbey. Is this because of the presence of Henry Burford or the fact that these idiotic people are going into that house of death? Or is it because of this strange young man who has come amongst them with his funny ideas? Perhaps it's a mixture of all three and much else to provide some entertainment before the era of television and 24 hour news.

Before we reach the door, it is opened by the Abbess saying, "You are well come, my Lord, sirs and Megan."

"Good day, Reverend Mother," chorus the four of us.

I am clearly settling into what is expected socially.

"All is ready. Is there anything I can do, sirs?" she adds.

Both Henry and Scabbard look at me. Megan just stands there demurely.

"Yes, Mother," I say, hoping this is the correct form of address. "Please take one large bowl of hot water into the sick room and arrange for four smaller ones to be waiting for us when we depart. All are to have soap with them."

"Yes, sir," replies the Abbess with her hands clasped in praying mode.

I then look at Scabbard and say, "Please hand over the muslin face masks."

Scabbard reaches into his large bag and gets out four strips of muslin which have been woven over, time and time again, in the manner I had directed. They're not perfect masks of surgical theatre standard, but they will probably keep out a few germs. They are tapered at the ends and I place one over my mouth and nose and tie it behind my head. I then tell the three of them to do the same. Although my voice is muffled through the muslin, they clearly understand and do the same.

The Abbess politely ignores the strange image we now present and leads us into the Abbey through a maze of corridors towards the sick room. As agreed, Henry, Scabbard and Megan wait at the door, but I can hardly get into the room as it is full of so many nuns, most of whom appear to be doing nothing at all except praying on their knees. I am horrified and in a loud voice exclaim,

"Everyone must leave the room except for two – only two – nuns with very good nursing skills."

There is a stunned silence and then a big kerfuffle as the room empties except for two nuns; one aged and one quite young.

As the room clears, I can see that the two sick nuns are on two beds, in the 'sheets' and covers and as far as I can tell, almost fully clothed. The stench is overwhelming and I'm glad I have on the makeshift mask, even if its only purpose is to filter the stink. My eyes quickly scan the room in the half light, as the curtains are also closed, and settle on a strange pile at the bottom of the two beds. I can't quite see what the pile is made up of, but in a fraction of a second that seems like minutes, I can see there are lots of different bundles in the pile that all appear to be roughly the same size. Eventually my eyes focus in and out as I slowly approach the pile, realising what I'm seeing, but then immediately dismissing what my eyes are telling me. I focus again, having to admit to myself that my eyes are not deceiving me. It's a pile of dead pigeons!

Taking a big step back and trying to hold my breath, I loudly demand, "Someone, remove all of these dead birds!"

The Abbess, who is at the door, starts to protest, "But, sir, they are there to help the recovery of the sisters."

"Remove them all immediately and clean the spot where they have been with very hot water and vinegar and then start to clean the rest of the room with fresh hot water; everywhere and everything!"

There is a stunned silence and Henry turns to the Abbess and gives a gentle nod. The Abbess looks at the two remaining nuns and the younger one leaves the room, presumably to get the hot water and vinegar. Once more I am reminded that without the authority of Lord Burford through his son, Henry, my words would have no effect at all.

I walk around towards the covered windows. These aren't curtains as I would know them, but merely cloth draped over a hole in the wall with a wooden shutter.

"Please take down these cloths and open the shutters" I tell them.

There is another gasp from those in the doorway, but this time the other nun immediately starts doing as I've bidden. Outside it is a warm but breezy day and immediately there is a blaze of light, soon followed by a rush of cool, fresh air. Straight away the atmosphere seems much healthier and the two sick nuns sigh as if a great weight has been lifted from them.

"And keep them open, except when it's raining hard or cold at night. Keep the door open as well to create a draught through the room", I say, turning towards the door only to realise that those who had been sent out, are still there, just outside the door and still all mumbling prayers.

"Look, oh dear, everybody except for the Abbess, please leave the area. The rest of you can get on with your usual duties. Go to the chapel if you feel the need to pray," I say in an exasperated and what I realise is a rather contemptuous tone, so I add sweetly, "God, will listen to you there."

There is a shuffling in the corridor and the Abbess says, "They are asking Our Lady for intercession."

I have no idea who Their Lady is but nod approvingly. I then stand still for a while, trying to compose myself and get my head around the enormity of what I've found. It is no wonder people don't recover and the disease spreads so quickly. Perfectly healthy people would die in circumstances like these. What on earth are the dead pigeons there for? What are they meant to do? Why fill the room with so many people when they know there is a fatal disease in the room? I tell myself it's probably because they believe that being nuns, and praying all the time, God would protect them. It's probably also because they feel the need to suffer and take risks. It's a bit like wearing a hair shirt or those painful garters Opus Dei members wear.

Henry, Scabbard and Megan have remained silent throughout my outburst but as if Henry can read my mind, he says gently to me, "The sisters had the shutters locked to keep out the miasma." It seems Henry has been greatly intrigued by his new, curious friend and has tried to get into my head.

Miasma? What's this? Not wanting to show my ignorance, I think back to my lessons on medieval history and have a vague recollection of a concept that disease is transmitted through the air in a medium they called a miasma.

Realising that my mouth is open, I regain my teacher-like

air and tell Henry, in a loud voice so that the Abbess hears, "The pestilence, or any disease, is not transmitted through a miasma. It is caught by touching the sick, or touching things the sick have touched, or breathing in the breath of the sick. This breath must be cleared from the room by clean, fresh air from the outside. It is not a matter of keeping the 'miasma' out but getting fresh air in to get the bad air out of the room."

Both Henry and Scabbard nod whilst Megan gives a serene smile, as I look at the Abbess to see her expression of disbelief slowly morph into resigned acceptance of what she must ensure happens.

Henry looks at Scabbard and asks him to get a couple of the makeshift masks for the two nursing nuns. To my surprise, Scabbard opens the large bag he has been carrying and takes out two masks. Once more I find myself in a difficult position as I can see Scabbard holding the masks in his hands that may look clean but are not germ free, and that is a concept I have no time to explain. As Scabbard holds up the masks, I turn to the Abbess and say, "Reverend Mother, please get another nun to take these masks and wash them in very hot water. Dry them outside and then give them to the two nursing nuns. When they have been washed, they must not be touched by anyone who has not just washed their hands. And, Scabbard, please get a couple more for them to use when the other masks are being washed, at least twice per day." Scabbard reaches into his bag again and extracts two more masks.

Now for another difficult order. I walk towards the door to speak directly to the Abbess. "Before the two nuns put on their masks, they must wash their whole bodies in as hot water as they can take, and wash their habits as well. Then, when they have put on new habits, find some sort of cloak to cover their whole habits. These cloaks can then be changed and washed twice per day. The nursing sisters must wash their hands every time they touch the sick patients."

The Abbess gives a bemused smile and beckons down the corridor to convey the orders.

At last there is an opportunity to do what I came for: examine the two sick nuns. Walking towards the stiller and quieter of the two patients, I gently roll back the blanket to reveal a still largely dressed woman, dripping with sweat and very smelly. In fact, the stench is overwhelming. I raise her arm and she winces with pain. I can see the large buboes in her armpit and they are oozing with pus. Leaning over the bed and trying not to touch her with my clothing, I pull her other arm up, causing her more pain, to reveal more oozing buboes. Obviously the nun's groin will also have buboes, but I don't think it would be acceptable for me to look with Henry, Scabbard and the Abbess watching. Anyway, what's the point in looking for the obvious? Her whole body seems to be covered in boils. Then I see them. Leeches! Lots of them. I take a deep breath – and wish I hadn't. I have no time or patience for diplomacy, so I blurt out, "Get all these leeches off her and never put another one on her – or anyone!"

There is a general hubbub and the Abbess begins, "But, sir..."

"I don't care, just get them all off and never put any more on her."

There is a further hubbub and I try to calm myself as I notice lots of cuts on her veins. They are presumably to bleed what little blood the leeches have left behind. This would be enough to kill even a healthy person, let alone someone suffering from a deadly disease. Gently I turn to those at the door and say, "It is an illusion that she has too much blood or bad blood. She needs every drop of blood to help her recover."

More hubbub follows and the Abbess says, "Yes, sir, I do understand and will ensure your commandments are carried out."

I then add, "So no more cutting to bleed her either."

"Yes, sir, I understand," she meekly concurs.

I pull up the bed clothes and turn to the other sick nun. She seems to be more restless but this is probably because she is not as ill. As I pull down the blankets and lift her arm, she has the strength to assist me, showing that she is the less ill of the two. Of course there are buboes, but they are not as big as the other sister's and not oozing as much pus. I pull up the blankets and turn around.

At this point, the nun who went to get the hot water and vinegar returns and I speak to both of the nuns, explaining in some detail how they must bathe the two patients' whole bodies in hot water and vinegar. As for the buboes, they must be bathed last and the pus must be removed with a clean cloth before they too are bathed. Then the cloth must be burnt – not washed, but burnt. If any pus gets onto on any of their clothing that must be burnt also. This is part of the reason for wearing the cloak over their habits. And any time the nursing nuns leave the room, they must wash their hands and anything else that may have touched the sick sisters. Also, the bed clothes must be changed at least once a day and be burnt. Anyone who comes in contact with any of these bedclothes must wash as well. The sick sisters must be bathed frequently in warm water, but when they become very fevered, they can be bathed in cold water. They should always try to keep the bed as dry as possible. I have to repeat a few things to ensure I get the point over but I think I make my expectations clear.

"Now, Reverend Mother, that hot water I ordered for us, please?"

As we leave I tell Scabbard, Henry and Megan to touch nothing on the way out until they have washed. I think about speaking to the two sick sisters but know there is little point in their fevered state. Instead I look at the two nursing nuns saying,

"Thank you for all you are doing."

The two sisters nod but look a little shocked that they should be thanked for doing their Christian duty and that they should be thanked by someone of such an obviously superior rank. Probably only the Bishop of Gloucester is of a higher rank than someone with the authority of Lord Burford.

As we all leave the room, the Abbess leads the way to the entrance hall where four bowls of steaming water await. Henry puts his hands behind his head to undo the strings of the mask but I quickly say, "No, wait a minute."

Looking at the Abbess, I ask for a cloth to wrap the masks in. The Abbess turns to another nun and just looks at her. She disappears. However, thirty seconds later she reappears with a cloth. I start to undo my mask signalling to the others to do the same. All of the masks are laid on the cloth and the other three start to wash their hands, faces and any other part of their bodies that have been exposed. Then I point to the cloth and the four masks, asking the Abbess to ensure they are washed, as directed, but only by the two nursing nuns so that no one else came in contact with them.

Suddenly the thought enters my head that I do not know the name of one of the two sick nuns, so I enquire of the Abbess, "I know one of the sick sisters is called Sister Cecilia, but what is the name of the other one, please?"

"She is Sister Florence, sir."

"Thank you, and what are the two nursing sisters called?"

"They are both called Sister Magdalene, sir."

"Oh, thank you, Mother Superior," I say with a nod and then wonder if this is how a 'sir' should behave towards an Abbess.

Feeling we have done all that's possible, we bid farewell to the nuns and the Abbess, who assures me that she and the other nuns will continue praying for the recovery of the two sisters, adding rather ominously that if they don't recover, they will pray for their souls. I just cannot resist saying, "Oh yes ,that will be very helpful."

The Abbess, however, takes me at face value and looks pleased that this vital contribution is being appreciated.

Outside the Abbey a large crowd is waiting for us to emerge. As we do, Scabbard and Megan divert from Henry and approach a man I don't know. At the same time, Henry says to me, "Are we going to other parts of the town now?"

"Well, I've had a rethink and I think we must now go back to Burford House to wash and change as we have instructed others to do."

"We will do that and I will give you some clothes to change into as you have lost all yours," Henry offers kindly.

"Thank you, Henry." I'm relieved at this as I haven't changed since I arrived, having expected to spend only a few hours on my 'travels'. Also, I'll fit in better with the 14th century scene, particularly as I assume he'll give me the clothing of a high-ranking Norman aristocrat. Then Scabbard catches up and tells us he has sent Megan off to set another two women to work on making more masks, and that he has ordered a few other things, such as two men to be in charge of setting up a permanent fire for any of the contaminated items. Once more Scabbard is showing his usefulness and Megan is beginning to play her part too.

Now it's back to Burford House where we can wash and

change. As we walk, I casually mention to Henry that it is a strange coincidence that both the nursing sisters are called Magdalene.

"It's not coincidence," answers Henry in a tone that shows his surprise at such a naïve comment.

"No? Why not?" I respond in all innocence

Henry looks uncomfortable and explains quite frankly that this is because they both used to be whores of some sort.

"Whores?" I exclaim.

"Yes, whores. Why else would they be called Magdalene?"

I look at him open mouthed as he continues. "If not actual whores, then loose women or young girls who liked boys too much. They probably became with child and that's how they ended up in the Abbey."

I look at Henry again and he adds, "You know, whores like Mary Magdalene?"

The significance of what he's saying begins to sink in and I remember the Catholic Church used to take pregnant girls – or those who had given birth or maybe even just had boyfriends and could possibly not be virgins any more – and lock them away in slave camps called laundries to punish them and 'cure' their sexual desires. In Ireland, this carried on until the very end of the 20th century.

I think about this and then observe, "So part of the reason they are called Magdalene is so that the world knows about their past?"

"Of course," responds Henry as if I have stated the blindingly obvious.

"And the reason why it is their job to nurse the two sisters is because their lives are worth less than the other sisters?" I ask rhetorically.

"Well, yes, but also because it gives them the chance to cleanse their souls and enter Heaven having spent less time in Purgatory."

"Oh, of course!" I add sarcastically, but Henry doesn't catch on.

At this point, we enter Burford House and the conversation ends as we go our separate ways. I've just had a hard reminder that the 14th century isn't just like the 21st century but without electricity.

CHAPTER EIGHTEEN

IT'S LATER THAN YOU THINK!

We go back into the house and the usual greeting party is nowhere to be seen. It seems the fear of where we've been is overpowering. Scabbard says, "I will organise hot baths for you both immediately, sirs."

I look at Scabbard and know I have to make sure he won't contaminate anything, or anyone, including us, by not cleaning himself first.

"Scabbard, I know you like to serve us but..."

"It is my duty, sir," interjects Scabbard with a very indignant tone in his voice.

I take a deep breath and chose my words carefully. "Yes, Scabbard, but in order to serve us, you must remain fit and well. You will be no good to me, Sir Henry or the Lord if you are ill or even dead."

I pause for a while and allow Scabbard to absorb this. "So, before you get our baths ready, I want you to take your clothes off and soak them in hot water, without anyone else touching them, and then have a hot bath yourself before preparing our baths."

Scabbard, confused, looks at Henry who gives him a slight smile. Scabbard then looks at me and says, "As you wish, sir."

Scabbard turns to leave and I add, "Oh, and give the same instructions to Megan."

"Yes, sir," he replies with a half-turn and then disappears leaving Henry and me to go to our respective rooms and wait.

I sit on my bed with a mix of emotions. They vary between being rather fearful of what I may have caught and boredom because of waiting for the bath. There's no TV to watch, no internet to play with, no Ipod to listen to, and not even a book to read. They have books in the middle of the 14th century, but Chaucer is a little young to be prolific yet and, anyway, I've read most of his stuff. Thinking of this, I begin to think that without this love of Chaucer, I probably wouldn't be here. Or if I were, I wouldn't understand people and would have no chance of making myself understood. Is this just luck or has some force brought me here for a reason? If so, why? The Time Lords would not allow me to do all the things I'm doing if it would alter the future. The philosophical debate about a man who goes back and kills his own grandfather, which he could not do because that would mean he would never have been born in order to go back and do it, keeps running through my head. No matter how much I rationalise things, I can't avoid thinking that this is all part of a plan. How else could it have happened? But whose plan and why should I be chosen to carry it out? Perhaps there is a God. If so, surely he has more effective ways of helping people through the Black Death? After all, he is omnipotent – allegedly! The Time Lords would not have approved, so who did? Or what? And why? Perhaps it was the fairies. That seems as reasonable as it being the Time Lords or God!

Suddenly I feel tired, probably because of the stress, and I lie on my bed for a rest. That's the last thing I remember until I become aware of loud knocking on my door.

"Who? What? Where am I? Oh, er, come in!"

"Sorry to wake you, sir," says Scabbard, standing in the doorway. "Your bath is waiting, sir."

"Em, yes, I'm coming. I didn't mean to fall asleep." I follow Scabbard to a room where a tub of almost boiling water is waiting.

"There you are, sir, and there are some of Sir Henry's clothes for you to change into.", says Scabbard pointing to a neat pile of clothing.

"Thank you, Scabbard," I say as the door closes behind him.

Cautiously dipping my toe into the water I realise it's hotter than I would get into at home. Having said that it should be as hot as possible, I can hardly complain but there's no cold tap. I lower one foot in and the water comes halfway up my calf. It's just about bearable but I pull it out again and look at the red mark. I put it back in and it's less painful this time. Now the other leg goes in and I'm standing in the tub. Slowly I lower my bottom until it touches the water. "Aah!" I yell and stand up again. It takes me at least five minutes to sit down and then I look around for some soap. There it is on a small table next to the bath tub. The tub itself appears to be made of wooden planks and held together with metal staves – rather as an old beer barrel would have been. It gently oozes water. Well, I find what I suppose is meant to be soap, although, what it's made of, I don't like to think about. It's probably some sort of tallow. Having washed my body I wonder what to do with my hair. I have no choice other than to use the 'soap'. By now the water is cool enough to put my head under, though there's not a lot of room to move in the tub. If this is what the very rich have to bathe in, what do the poor use? They probably have nothing at all. Once I've wet my hair, I begin to work the soap into it. Then there's a knock at the door.

"Come in."

The door opens and Scabbard stands there with a sort of sheet in his hands.

"I've come to get your clothes to wash, sir."

"Oh, yes, thank you, Scabbard."

He comes in and picks up the clothes in the sheet, being careful not to touch them. He's clearly taken on board my instructions and this time I can't help but notice how clean he looks. He walks towards the door with his bundle and turns to say, "Thank you, sir."

I give a little nod, slowly learning that I've probably been treating Scabbard with more respect than our respective class positions would dictate. Scabbard goes out again, leaving me to finish off washing my hair and then I lie in the bath and soak for a while – the most luxurious feeling I've had since I arrived.

After a long while, the too hot bath begins to get a little cool, so I stand up and look at my lobster-like body. No permanent harm has been done, though. It was just a very hot bath. Sorting through the clothes Scabbard has left behind, it's difficult to work out what goes on first and where. Suddenly I realise that Scabbard will be a little confused when he sees my underpants. Oh, sod it, I think. It's too late now anyway and they can't be more confusing than many other things about a man from the 21st century. In the pile of clothes I find an undershirt, a tunic, a sleeveless jacket, long socks (or stockings) and, to my surprise, a pair of basic briefs. Donning them all I feel a bit like a pantomime character but, also, more comfortable knowing that I'll fit in better in the 14th century.

I step out and into the reception area, which is empty, and now I have no idea what to do as this is the first time I've been alone, except in my bedroom. Hopping from foot to foot for a while, I decide to wander around the house. No sooner have I taken a few steps than one of the kitchen staff comes out of a door and stops, staring at me.

"Hello. Oh, uhm, good day", I say correcting my 'English'.

Her eyes move up and down and after apparently realising that I'm wearing different clothes, her expression of apprehension turns to a smile. "Oh, there will be some food served soon, sir."

"Oh, thank you, I'll be upstairs."

Back in my room, I'm once more filled with the sense of a lack of entertainment. It's difficult to cope without the 21st century's distractions. How would Henry cope in the 21st century? We will never know! Looking out of the window and across the estate I can see a bath being filled outside. What's going on? Is someone else having a bath? Looking out towards Swinbrook, I can see the small village which only consists of a few houses, but I can't help but think that it doesn't grow much over the next nearly 700 years. As I look around and time passes, a number of buckets of hot water are brought out to the bath and then a naked man emerges from the house and dips his toe into the bath just as I did earlier. As I watch, feeling a bit like a pervert, there's a knock at the door.

"Come in."

"Sir, are you ready for dinner?" asks Scabbard as he opens the door.

"Oh, yes. I'll come down now."

Scabbard waits at the open door and I follow him down to the dining room where he holds the door open for me.

Henry is already sitting at the table and I walk in to his greeting of, "Come in. Sit down." He gestures with his hand to the place opposite him.

As I sit down, I notice four places have been set. Henry and I now begin to chat like two old friends who are very close when the door opens and in walk the Lord and Lady. Standing up I give a slight bow and sit again as they take their seats. Clearly the Lord wants a report on the morning's proceedings, so we both start talking. The table is still bare of food and as Henry and I are recounting the day's events, the door opens again and in walks Megan with a large tray. I'm seated opposite the door and glance up and then turn towards Lord Burford again, only to look back at Megan as my jaw drops at the vision of loveliness that has just walked through the door. For the first time, I'm seeing Megan with her hair clean and brushed. Previously I thought I would fancy her if she were cleaned up but I never thought she'd be this gorgeous. Being slim and young she looks good without a bra, but I've previously noticed how older, bigger women look saggy and shapeless without a bra. I become aware that I'm staring, so I close my mouth and force myself to look away. Megan puts the food down as she shyly catches my eye. Previously she hasn't flirted in Lord Burford's presence, but she must have realised I am staring and can't resist responding. Having placed the food on the table she walks towards the door and gives a quick look back as she leaves, just to make sure I'm still looking. I am.

Struggling to get my mind off the lovely Megan, I join Henry in telling them about our visit to the Abbey. As Henry had not been shocked by what we found and it was no more than he had expected, he leaves it largely to me to tell about the horrors of the dead pigeons, bloodletting, closed windows and leaches. Lord Burford takes a deep interest in the 'funny' ideas I have and seems to be convinced by my argument that blood is necessary for good health and reducing it is not a good idea at all. As for the dead pigeons, he doesn't appear to be at all convinced as to the efficacy of this 'treatment' anyway. What is more difficult to get over, though, is the concept that there's no such thing as a miasma.

"Surely there must be," says the Lord, "or else how did disease get transmitted from one sick person to another?"

Not feeling able to go into detail about oxygen, nitrogen and carbon dioxide, I restrict myself to saying that little animals inside the sick person are coughed, or sneezed, out and then go onto other people. "Yes, we can see little drops flying around when people cough," the Lord adds helpfully.

"Ah, but that is not only liquid. The tiny animals are inside the droplets," I reply, restraining myself from talking about how viruses cause the body to cough or sneeze, just so that they can spread themselves to other hosts.

The idea of a tiny animal that could think for itself would just be too much for a medieval man, even if he clearly does have an intelligent mind. Anyway, I'm obviously winning over the most powerful man in town so there's no need to over complicate the issue. At this point, I remember an expression my father has used ever since I can remember. It's 'coughs and sneezes spread diseases', so I repeat it a couple of times for effect.

Lord and Lady Burford like this, as does Henry, so I latch onto it and repeat it many times. There is a pause and I cannot resist asking, "Is this chicken?"

"No, it is goose!" says Lady Burford, surprised that I don't know the difference, but I have never eaten goose.

"But what can we do?" asks the Lord, wanting to get to the cure rather than the theory.

"Well, we must impress on everybody not to sneeze on anyone else and to blow their noses on rags. Those who do have kerchiefs, must wash them very often and replace them with new ones as often as possible. This really is vital if we are to stop the spread of this pestilence or any other disease." I toy with the idea of asking him to stop people constantly spitting in the street, but refrain from doing so, as I feel this would probably be asking too much. He may simply ask where else they should spit and I'll have no answer.

"Mmm," replies the Lord. He picks up a small bell on the table and shakes it. Within seconds Megan appears at the door. She must have been waiting outside. She enters, curtsies and asks, "My Lord?"

"Oh Megan, ask Scabbard to come here, would you?"

"Yes, my Lord." She curtsies again and leaves the room.

At this point, I can't help but note how relatively polite Lord Burford is to a person of such a low social order. She is not just a maid but also probably not free, either a serf or a villein, and even worse, she's Welsh!

Soon Scabbard appears and the Lord indicates for him to pull up a chair near to the table; not actually at the table.

"Edmund, would you repeat to Scabbard your explanation about coughs and sneezes?"

"Yes, sir," I oblige and off I go repeating what I had said before but this time a little more succinctly. I also get Scabbard to repeat, "Coughs and sneezes spread diseases! Coughs and sneezes spread diseases! Cough and sneezes spread diseases!"

Then Lord Burford adds, "Now make sure everybody in the town knows this."

"Yes, sir," Scabbard says as he departs.

I'm impressed that before the 21st century's age of mass media it's still possible to spread health education.

The conversation moves on and Lord Burford asks the awkward question I've been fearing. "Will the sisters survive?"

I take a deep breath and say, "To be honest, I don't know, but their chances will be increased if the Abbey follows my instructions. More importantly, it will increase the chances of other people not getting the disease, which is far more helpful."

"Mmm, yes. I have issued instructions that if anyone else is afflicted they are to be kept in their homes by boarding them up along with their family."

I'm shocked to silence! Then I choose my words carefully and, as respectfully as I can, offer some advice. "May I suggest that only the sick person is boarded into his or her home and that the rest of the family is moved elsewhere and kept separate from the rest of the townsfolk?"

There is another silence – a thoughtful one – as Lord Burford decides whether or not this is a good idea or even possible. After a few seconds, he looks at me so I add, "If we board the whole family into the house, inevitably almost all will get the disease, but if we isolate the other family members they are likely to survive but won't infect others."

"Mmm, alright.", he says with a decisive tone of voice, "When Scabbard returns I will tell him to arrange for one of the barns to be used for these people."

Barn, I think, but keep quiet. After all, it's summer and the alternative is much worse. I allow myself a warm feeling and then add, "The rest of the family will be quarantined".

"Quarantined?" asks Lord Burford thoughtfully. "Ah yes! As in the Italian Jewish quarter of the town where they are kept away from the rest of the people."

I hadn't thought of this when I used the word "quarantine" but it makes sense and I've learnt something from a 14th century man about the root of a 21st century 'English' word.

At this point, there's a knock on the door and Megan enters with another little curtsy and I wonder how old people behave when their knees are too stiff to do regular curtsying.

"Sir, Father Mackenzie is here and wishes to speak to you, sir."

"Oh, send him in, Megan."

She disappears and with a raised eyebrow Lord Burford asks rhetorically, "I wonder what he wants?."

Father Mackenzie enters and with his hands together in prayer mode gives an obsequious smile and bow, saying, "My Lord, my Lady, Sir Henry, Sir Edmund."

Sir, eh? I think to myself. At least he knows his place!

"Yes, Father, what do you want?" asks Lord Burford rather curtly.

"Sir, I have heard of the good work being done today in the Abbey." He pauses.

"Yes?" Lord Burford encourages him to go on.

"So I would like to say a Special Mass in the church tonight to ask the Lord our God to give his blessing to the work being done in the temporal world."

"Oh, yes, Father. What time do you suggest?"

"It's entirely up to you, sir," Father Mackenzie replies, becoming even more obsequious.

"Shall we say the eighth hour, Father?"

"Yes, that would be perfect, sir," the priest replies as he shuffles backwards and out of the door, bowing so low that I wonder if he was ever in a yoga class.

As the door closes, Lord Burford lowers his head and says. "And a good donation from me for another Special Mass, no doubt!"

I understand I have a greater ally in Lord Burford than I

realised. There's no doubt that he believes there's a family of Gods in the sky pulling the strings but he seems aware of the self-serving nature of the Church.

The eighth hour, I think to myself and glance out of the window to see the lengthening shadows and realise it's a lot later than I thought. How long did I sleep for after returning from the Abbey? The idea that Henry and I would go around town this afternoon will now obviously have to be left until tomorrow. At this point there's a knock at the door and Megan enters again with another tray of food and puts a bowl in front of me. As I begin to eat, it appears to be some sort of pudding made with flour, honey and plums.

"Ah, fruit," I say, more to myself than anyone else.

"You like fruit, do you, Edmund?" asks Lady Burford.

"Yes, I do and this is really delicious," I reply quite genuinely.

"Good," Lady Burford says with a glow of pride.

Even though she has probably not cooked it, she obviously feels she's being complimented. As we're finishing our meals, I look at the Lord and enquire, "Did I, erm, see a bath being prepared in the garden earlier on?"

"Yes, we thought as Megan and Scabbard were bathing, the rest of the staff may as well do so as well. After all, it is such a lovely summer's day", explained Lord Burford. I hope that this idea might catch on!

Soon the meal is over and we all leave the dining room. Henry and I walk together and I ask, "Do you have anything I could read please, Henry?"

"Yes, of course," says Henry turning in his stride and going back the other way. Coming to a large, heavy door, Henry opens it to reveal a library full of books. I beam and start to look along the shelves.

"I'll leave you to it," says Henry, disappearing.

I look at the hundreds of books, all made of materials that don't seem like paper – or if it is, very rough paper. There are hundreds of titles and names I've never heard of, even though I spent years studying medieval literature. Finally a title catches my eye. The Divine Comedy by Dante Alighieri. This is a book I've heard of but never read. Plucking it off the shelf I hurry to my room to read this gem of poetic literature. Once I'm in my room, I fling myself on my bed and begin to read. What would my English teacher, Miss Stables, think of this? Not only am I reading the famous Divine Comedy, but I'm reading it in its original medieval English translation in a genuine medieval book. So entranced am I that I don't notice the passage of time and feel deprived when Henry knocks on my door and walks in saying, "Time to go, Edmund."

The two of us walk to the main door of the house and Henry asks, "Are you enjoying the book?"

"Yes, I am." That little gremlin once more appears on my shoulder, so I add, "But I have not yet reached The National Express or The Frog Princess."

"Er, I do not remember those."

"Oh, never mind."

"That was another of your obscure comments, wasn't it?", Henry observes with a knowing smile.

I just smile as we reach the great door where it seems the whole Burford household is waiting. I feel a little guilty as I'm sure the Lord and Lady should not be kept waiting.

"Sorry to keep you all waiting," I say a little nervously.

"Pay that no mind," says Lord Burford kindly and the others mumble in respectful agreement.

Off we all go and just before we reach St John the Baptist's church, the Lord comes up to me and says quietly, "You will be careful, won't you, Edmund?"

"Yes, sir, of course I will." Lord Burford nods and we enter the church.

This time the service, or ceremony, I'm not quite sure what it is, passes relatively quickly as the priest stands at the front apparently talking to himself and all the others chant when required. I join in too as I'm getting better at this ritual. Soon it's all over and Father Mackenzie hurries to the door to do a bit more grovelling as Lord and Lady Burford pass through. By the shadows outside I estimate we've been inside for about half an hour. I don't know how much of a donation Lord Burford would be expected to give, but guess it will be quite a lot for half an hour's work. Oh well, what price could be put on God's blessing? I think to myself. As we walk away from the church, Father Mackenzie watches us. Then he turns to another priest and says, "We must watch that one. I think the Bishop of Gloucester should know."

Back at Burford House, Henry says to me, "Have another read. There will be some supper just before dusk."

At a guess it is now about the ninth hour, so I assume I have about one hour to read my new-found love, as it is still virtually midsummer and remains just about light enough till around ten. I'm engrossed in the book once more, but when there's a knock on the door, I call out, "Come in."

The door opens to reveal Megan with a bowl and a towel. "This is for you, my good sir, and supper will be ready when you have washed."

"Thank you, Megan."

She puts down the bowl and just seems to hang around. I don't know how to take this and stumble to say, "Thank you for your help today. It was very useful."

She smiles and gives a nervous little curtsy. I'm sure she's doing more than just flirting, but I simply don't know how to get off with a girl from the Middle Ages, especially as she's nearly 700 years old. Eventually the conversation grinds to a halt and Megan edges towards the door and closes it behind her. Oh my God! Have I blown it? But if I do make a move, what about later on? It's probably best I don't.

I quickly wash and go downstairs to the dining room. No one is there yet but on the table there's a sumptuous choice of breads and cheeses, plus, of course, the ubiquitous beer. I had quite a lot of beer at the previous meal and perhaps that was why the Special Mass seemed to pass so quickly! Soon Henry walks in and we sit and chat about the day and nothing at all really. The breads are all a little too heavy for my liking but the cheese is lovely and very flavoursome. The conversation goes on until it is completely dark, which I estimate is about half past ten. So Henry and I withdraw to our respective rooms and I slip my clothes off and fall on the bed. There's no time to think about the day as sleep comes almost instantly.

CHAPTER NINETEEN

AROUND THE TOWN: MORNING

I get up the next morning and go down for breakfast. Having been here – or is it there – for a few days now, I'm beginning to experience it all as normal. Rising, washing in the water brought by Scabbard, and having breakfast seem no surprise and of little consequence. Henry is already waiting and the two of us chat about the day ahead.

Meeting Scabbard and Megan at the door, we head off towards the Abbey. Before we get there I stop and turn to the other three. "We will not go into the Abbey, we'll just speak at the door" I say.

"Is that to avoid the pestilence?" asks Henry.

"Yes, partly. There's no point in taking unnecessary risks and, also, we don't need to go through the same procedure as yesterday unless there is a problem we need to go in for".

"Alright."

Then Megan opens her mouth as if to speak and closes it again.

"Yes, Megan, what do you want to say?" I ask.

"Well, sir, I was just wondering... if..."
"Yes, Megan, get to the point, please."

"Well, sir, I thought it might be good if I went into the Abbey to check if everything is being done properly."

I look at her.

Then she gabbles, "Oh no, sir. Sorry, sir! I didn't mean to be presumptuous, sir. It's just that, well, I think I know what you require, sir, and I thought I could be of more help to you, sir, but I didn't mean to... Oh, er, sorry, sir."

I gather my thoughts and say, "Yes, Megan, that is a very good thought." There is a long pause. "But you are aware it increases your chances of catching the disease?"

"Yes, sir, but if it will help the nuns..."

"Very well I will speak to the Reverend Mother and explain things. You are only to go in and see what's going on and give instructions. Do not stay longer than is necessary. Is that okay?"

There was another long silence. "Sir, I don't know what the word 'okay' means?"

Henry jumps in by saying, "Yes, I have also been wondering about that, Edmund. You keep on using the word."

Suddenly realising I've been using a word that is not used in the 14th century I try to explain it away. "Oh, er, sorry. It's a word we use at home. It means 'Is everything good?' or 'Are you happy?' It's used to confirm something or as an interrogative."

"Oh, I see," says Henry.

Quickly moving the conversation on, I tell Megan, "I want you to come to the door with me and I will tell the Reverend Mother you are here to oversee my instructions and then you are to leave."

"Okay," replies Megan with a smile and we all approach the Abbey door, watched by a gathering crowd like yesterday. Before we can get there, however, it is opened by a nun saying, "Come in, sirs."

"No, Sister, we will not all come in today, but may I speak to the Reverend Mother?"

"Yes, sir, she is on her way."

"Thank you."

There then follow a few seconds of nervous waiting as the nun hops from foot to foot. Then the Abbess arrives. "Good day to you all. Please come in."

"No, Mother. I spoke yesterday before about unnecessary risks, so we will not all come in, but Megan will go in to see how the sisters are..."

"Oh, they seem more comfortable..." interjects the Abbess.

"Good! So, Megan will carry out my wishes and then leave," I say, trying to adopt an air of authority.

The Abbess looks at Megan rather questioningly but says, "Come in, Megan."

Megan bends down, opens her bag, takes out her muslin mask and begins to put it on. The thought passes through my head that I should check whether it has been washed or whether it is a new one but I restrain myself realising that Megan is an intelligent girl and she is proving a great asset to me in this situation. I get the impression the Abbess is rather put off by the idea of such a young girl being put in charge, but further admires Megan for her courage and maturity. As she enters, I say, "Thank you, Reverend Mother. Megan knows what is required." I'm trying to give Megan a bit of back up and then turn to walk away. Henry and Scabbard follow.

As we walk I turn to Henry and ask, "Is the Abbess a bit put off that such a young girl should be delegated to giving orders?"

There is a second's pause and Henry says, "I suppose by 'put off' you mean a little insulted?"

"Yes," I reply, realising I've done it again.

"That is one reason, yes, but I think the main reason is because she is only a serf."

I had not thought of this but remember once more from the Domesday Book that the word 'serf' and 'slave' are used interchangeably. It dawns on me that Megan has no rights whatsoever. She owns nothing and can do nothing, or go nowhere, without permission of the Lord of the Manor. She may not be in shackles but legally is no freer than a Negro on a sugar plantation. But where would she go anyway? Her parents were killed in one of the wars in Wales, so she's probably lucky to be alive and have a place to live and food to eat. There are no Social Services that would look after her in Wales, and there probably are hundreds of Welsh children in the same position who simply starved to death. Such are the Middle Ages!

"Sir Edmund," says Scabbard and I turn to look around, realising he is hanging back. He probably wants a talk, rather than the odd word, so I stop and listen along with Henry.

"I have been around the town and at any house where there is some sort of sickness, someone will meet us and tell us the problem."

"Oh, good. You have done well, Scabbard. That will save us wasting time."

"And, um, the blacksmith humbly requests you go into the forge to discuss something he is doing for the Lord", Scabbard adds.

"Oh, well, yes, we can do that," I reply, wondering what that is all about.

As usual, the town is full of market stalls and business being conducted. An uncomfortable thought crosses my mind and I turn to Henry and ask, "How do all these products get into the town?"

"They came in through the official points and all care has been taken to check where they came from."

"Good, but I am concerned that the sisters probably got the infection from some of the clothes brought into the town."

"If I may help there, sir?" offers Scabbard.

"Of course, go on, Scabbard."

"We now know that the two sisters visited a sick household in Alvescot and that must have been where they got the sickness from."

"Oh, I see! Well, that's good to know. At least now we understand how it got into the town. But it shows how careful everybody needs to be."

"Yes, sir, but the nuns must visit the sick, if only just to pray for them."

I nod. What else can I do? The nuns are, knowingly, risking their lives to help these people. I can hardly tell them they should not. They may be of some help and even the prayers may give help and some solace to those who believe – which, of course, everybody does in the Middle Ages. Probably the most effective medicine they have is the placebo effect. Anyway, what use are nuns if they do not help the sick and pray for them? Without that belief, there would be no point in being a nun.

We carry on with business and walk up the road. A woman stands in the road and approaches Scabbard as we pass. Why Scabbard? It's probably because she's too humble to approach the Lord's son. This woman is one of those who was to wait outside if they wanted a visit from the strange 'doctor'. Scabbard looks at me and tells me that the woman's husband has been ill for few days.

"Well, tell me your husband's symptoms, Madam?" I ask the woman.

"What, sir?"

"What is wrong with your husband?"

"Oh sir, he has been ill for a few days."

"Yes?"

"He is very weak, feverish, often sick and keeps shitting."

"Alright, we will come in and see," I say, consciously avoiding the term 'okay'.

All three of us don our makeshift masks, which causes the woman to look at us quizzically, and follow her into the house. In a chair sits a middle aged man, fully dressed and soaked in what is probably sweat.

"John, John," says the woman. "Sir Henry and Sir Edmund have come to see you."

"No, no, I'm alright, I haven't got the pestilence.", John insists.

Clearly the poor man is more concerned with the consequences of having the plague than anything else. He doesn't want his house to be boarded up with his family inside, all virtually facing certain death.

"It's alright, John," I say reassuringly, "just let me have a look at you." Turning to the woman, I ask, "What's your name, Madam?"

"Oh, it's Maria, sir, and my children are.."

"Yes, yes, Maria. Can you help me take his top clothes off?"

"Oh, certainly, sir."

The two of us struggle to get John's top clothes off as he continues to protest his perfect health. When his chest is exposed, I lift his arm whilst asking Maria,

"How long did you say he has been ill?"

"Oh, two or three days now, sir." This is reassuring, as any symptoms would have become apparent by now if it were the bubonic plague.

On lifting his arm I'm hit by the smell of stale sweat, but nothing at all to compare with the stench that surrounded the sick nuns. Mind you, there are no dead pigeons either. Looking into his hairy armpit is not a pleasant experience, so I lower it as quickly as possible. Then I turn John around to look at the other armpit.

Lowering the second arm, I look at Maria and say, "I don't know exactly what is wrong with John, but I am as sure as one can be that he does not have the plague." There is a cry of joy from Maria and a string of names erupts from her as ten years appear to disappear from the woman's face. In through the door comes a stream of children of varying ages all running to their mother and father who fall into what looks like an oversize tubby cuddle.

"Woe, woe, woe!" I exclaim. "I said he doesn't have the plague but that doesn't mean he's not infectious."

"Oh, sir?" responds the mother, looking confused.

"D and V can be very contagious, so keep yo..."

"What, sir?"

"Diarrhoea and vomiting."

"Eh?"

"Shit and sickness!"

"Oh, er, sir, but he's not going to die?"

"Probably not, but the children must keep their distance until he starts to get better and you may tend him by washing him frequently with cool water. Try to get him to eat as much as possible. Maybe some soup."

"Soup, sir?" she asks as she looks around nervously at the fire with a pot on it.

"We only have pottage, sir."

I move to the fire and look at the blackened pot with some sludge in it.

"What is in this?"

"Oh, root vegetables, peas, oats and anything else we have, sir."

I realise then that this is their main diet, so I say, "Give him some of the liquid until he gets stronger. Then you can give him the thicker bits. And, er, keep the…" I look around for windows but there are none really, just holes with wood in them. "Keep the, er, door open as much as possible. Take his clothes off and put him to bed till he can stand easily. Then wash his clothes and the bed he's been in."

"Oh, yes, sir, that I can do now. It's the middle of summer."

"Good."

"Are you sure he will not die, sir?"

"Not if you follow my instructions, Maria."

"Oh, I will, sir. Out you go children! Get on with your work and I will bring you some food later. Oh, thank you, sir. Thank you. Thank you. Thank you!"

Henry, Scabbard and I hurry out and I remove my mask, as do the other two.

"I want to wash," I say to no one in particular.

"There is a trough up here, sir," Scabbard offers.

A trough! Oh dear, where can I start, I think to myself. Oh well, it's better than nothing I suppose. When we get to the trough, I say to Scabbard, "Use that little bucket to pour water onto my hands so that the water does not go back into the trough". This Scabbard does for me and then for Henry. Finally, I pour water onto Scabbard's hands, but he seems very embarrassed that I should serve him.

On we go, followed by a growing crowd, to a large building that's emitting smoke and a funny smell along with it.

"This is the foundry," says Henry and we turn to go in.

As we enter, we are hit by a wall of heat. Men are running around all over the place and sparks are flying. I think to myself that I have never been big on health and safety but a few goggles wouldn't go amiss. Work virtually stops as the foundry workers look at us and the usual bowing and scraping commences. A man who appears to be some sort of foreman approaches us and begins to talk to Henry. He has an old, lined, ruddy face that's probably the result of working next to such heat. I can't help but notice that the man's hands and arms are covered in scars, probably caused by sparks from the furnace or drops of hot iron. He looks to be in his 70's or 80's but I wonder how old he really is. I'm so intent on working out the man's age that I hardly hear him tell Henry that the reason why I'm wanted is in the next section.

Henry, Scabbard and I file through the foundry and into the next area where there is another furnace. It immediately becomes obvious that this section is not an iron foundry but a glass making factory. Two fires are burning and spitting, and on them are two large pots boiling with a substance which is obviously glass. Once more, work virtually stops as we enter and, much to my relief, we stop at the edge of the working area as a man approaches us. He too is covered in little scars but does look younger than the other man. More bowing and scraping follows and then Henry says to me, "This is Harold, the chief glass smith and he would like some help on making the right sort of glass for the star looker."

Oh my God, I think. He thinks I know what I'm talking about! Oh well, better try to blag it like I have with virtually everything else since I've been here. I turn to Harold and ask, "Have you got some examples of glass that have not come out perfectly and have distortions in them?"

"Oh, yes, sir, we've got plenty of those. If you'd like to come outside with us..."Henry and I nod and the man walks towards a side door followed by Henry, Scabbard and me.

At the door there is a little bit of confusion as Harold opens the door, goes through it, and immediately scurries back to hold it for his betters as we go through. Once outside, he directs us towards a few large boxes all filled with broken glass. Looking in, but not wanting to put my hand in, I look for a good piece of distorted glass and then lean forward to carefully pick it up.

"Oh no, sir, you let me do that, sir," says Harold, quickly going to pick up the piece. Taking the piece from him and holding it up I lower myself slightly to look through the distorted bit. Then, getting into my role of a Norman aristocrat, I say, "Could you pick out a few bits like that, my man?"

Harold quickly produces five or six similar bits of broken glass and I say, "You see how, as the light passes through the distorted part, things on the other side look bigger and misshapen?"

"Oh yes, sir, I have noticed that before, sir."

"Well, that's what we want, but without the misshapen bits, so try to make it as good as possible."

Harold looks a bit confused and grunts, so I try to clarify the point by saying,

"Try to make it convex."

"Eh, sir?"

"Try to make it so it is thicker in the middle than it is at the edges."

"Oh, I see, sir."

"Polishing the glass as well would probably make the image clearer," I add, thinking they must know what polishing is as they work with wood. There is a pause then Harold asks, "The im–idge, sir?"

"Yes, what you see on the other side of the glass," I tell him, hoping that will be enough. It seems it is, so I ask, "Do you think you can do that, Harold?"

"Oh yes, sir, I can certainly do that, sir. Oh yes, sir, don't you worry about that, sir.", he assures me.

"Good. Then get two bits of tubing, one sligh..."

"Of what, sir?"

"Tubing!" There was no response. "Piping?"

"Oh yes, sir, I can do that, sir."

I think and then add, "But not made of pottery or terracotta. It needs to be very thin and very light in weight."

Harold looks thoughtful and then smiles and says, "Oh yes, sir. I think I can do that, sir."

"Good. One must fit very tightly inside the other so it slides in and out. Then you put the glass at each end and slide in an out till you get a good focus on the moon."

"The moon?"

Realising my literal interpretation, I say, "For example."

Still there's no reaction.

"Or a star."

"Oh yes, sir. Yes, sir, yes, sir."

"Then you need to just keep trying different sorts of glass and length of tubing... er, piping, till you get a good picture of the moon or whatever."

"Yes, sir, uhm, er, how do I get the glass to stay at the end, sir?"

Realising I could be there all day, I start to move off saying, "I'm sure you can find a way, Harold. I have total faith in you, Harold."

"Oh yes, sir. Yes, sir. Oh, er, this way out, sirs. This way out, sirs," Harold says as he leads us out around the side of the foundry to the road. "It will mean you don't have to go through the heat, sirs."

This pleases me and I'm relieved to reach the street again.

Then Henry says to Harold, "Good day, Harold."

Harold clearly understands this means he is to clear off now. We start moving up the road and although I'm pleased to have avoided the heat, I rather wish I'd taken more notice of how the foundry and glass works operate.

At this point, Scabbard comes up close behind us and begins to speak to us both. "There is a family here who would like to talk to you, Sir Edmund."

"Yes?"

"Not because they think they have the disease, but the son has a strange sort of, er, er, er, possession."

Scabbard seems to whisper the word 'possession' as if it is something dirty and unmentionable.

"Oh well, we had better have a look."

"The house is here, sir."

As we turn towards the house I become aware that there are men in the street shovelling up the piles of horse shit. Wondering what they will do with it, I realise it will be spread on the land around the town as manure. There will certainly be fewer flies. Then my mind turns to the fact that Scabbard always manages to remain a respectful distance behind. What a degrading, feudal culture. I remember that Phil always keeps a respectful distance behind Betty and he's been doing it for decades. A degrading feudal culture, indeed!

Before we reach the door, it's opened by a bedraggled little man who is dirtier than most and looks as though he could do with a good meal. Scabbard walks up to us and says, "Sirs, this is Edward. His son, also Edward, is the afflicted one."

"Alright, we had better see him."

"Sir, sir," says Edward "He appears well, but sometimes..."

"Yes, Edward, let me see him.", I cut him off to get on with things as quickly as possible.

We step into the house for which the word 'hovel' seems to have been coined and there's a very unpleasant smell. The smell of poverty! There is young Edward sitting on a stool and standing in a dark corner is a woman, presumably the wife and mother.

"Do you think we could move closer to the door way?" I ask. "There I will be able to see better." I need any excuse to get away from the smell.

"Now, Edward, tell me what is wrong with young Edward?" Looking at the lad, I think he looks about ten or eleven.

"Well, sir, most of the time Edward is very well and then sometimes he... he... throws himself to the floor and, er, twitches and there is nothing we can do to stop this. Then he wakes up and seems... and seems... normal but he is always very tired and has no memory of what has happened."

"Mmm! Scabbard, may I talk to you?"

"Of course, sir."

I lead Scabbard outside, followed by Henry who is equally pleased to leave the smell. "Scabbard, I assume you know the family?"

"Yes, sir, I know all the families in the town."

"And what can you tell me about the boy?"

"What do you want to know, sir?"

"How old is he?"

"Fourteen years old, sir."

"Fourteen?"

"Yes, sir."

"They, uhm, seem very poor."

"That is because Edward cannot get much work because young Edward is possessed, sir." The whole family is cursed by young Edward's possession.", Scabbard explains.

"I see. Of course.", I say reassuringly.

"Come back in with me, Scabbard, and listen carefully to what I say as I want you to make sure the whole town knows what I have to say."

Inside, the family looks anxious and Henry, sensibly, stands at the door. The woman is standing by the doorway as I re-enter, so I ask her, "And what is your name?"

"Marie, sir," says the mother with a little curtsy.

I proceed to try to explain to the family, Henry and, most importantly, Scabbard, as he will have to put the word around town.

"Edward suffers from what is known as epilepsy."

Silence fills the room.

"That means he..."

"We have had many Special Masses said for him, sir," interjects the father.

This gives me a moment to think. There's no point in my explaining about electrical convulsions in the brain. Eventually, I find words I hope will put the point over.

"You know when people sometimes get cramps in their leg and it is very painful, with no control at all of the leg?"

"Oh yes, sir."

"Well, Edward gets cramps in his brain... inside his head, and that means he has no control of his body for a while, just like someone who has no control of their leg for a while."

There is a long silence and then Edward asks, "What can we do about it, sir?"

"Nothing at all, just as there is nothing you can do for someone who has a leg cramp." A sense of despondency descends upon the house.

"But I have no doubt that Edward is not possessed by demons or the Devil."

"Not possessed by the Devil, sir?"

"No, Edward. It is probably congenital... in the family. There's probably another person in the family who had the same problem."

Marie 'whoops' and hides her head in her hands. Edward screams, "You knew, Marie. You knew!"

"Edward, listen to me and listen carefully. It is not Marie's fault! It is not Marie's fault any more than it is Edward's fault. There is no possession going on. We will tell the world and from now on your life, and the life of your family, will get much better. You will be able to hold your head up in the town and all will know you are good people." There is a slow realisation as the parents and the child begin to understand. As I walk towards the door, I say to Scabbard, "You know what to do, don't you?"

"I think I do, sir. Yes, sir."

I know Scabbard well enough by now to accept he will carry out his duty and put the word around the town that neither Edward, nor any of his family, are possessed by anything. I already have a high opinion of Scabbard but it's now greatly enhanced by the thought he went out of his way to get the strange 'doctor' to visit someone whom he knew did not have the illness, just so that Edward and his family might be helped. Then I remember what Edward said about having Special Masses for young Edward. These Special Masses had to be paid for. The family is destitute, yet the church is making money out of their fear and desperation. Shameful.

CHAPTER TWENTY

AROUND THE TOWN: AFTERNOON

Looking up at the sun I can see it's about midday now and that, for the first time since I arrived, there are clouds building in the sky. As we move on, I notice another building with steam, smoke and a rather unpleasant odour coming from it. I turn to Henry and ask,

"What goes on here?"

"Aah, that's where they make vellum."

"Oh, really? Very interesting."

"Well, uhm, would you like to go in and have a look around?"

I think for a moment and then, without realising the significance, say, "If Scabbard doesn't mind?"

Turning to Scabbard, I can see his confused expression and realise I've made a mistake again by treating Scabbard as an equal.

"Oh, here's Megan, sirs," says Scabbard, conveniently changing the subject, and sure enough Megan is coming up the hill carrying a large basket.

"Ah, food. Good girl, Megan," Henry calls as she approaches.

Megan smiles. "Good day, sirs. I've finished at the Abbey and been back to have another bath and a change of clothes," she said coquettishly, tossing her head to show her lovely washed locks.

"Oh, I am pleased, Megan. Come and tell us all about it," I say.

Scabbard has already moved over to a grass verge and now takes the basket from Megan and starts to unpack the food and a jug of small beer.

As we settle onto a blanket which had been over the top of the basket Megan was carrying, I look at her and she begins to relate her visit to the Abbey.

"I went into the Abbey and immediately there was a strong smell of vinegar, so I knew things had been scrubbed and all the surfaces looked very clean. I asked about the cleaning, about the hand washing, about staying out of the room, about the wearing and washing of masks and not touching anything unnecessarily, and the windows were all open, and they had changed the bed clothes, and there were no dead pigeons around, and there had been no blood-letting, and... er... there was something else, but I have forgotten."

She drops her head. "Sorry, sirs."

"No, no, that's quite alright, Megan. You have done really well," I say quickly, not wanting to dampen her enthusiasm. A smile returns to her face as she lifts her head and swells with pride. It's probably the first time in her life that she has been trusted with an important job, and she hasn't failed.

Then she looks at me and adds, as if as a casual afterthought, "And then, of course, sir, I went back to the house and had another bath to make sure I don't infect anyone." She flicks her lovely newly washed hair with her fingers and gives me a flirtatious smile as I think this is probably the first time in her life that she has ever had a bath two days on the trot.

"But, Megan, there is just one little thing you have forgotten to tell us," I say teasingly. Megan's mouth opens and her eyes dart from side to side. Henry, Scabbard and I gaze at her for a couple of seconds in mock reproach, but then I can bear the cruelty no more and ask, "The two nuns..." I pause once more. "How are they?"

"Oh, Sister Cecilia and Sister Florence? They are still alive and seem to be less feverish. Sister Cecilia has even been able to eat a little food."

Her audience of three heave a sigh of relief and I wonder at Megan's casual attitude towards the improving health of the sisters. All I can think is that the assumption that I, Edmund, would make them well, has had the 'white coat effect'. My father has often talked about the placebo effect a pharmacist wearing a white coat has and he often says, "Don't knock it; it works!"

At this, my mind wanders to my father, my mother and my sisters. What must they be thinking? They haven't heard from me for days. They must be worried. When will I be able to talk to them again? Will I be back in the 21st century before they return from Australia? Will I ever be back in the 21st century again? I shiver at this thought and become aware that the other three are expressing their joy at the news of the sisters, and making Megan feel good about her part in their partial recovery. I join in the congratulatory noises and we all sit and eat our food with a warm sense of achievement. When I have had enough to eat, I move up the bank a little and rest my back against a tree, soaking up the midsummer rays. Once more I become aware of the fact that the picnic is not very private and that a lot of the inhabitants of Burford are watching us in a not so subtle way. Henry is obviously used to this, but I find it very disconcerting.

As I top up my suntan I notice a group of children across the road and down the hill. They have a ring shaped object they're throwing against a wall. Turning to Henry I ask, "What is that game those children are playing?"

"What, those girls down there?"

"No, those boys," I reply, pointing to the group of children.

"Boys!" exclaims Henry sounding rather confused. "They're not boys, they're girls."

"Girls! Surely they're all boys?" I ask.

There's a long pause and eventually Henry rationalises the situation by saying, "I think we have a translation problem here Edmund. 'Boy' is a term used to a servant as in, "bring me some wine, boy." Those are all girls. They are all knave girls. There are no gay girls there. They are playing a game called coyts.

"Oh!" I say, trying to terminate the conversation. I've learnt what their game is called but I'm now a lot more confused. It seems boys are waiters, or servants, and all children are girls. Male children are called knave girls and female children are called gay girls. I just can't cope with this concept. For the first time the difference between 14th century English and 21st century English is just too much for me to get my head around.

When we've all finished eating, Megan begins to pack up the picnic and place things back in the basket. Henry looks at her and says "Megan, we're going to look around the vellum makers. Edmund is interested in it. We will continue looking for any ailments around the town thereafter, so you may either go back to the house and continue your duties, or you may accompany us."

Megan looks at Henry, then at me and then back at Henry again.

"Ooh, er, sir, if you don't mind me coming with you… if you think I can be of any use to you, then yes, sir, I will accompany you, sir."

"That's settled then," says Henry and begins to move towards the vellum makers.

As we enter the vellum makers, a man looks at us, sees Sir Henry and literally runs away. Thirty seconds later, he reappears behind another man who comes hurrying up to Henry saying, "Good day, Sir Henry. Good day, Sir Edmund, Scabbard." He just looks at Megan. "What brings you here, sir? How may I help you?"

"Edmund, this is Cedric, the vellum master and owner."

"Good day, Cedric," I say and the man gives a little bow.

"Edmund has expressed an interest in seeing how vellum is made and I told him you would be proud to show him the process."

I smile, thinking that Henry had said no such thing.

"Oh yes, sir. Oh yes, sir. I would be very proud to do that. So, er, shall we start by looking at the hide selection process?"

"Thank you, Cedric," says Sir Henry and the four of us follow Cedric into a large sort of warehouse area where there are piles of animal skins, all laid one on top of the other.

The room is full of steam and there are some giant pots boiling along the side of the room. There's a very unpleasant stench that gets to the back of my throat.

"This, sirs, is where we sort out those skins that are good, and those that are not good enough go in this box here."

Henry and I look in and mutter. Then Cedric takes us over to the three giant pots, all on their own iron grates with a fire under them. A man is busy running around stoking all the fires and putting more wood under them. I get the distinct impression the man is trying to look busy.

"Here is where we boil the hides in lime to get the fur or wool off them" explains Cedric.

Ah, lime, I think. That explains the discomfort in my throat, but it's not the only smell. There's also the stench of the boiling hides. Above the giant pots there's a large, long hole in the wall which, presumably, serves as a window and a chimney. Once more the thought of health and safety in the 21st century enters my head.

Then Cedric adds, "The best skins are from stillborn goats. They produce the smoothest parchment. Of course we need a lot of kids to make any small book with them."

I wonder how many stillborn kids are found naturally or how many pregnant nannies are slaughtered to get at their unborn kids?

"This way now, sirs."

The party leaves the building through another door and into the open air. All five of us, including Cedric, take deep breaths of the fresh air to clear our lungs of the foul, acrid stench. I think of the man inside who probably has to work there day after day, week after week, month after month, year after year. His lungs must be in a terrible state. Cedric points to a few washing lines that all have skins hanging on them. Apparently this is the next stage in the process.

"In here, sirs," says Cedric, opening a door to another building.

Inside is another large room with a different smell to it. As we enter, there is a flurry of excitement as the unexpected visitors are noticed. Henry turns to Cedric and says, "Tell them to just carry on."

Cedric waves his hands about and the workers carry on with their jobs. All around the room are wooden frames with skins tied to them. Three men are working on the skins with curved knives, scraping them. Henry looks at Cedric who takes his cue. "This, sirs, is where we stretch and scrape the skins."

There is a long pause as we look around.

"Then we tighten them again, scrape then again and stretch them again until they are the right thickness to be used."

The group spends a little time looking around, and we are then led out across a courtyard with wagons and couple of tethered horses, to a sort of shop.

"And this, sirs, is where we send them off to whoever wants them, and some even come in from the street to buy them."

We have a quick look around and soon we are back in the street giving our thanks to Cedric, whose reputation in the town has probably been enhanced greatly by our visit.

"Now, where to, Scabbard?" asks Henry.

"Sir, I only know of one other family where there is definitely a sickness amongst most of the family."

"Off we go, Scabbard."

I added, "Lead on , MacDuff."

Henry and Scabbard give me a quizzical look but I'm getting used to this. I look towards Megan but her eyes say something different. It makes me think of the adoring, well-practised gaze that the wives of American presidents give their husbands at their swearing in ceremonies. We set off down the hill and into a short side street. Scabbard is leading the way and he stops outside a little house, turning around and saying, "This is the home of Iain and Agnes and their family."

Once more the masks are passed around and tied over our mouths and noses.

Scabbard knocks on the door and it is opened by Agnes, who is clearly expecting guests and ushers us in. She looks bedraggled and not too healthy, but then again, it is always difficult to tell how old or how healthy the poor of the Middle Ages are. Inside is the usual musty, sweaty smell I've almost become used to, and there I see Iain slumped in a chair. I approach him and ask the usual trick question used by medical people, "How are you, Iain?"

"I'm fine, thank you, sir," he croaks in a voice that clearly suggests he's in a lot of pain. Even with his hoarse voice, a clear Scottish accent is noticeable.

"How long have you been in Burford, Iain?" I ask.

"Oh, many years now, sir. We came down to England during the famine to look for work."

"I see."

Then Iain adds, "Burford has been good to me and my family."

I can see Henry, Scabbard and Megan smiling with pride at the compliment from this incomer.

Everybody in the room is coughing and spluttering. Iain is feverish and smells of sweat. The family are clearly ill but is it the pestilence?

"Please remove your top clothes, Iain."

Iain looks confused but complies with the wishes of his better. Reluctantly I lift his dirty arm and inspect his arm pit.

"Who was the first to get ill?" I ask.

"I was," says Iain. "Five days ago. I haven't been able to work since."

This is long enough to assure me the buboes would have developed by now if it were the Black Death.

"Open your mouth please, Iain, and say aah."

He looks confused again but opens his mouth and makes the required noise. Looking into his mouth, I can clearly see spots all over his throat and tongue. "Alright, Iain, you may get dressed again." I then have a quick look at all the children and Agnes but am only interested in looking down their throats.

"You have all got tonsillitis," I tell them with a smile.

Silence!

"What, sir?" asks Agnes.

"Ton-sill-eye-tis," I say again. "It is a virus and not the pestilence."

Many sighs of relief and hoarse 'whoops' of joy follow.

"I expect you have had the same thing before?"

"Oh yes, sir, I have and I told people that but no one believes me."

"Mmm, it will go away, but you need to drink honey in warm water to ease your throat. Megan will bring you some willow herbs as well and you must take the wood out of the windows and get outside as much as possible."

Turning to Agnes, I say, "All of the kerchiefs must be washed as often as possible and get some clean clothes as well."

Agnes looks embarrassed and I realise the problem is that they probably don't have a change of clothes, so I add, "It is summer, so little clothing is needed. You can wash the children's clothes on a sunny day."

Agnes looks reassured.

"Megan can stay behind to give you advice on other things you can do. And if you could all have a bath that would aid your recovery."

Agnes and the children mutter, and then Agnes says "We can go to the river, sir, but …". I reassure her by saying "I'm sure Megan can sort something." I look at Henry and he looks at Megan with a nod. Megan gives one of her beaming smiles, and she stands to her full height and nods that she has understood.

As we are leaving, Agnes says nervously, "Excuse me, sir, but we can't go out because other people run away from us."

"Don't worry, Agnes, Scabbard will make sure everybody knows you are all not suffering from the disease."

Scabbard looks at me and says, "I will start immediately." Then he goes to the house next door and knocks on the door.

Henry and I walk off towards Burford House, our day's work completed, leaving Scabbard and Megan to carry out their allotted tasks. I look up at the sky which is darkening by the second as the clouds move in and begin to billow. I remember the old adage of an English summer: three hot days and a thunderstorm. I'm not particularly looking forward to the bath tub experience again, but I know I have to set an example if I expect others to do the same. As we pass the church, we are unaware that once more we are being followed by the eyes of Father Mackenzie.

CHAPTER TWENTY ONE

NORTHLEACH

The next couple of days just fly by as we again visit the sick in the town and the surrounding villages. This means I have to get on a horse again and pretend I'm a better horseman than I actually am. Anyway, it's all good practice. One of the villages to be visited is Northleach. I've been there many times before in the 21st century and have always been impressed by the large church for such a small settlement. As we approach the village, there's a road block, as there is at all the entrances to Burford.

"Stop there please, sirs,." calls one of the men at the road block.

Both Henry and I rein in our horses and Henry calls back, "I am Sir Henry Burford, son of Lord Burford, and this is Sir Edmund de Covny. We are both skilled medical practitioners."

The guards go into a conflab and then shout back, "Are you both healthy?"

"Yes, we are and we have come to see how the village is doing and to see if we can offer any help."

Another conflab ensues and the men begin to draw the barrier aside. As the two of us ride in there is the usual forelock tugging and words of welcome.

"Is there any pestilence in the village?" asks Henry

Silence!

Then one man who appears to be in charge says, "Well, er, we have two houses nailed up but we don't really know."

"Take me to them, now."

"To the house of sickness, sir?" he asks in surprise.

"Yes, now. Quickly, man!"

The man runs ahead, but not far into the small town, to a house next to the beautiful church, which looks quite dramatic in the village of the 14th century even though it has not changed much by the 21st century. The streets are still recognisable but there are fewer of them. The man stops by the house which has a guard outside and is literally nailed shut. By now it has become clear to me that Henry has taken control because his name carries weight that mine doesn't. I also realise that Henry has been very humble over the last few days, leaving me in charge in Burford.

"How are these people being fed?" I ask.

"Through here, sir," says the man, pointing to a small open window with a tray on the sill. Henry and I look through the hole as the stench floods out.

"Open the door!" says Henry forcefully.

"What, sir?"

"Open the door, we're going in!"

It seems that even the birds fall silent.

"Now!"

The men jump and begin to pull the boards off the front door as I open the bag to get out our masks, again being watched in amazement by the men and a gathering crowd.

When we enter, we see the family cowering and covering their eyes from the sudden light. There are two adults and four children, who clearly have no idea what's going on. Henry says in a calm but forceful voice, "I am Sir Henry Burford, son of Lord Burford and I command you to take off your top clothes."

No one moves and after a few seconds, Henry says a little louder, "Now!"

They begin doing as they were told, still having no idea why they should. First I go to the father and lift his arms, one after the other to look for buboes. Having looked at him, I then move on to the children who are looking very afraid, but can now see what is expected of them and that nothing bad has happened to their father. Finally, I approach the mother who has, naturally, been reluctant to take her clothes off. Once more I lift up both arms and inspect her armpits.

"You can all put your clothes on again," I say and we both leave as quickly as possible to take deep breaths of fresh air.

The men outside back off as we emerge and I address them saying, "None of these people have the sickness!"

Mumbling ensues and Henry takes over by saying, "None of these people have the sickness and they are no longer to be nailed up."

A sharp intake of breath is heard and Henry adds, "They are all ill and probably infectious, so you should avoid touching them until they are recovered, but they will recover. They will stay in the house but all the doors and windows are to be opened."

More intakes of breath and mumbling follow.

"A servant girl will come tomorrow and she is to be given everything she asks for and all instructions she gives are to be followed," instructs Henry.

"Now take us to the other house," I command, trying to don Henry's mantle of authority.

As we are being taken to the other house, I ask, "How long have that family been in there?"

"Oh, eight days now, sir, but the other family only since two days ago, when the father returned home ill."

"Mmm. How many are in there?"

"Three children and their parents, sir."

Soon we arrive at the other house and Henry demands the house be opened. This time the instruction is carried out immediately as Henry and I don our masks once more. As the door is opened this time, the man in charge calls in, "This is Sir Henry Burford and Sir Edmund de Covny and you are to do as they tell you."

Inside the smell is even worse than in the last house. On the floor in a corner a man is lying motionless. I look at the mother and kindly ask, "What is your name?"

"Daisy," she replies in a weak voice.

"Please remove your husband's top clothing."

Daisy looks very confused and frightened but begins to do as she has been told. The man does not respond and when his chest is revealed, Edmund tells her to now help the children remove their clothes and then her own.

I approach the man with great trepidation and lift his limp arm. Immediately the stench increases and I can see the pus running down his side and arm. There's no doubt that he has the plague and he seems to be completely lifeless. I just look at Daisy and she begins to weep saying, "He died this morning, sir."

He's clearly dead and I look at Henry saying, "I need water before I touch the others."

Henry walks to the door and calls for a bucket of water. Soon it arrives and is dropped at the door. Henry picks it up and walks over to me and I wash my hands in it before approaching the children. I inspect the first child and there are no apparent buboes. Then I inspect a girl of about six years old. She's sweating and seems to be in pain. As I lift her arm, the small buboes became apparent. I say nothing but walk over to the bucket to wash my hands once more. Then I approach the final child. Lifting both arms I can see nothing, and the child seems relatively healthy. Well, as healthy as any poor child can be expected to be in the Middle Ages. Turning to Henry I say, "We must get this dead man out of here and there is no point in anyone else touching him." Henry nods as I begin to pull the dead man by his arms. Daisy and the three children burst into tears as Henry goes out ahead.

Outside the crowd literally runs away as I pull out the body. Henry washes his hands once more and then empties the water into a nearby gully, calling for fresh water. No one touches the bucket, which is just as well, but soon another bucket of water arrives and I indicate to Henry to wash again first, ensuring no water drips back into the bucket, before I wash in the fresh water once more. I speak quietly to Henry. "Who is the man in charge?"

"He's the town reeve."

"The town what?"

"The reeve."

I look confused so Henry explains, "You know, the man in charge of organising the village, planting, harvesting and anything else like these circumstances."

"Oh, I see," I say, realising this is a word everybody would know during the Middle Ages. Telling myself that Henry will probably attribute my ignorance to my being 'foreign', I begin to think that the 21st century name Reeve, or Reeves, is probably derived from this position in the Middle Ages.

"Would you tell him to arrange a quarantine house for the two children and the mother?" I say. "Daisy may come back and forth to the child in here if she wants to, but if she does, she is not to have any contact with the other two children afterwards. Megan will know what to do in terms of cleaning and the washing of clothes. Tell them to also open windows and doors but to have no contact with anyone. This must continue until either the child recovers or… dies. Oh, and ask what the child's name is"

Henry speaks to the reeve as I wait. When he returns he tells me the child's name is Matilda and she is six years of age. I would have thought she was only four or five years old but I'm getting used to malnourished children looking younger than they actually are. Having finished our work in Northleach, we both mount our horses once more. As we turn to ride away, the two children and Daisy are emerging from the house to be taken to quarantine. As we trot off, the sound of a very distraught six-year-old's screaming rings in our ears. This is heart-rending for both Henry and me but it's the best we can do for the benefit of the rest of the family. Soon we're galloping along what will become the A40 back towards Burford. At the barrier outside the town we're greeted by Scabbard who has been left behind, along with Megan, to carry out my instructions around the town.

"A bath and clothes for us both," orders Henry and the two of us ride down the hill to go through the usual process.

Having bathed and changed yet again, Henry and I call for Scabbard and Megan to give them instructions. They arrive very soon, clearly enthusiastic to help in any way necessary.

"Megan, in the morning you can go to Northleach and do the same things as you have done in the Abbey," I tell her.

"Sir, there are a few hours of light left, so I could go now and be back before midnight?"

"Well, if you don't mind," I reply, realising once more that Megan is not used to being asked if she minds being told what to do. Even so, I'm once more impressed by her enthusiasm, commitment and maturity.

By the time Megan returns, both Henry and I are fast asleep.

CHAPTER TWENTY TWO

ALVESCOT AND CLANFIELD

At breakfast the next morning, Henry and I are joined by Lord Burford. He wants to know what happened in Northleach and I leave most of the explaining to Henry, who I think is coming into his own. This greater role for Henry is something that pleases me, not least because I'm hoping to get back to the 21st century as soon as possible. How this is to be achieved, though, I have no idea at all. Fortunately, I've been too preoccupied with the problems of the 14th century to have given much thought to whether or not I will ever be able to get back. Now that I've been here a few days, I'm concerned about what my friends in the 21st century will be thinking. Most of all, my family, now in Australia, must have called my home and my mobile many times and will be upset and concerned at getting no reply. One possibility of 'escape' has crossed my mind, and that is to take a horse when I'm on my own and simply ride to where I left my laptop. All I'll have to do is to disappear as I arrived, and the horse is bound to return home to where his food is. That would mean my conscience will be clear about the horse but I'll feel guilty about just disappearing on people who have been so good to me. Most of all, I'm concerned about my good friend Henry. Alternatively, I could tell Henry the truth and ask him to assist in my return. No, there is no alternative!

All these thoughts are racing through my head as Henry is relating yesterday's events to his father, and Henry's words rather fade into the background. So, when Lord Burford asks, "Do you think the young girl will survive?"

Instinctively, I just say, "What?"

There is a pause and Lord Burford asks, "Do you think the young girl with the disease will survive?"

Pulling myself back to the 14th century. I reply, "Er, that depends on many things. I am sure Megan will be able to help her a lot and I need to talk to her to see what happened last night when she went to Northleach."

"Your wish will be granted soon, Edmund, as I have told both Megan and Scabbard to be here after breakfast."

As soon as Lord Burford stops speaking, there is a knock at the door and in walks Scabbard on his own. "Ah, Scabbard, is Megan not with you?"

"No sir. I have only come to tell you that Father Mackenzie is here to see you, sir." Lord Burford raises his eyebrows, saying, "I wonder what he wants. You'd better show him in."

"Yes sir." Scabbard leaves.

A minute later, Scabbard shows Father Mackenzie into the room.

"Good day, Father Mackenzie, what can I do for you?"

"Good day, Lord Burford," he says with a bow. "I have some business to attend to with the Bishop. Er, nothing important, you see, but I have come to beg your permission to leave the town to go to Gloucester."

"Yes, Father, of course you may, but you will be careful, of course?"

"Oh yes, sir. I may stop in Cheltenham if I can find a safe inn but I will take great care, sir."

"Good, your trip could be useful to me as you can let me know how the pestilence goes in Gloucester on your return."

"I would be honoured to be of use to my Lord," he replies obsequiously, with more bowing and clenching of hands.

"In fact, I may not be here when you return as I am going to Windsor to see the King for a few days.", Lord Burford informs the troublesome priest.

"Oh, I'm sure Burford will be the less without you, my Lord."

"Yes, Father, good day to you."

"Good day to you, my Lord." Father Mackenzie grovels his way out backwards.

"Oh, Scabbard, come straight back in with Megan when you have shown the Father out."

"Certainly sir."

As the door closes, Henry looks at Lord Burford and says, "I didn't know you were going to Windsor, Father."

"Yes, and that's part of the reason why I want Scabbard and Megan to be here."

Two minutes later, Scabbard and Megan enter and Lord Burford tells them to sit down. Megan looks uncomfortable at this and I think it's probably because she has never been invited to sit at the same table as the Lord before.

"So, Megan, tell us about your trip to Northleach last night"

"Well, sir, when I arrived they were obviously expecting me and they gave me all I asked for and did all I asked."

There's a long pause. "Yes, go on, Megan"

"So, I went into the house with Matilda."

"That's the young girl?" interjects Lord Burford.

"Yes sir. And I bathed the girl, with the hot water they gave me and I covered her boils with honey. I made sure she ate something. And, er… I am afraid I, er…"

"Go on Megan."

"I, er, gave her a cuddle. Oh, I am sorry, sir, I really am sor…"

I feel the need to defend Megan to her Lord and 'owner' so I quickly come into the conversation with, "Megan, I know I said to have as little contact as possible with the sick but Matilda is a young child and showing her love is as important as anything else."

"Oh, thank you, sir. Thank you. I did have my mask on, of course, and I washed my clothes and had another bath when I got back, sir."

"Good girl, Megan," reassures Lord Burford.

"Then I called for Daisy, little Matilda's mother, and told her how to go about cleaning Matilda and cleaning the house with hot water and vinegar. I also told her she could come and go between the houses but not to have any contact with her other children once she had been with Matilda. She had to choose between her children," Megan says sadly.

"It will only be for a few days, Megan, because either Matilda will get better or she… won't", I remind her, trying to be as sensitive as possible.

"Then I went to the quarantine house and there was no comfort there, so I told the reeve to do whatever he could to make their lives better."

"Well done, Megan," praises Lord Burford. "And have you been to the Abbey today?"

"Yes, I have, sir. And the sisters are progressing well. In fact,

Sister Cecilia can sit up in bed now."

The little gremlin gets on my shoulder again and I can't help but ask, "Are the other sisters still praying for them?"

"Of course they are, sir."

"Well, let's move on to other matters," Lord Burford concludes.

"As some of you now know, tomorrow I am going to see the King at Windsor and I intend to tell him about what we have been doing here. I was going to take Scabbard with me but I would now also like Henry and Edmund to accompany me."

Henry sits up straight and glows at the thought of being presented to the King. I drop my head thinking, how on earth am I going to handle this one? Lord Burford turns to Megan and says, "You, my girl, are too important here to come with us."

"Oh, thank you, sir, thank you."

"And what are you two intending to do today?" the Lord asks, turning to Henry and me.

Henry once more takes command by saying, "There are a couple of important places left we need to visit – Alvescot and Clanfield – where we know people have the disease, because Clanfield was the first local village to get the disease and Alvescot is probably where the sisters got the sickness."

Lord Burford's eyes drop at the thought of his son and heir putting himself at risk once more in a place known to have the plague. Northleach was different, as he didn't know before his son went that the sickness was definitely there.

"Well, if you are both sure it is necessary, then you must go. Tonight there will be a small celebration for the whole household."

"Oh, Father, that sounds wonderful." Then Henry looks at his father with a serious face once more and asks, "Could you spare both Megan and Scabbard today as I believe we will need their help and their horses' carrying capacity?"

"Of course they can accompany you. Scabbard, Megan, I think you both know what is expected."

"Yes, sir," they chorus.

With that they begin to leave the room but I catch Scabbard's arm. "Look, I have made a drawing and I was wondering if you could have something like this made for me?" I give him a drawing of a basic toothbrush and point to the brush end. "If these could be made of the hardest bristle possible, it would be good. The whole thing should be about as long as from the tip of your middle finger to your wrist"

Scabbard looks at it and smilingly assures me, "I'm sure this will be possible, sir."

"Good, and please make the handle as smooth as possible; I don't want any splinters."

"Of course, sir."

"Just one more thing, Scabbard... Can you get Cook to make me some sweet jelly, and then get a clean chalk stone and grind it well in a pestle and mortar and add it to the jelly in a ratio of about one to three?"

Scabbard looks at me for a while and then asks, "A what of one to three, sir?"

"A ratio: one part ground chalk to three parts jelly."

"Certainly, sir," replies Scabbard, far too polite to show his disbelief that I want chalk-flavoured jelly.

Half an hour later, all four of us are on our horses and heading up the hill out of Burford. Henry is in the lead and thus dictates the route that takes us across fields and not via the route I'm used to driving along. I know we're heading south and slightly to the west of where Carterton will be established 550 years later. As we ride along, I look to my left just to see if I can see the blue windmill I left to mark the spot where I hid my laptop on that first day. It's raining a little and rained a lot during the night. I think of the laptop inside that plastic bag I left it in, hoping that it will be enough to keep it dry. I can see nothing resembling anything blue and although I knew we are quite far away from where I left it, I still worry about whether or not a sheep has eaten it, or if a passing human has perhaps picked it up thinking, What's this? Anyway, there's no point in worrying now.

Soon the church is in sight, and as we approach the village, we can see there are no roadblocks to keep people out and no signs of life. The company slows as we enter the village and stops near the church. There is silence except for birdsong. Suddenly a voice rings out, "If you are not sick, leave as soon as possible."

We all look around but can see no one. "Don't you know what has happened here?" the voice asks incredulously.

Henry turns towards the church, where he thought the sound was coming from, and replies, "Show yourself and tell me what has happened here!"

Silence.

"I am Sir Henry Burford, son of Lord Burford and we have come to see what we can do to help."

Still there is only silence. A man finally emerges from the shadows of the church. It's the priest. "God has sent his retribution for our sins. Many are dying of the sickness or are starving to death. There is a lack of food coming into the village and we cannot get out to find any. Those who are not sick or starving are already dead!"

Henry dismounts and the rest of us follow. "Come here and speak to me, Father Eugene. None of us has the sickness."

"Then you must leave as soon as possible, sir," the priest replies as he slowly approaches us.

"We will leave only when we have assessed the village. Now tell us what the situation is here?"

The priest clearly recognises Henry Burford and begins to do as commanded, telling us that many households have the sickness and others remain in their houses for fear of getting the plague or being killed if they tried to go to another place. There is no point in visiting each house now, but a large barn is requisitioned and the priest goes to find some men who are not ill. They come to the barn looking fearful and confused and are instructed to bring tables, beds and cooking equipment from houses where there's no sickness. Then orders are given for those in houses with the sickness, but who think they are not ill, to come to the quarantine barn. Megan soon sets to cleaning everything with vinegar and ordering fires to be set for hot water. I'm struck by the difference between the nervous young girl in the presence of Lord Burford and the confident, commanding young lady in her important role. It is not surprising really. Not only is he her Lord but he literally owns her. Added to which she probably owes him her life after her parents were killed in the Welsh wars.

A few hours later, the village has been organised into sick houses and quarantine barns and houses. Henry, Megan and I all take on the task of assessing whether or not people have the sickness, while Scabbard takes command of ensuring that Sir Henry's other instructions are carried out. By the time we've done all that can be done, the village seems in a much better state. Most importantly, the sense of despair and inaction has been replaced by a sense of hope. I have assured the villagers many times that not all of them will die. Eventually Henry,

Scabbard and I leave, leaving Megan behind to continue doing what she's now used to doing.

"You are to be back long before nightfall, Megan, as the house celebration is as much for you as anyone," commands Henry. The final words of Sir Henry to the village are, "Scabbard will return tomorrow with more food and provisions."

This is greeted with loud cheers by the villagers, who seem transformed within the last few hours.

"But those of you who are well must tend your fields if we are all to survive the winter."

With this the three of us turn and ride on towards Clanfield.

Within a few minutes we are approaching the small village and we can see a barrier across the road, but there are no guards to prevent our entrance. We easily ride around the barrier and stop at what I recognise as the junction between the Alvescot and Bampton roads, but there's no Clanfield Tavern to my left. For about a minute the three of us sit in silence listening to the silence. Then Henry turns to me and says, "We think this is the first place in Oxfordshire where the plague struck."

"Oh, I see! So, why does there appear to be no one here?"

"I can only assume it is because everybody in the village is either dead or has fled."

The full enormity of the effect of the Black Death suddenly hits me. This is what will happen to any village where the bacteria gets a hold before any steps are taken to prevent its spread. No one would stay here once they knew what was happening.

There are not even any animal noises and it seems even the birds have left.

"So, where are all the livestock?" I ask Henry.

"I imagine they were all set free before the last few people of the village left, probably in the hope they would survive and would still be around when the owners returned."

As if in answer to Henry's assessment, we hear the distant sound of a cow further down the road towards Radcot. Henry looks up towards the sound and says,

"Let's go and investigate." Then he squeezes the flanks of his horse to move on.

Slowly we move through the few houses that constitute Clanfield in the 14th century. Soon these dwellings peter out and in a field to our left we can see a cow. She's continually mooing but the sound is not what I'm used to hearing from a cow – not that I've spent a lot of time listening to cows mooing in the 21st century! We turn off the road towards her and as we approach, she begins to move away, so we reign our horses in.

"Why is she making that strange noise?" I naively ask of Henry.

"It's probably because she has not seen men for a few days and because she needs milking. I expect she is in a lot of pain."

Of course! Henry must think I'm really thick. Everybody in an agricultural society would know that.

"Couldn't we try to catch her and milk her?" I ask with more naivety.

"Ha, ha! Well, we could try, but I doubt if she would let us catch her. She doesn't know us."

I feel I have to try something, so I pass my reins to Henry saying, "Please hold these."

I dismount and walk slowly towards the suffering beast. She's clearly a cow but doesn't look like a Jersey or a Friesian. As I approach, she moves away so I crouch down trying to appear smaller and less threatening. I try this many times but can never get close enough to touch her, let alone catch her and milk her.

Eventually, it's clear I'm wasting my time and give up. As I return to my horse and pull myself back on, Henry hands me the reigns with a smile that says, 'I told you so!' Scabbard remains silent and his face says nothing. He knows his position and it is not to express an opinion on the behaviour of his betters. As we turn away, I give one last look back to her and think that if I had a 21st century rifle, I would shoot her through the head to end her misery. Clearly there's nothing to be done in the village of Clanfield. In those houses there are probably dead people but there's no point in going to look. That really would be an unnecessary risk. We turn our horses and head back towards Burford. My legs are aching a little but I'm obviously getting used to riding. Before long we're approaching our destination.

As we come towards the town we go through the usual procedure, as the barriers are moved aside and everyone keeps their distance from the potential death we've brought with us. Then we ride down the hill, over the bridge and into the grounds of Burford House. As we dismount, Henry tells Scabbard not to rush the cleaning of the horses, saddles and bridles as he should do it properly. The other household staff can cope with the arrangements for the celebration.

"Certainly not, sir," he replies.

Once we're in the house, there are baths and changes for all, and even I'm getting a little fed up with this routine, as it's not as easy as having a quick shower in my own house. Then Henry and I meet again for a brief snack before the evening's festivities. We haven't eaten properly since leaving in the morning and we're very hungry. When the meal is finished I say to Henry, "I am going to my room to lie down, so I'll see you later."

"Okay," replies Henry self-consciously as I disappear.

In my room I throw myself on my bed.

CHAPTER TWENTY THREE

THAT NIGHT

"Sir! Sir! It's time to get up, sir!"

I open one eye and Scabbard slowly comes into focus.

"Thank you, Scabbard."

Scabbard turns to leave, but as he's going out, I ask, "Oh, Scabbard, did you have that toothbrush made for me?"

"Yes, sir, it's waiting for you with the jelly Cook has made for you."

"Good, could you bring them up, along with some water please?"

I still cannot prevent myself from adding 'please' to any request I make to a servant.

"Certainly sir."

I lie there for a while trying to guess the time from the fading light outside and wondering why I'm so tired. I had plenty of sleep last night, yet had obviously fallen asleep when all I intended was to lie down for a brief moment. Is it the stress of being in this situation? The fear of catching the Black Death, or the fear of never getting back to the 21st century? Or is it the physical stress of having to do so much horse riding? It's probably a bit of everything. Then Scabbard reappears with the toothbrush and toothpaste. He puts it down on the table and turns to walk out.

"Thank you, Scabbard" I say, jumping off the bed eager to clean my teeth properly for the first time in days.

Before Scabbard reaches the door he turns back to me and says, "Sir, the barber is in and I wondered if you might like him to give you a shave?"

"Er, yes, Scabbard, that would be good." I now have a thin beard and although I couldn't grow a full beard yet, I have to admit it does look a little untidy. Obviously the Lord does not go to the barber; the barber comes to the house! He's presumably been called in because of the celebration tonight. Then I remember that I'm going off to see the King tomorrow! This must be another reason why we must all be shaved. There's only one bowl of water, so first I wash my hands and face as I will have to spit into the bowl when I have finished cleaning my teeth. The toothpaste isn't too bad at all, and neither is the brush, although the bristles could have been stiffer. There is another knock at the door.

"Come in."

The door opens and a man enters with a large tray on which is a bowl of steaming water and various instruments. Around his neck are a few towels. Obviously he's the barber.

"Ah, yes, er, where would you like me to sit?"

The barber looks around at a high-backed chair and says, "Here would do nicely, sir."

I've been shaving for the last few years, at first rather unnecessarily, but I have never been shaved. First my face is washed in the hot water and then I'm lathered, not very effectively, with some form of soap. A thin, very sharp knife is produced and the shaving begins. It's a little painful but a not unpleasant experience. When I think it's all over, the process begins again. Finally, my face is washed again and patted dry. Once more I find myself feeling uncomfortable. Should I pay the barber? And if so, what with? I've never had any money since being here. Fortunately, the barber packs up, gives a little bow and leaves.

From the noise throughout the house it's obvious things have started and I arrive just as people are sitting down to eat at the large table now laden with food. A tankard of beer is thrust into my hand and it soon becomes obvious that I am the centre of the celebration. It dawns on me that this is the first time since my birthday and passing my driving test that I'm free to drink alcohol: even though I've been drinking small beer since I arrived. Now's my chance to let my hair down a little. I empty the tankard and soon it is replaced with another one as I sit down at the table in the place left for me next to Henry. There are people here I have not seen before and I am introduced to them all, but by now the beer is beginning to take its effect and it's clearly not like the small beers I've had up to now. Then Megan walks in carrying a large tray of more food.

"Megan, you're back!" I exclaim in a voice much louder than I should have. She smiles and begins to unload her tray around the table, skilfully making her last stop next to me.

"So, did all go well in Alvescot after we left?"
"Yes, sir, I carried out all your commands and I will return tomorrow after I have been to see Matilda in Northleach."

"Good, and your hair looks lovely again, Megan."

She coyly smiles and tosses her head and then becomes aware that others have heard this – something I seem completely unaware of. She smiles once more and backs out.

On the table there is wine and this is the first time I've been offered wine since coming to this time. It flows freely and I soon lose track of how much I'm drinking. Inevitably the conversation soon turns to the plague that is being visited on the world and it's incumbent upon me to express my views as to its progress. "It will sweep the whole country this year and then become less virulent during the winter as the cold kills off the bacteria" I tell them.

"Bacteria," echoes Lord Burford. "Yes, you have used this word before. If I remember correctly, they are the little animals that get into people and make them ill."

"Yes, that's right. Very little, so small that they are carried inside the little fleas on the rats and they get into people when the fleas bite them. That's why we must kill as many rats as possible."

"Scabbard, how's the rat killing going?" asks the Lord as Scabbard is attending to the guests.

"Oh, very well in Burford, sir, and I have set the men to do the same in Northleach and Alvescot." The conversation moves on and the wine flows more and more.

Later the subject of the plague comes up again and this time Henry asks, "Will the sickness return again after the winter?"

"Yes, it will. Even though you have had very cold winters during the last few decades..."

"Yes, I had noticed that," Lord Burford throws in.

"It will come back again. You have had colder winters, and summers, actually, because you are in what is known as the little ice age."

I'm aware that the alcohol is making me say things that no one in the middle of the 14th century could know, but, because of the alcohol, I just don't care.

"In fact, by 1350 the population of England will be only two thirds of what it was in 1347, and by the end of the century the population will be only half of what it was in 1347."

This information is received with a mixture of shock and disbelief, followed by embarrassed laughter.

"After that, the plague will come and go for the next three hundred years and it will not be until the 16th century that the population recovers to where it is now."

Fortunately, many have consumed even more wine than I have and this is all now being treated as drunken banter. A man down the end of the table, whose name I don't know even though I have been introduced, asks, "So, after a few hundred years, will the pestilence never return again?"

"Not after 1665, no. Well, not in England anyway."

"Why   not?"

"Ah, now that is a good question!"

There is silence and all eyes are on me as they expect me to pontificate further. "There will be a number of reasons..." I begin.

My head is swirling and I have to try to get my thoughts together. Something tells me to shut up but I'm in the flow now and enjoying it so much that nothing is going to stop me. I force myself to go on.

"There will be better hygiene, as I have tried to teach you here, and the black rat will largely be replaced by rattus norvegicus..." If only I could hear myself sounding so self-important.

"By what? A brown rat." asks Henry while showing his knowledge of Latin once more..

"Rattus norvegicus, the brown rat as opposed to the black rat that is around now..."

"How will that make any difference?" asks Henry.

"Well, because they carry a different sort of flea that doesn't carry the Black Death."

There's general laughter at the idea that there are different sorts of fleas, let alone that different sort of rats have different sorts of fleas.

"And, of course, the population in general will start to develop a natural immunity to the disease."

More loud laughter. At this point, I allow myself to drift off into my stupor and continue to stuff my face with food and wine.

Later the conversation turns to the imminent visit to see the King in Windsor. Lord Burford is the centre of this discussion and says, "I believe Edward of Woodstock…"

"Edward of Woodstock? Who's he?" I ask, jumping in rudely, as I've been told not to do, in another unguarded moment..

"Edward of Woodstock, Prince of Wales, Duke of Cornwall, Prince of Aquitaine…"

"Oh, him? The Black Prince!"

"The Black Prince? Why do you call him the Black Prince?"

Fortunately I still have just enough presence of mind to say, "Oh, er, that's what he's known as in Saxony."

"But why the Black Prince?"

"Er, I don't really know. It's just what he's known as."

"Ah! You have heard of his great victory over the French at Crecy, haven't you?"

"Yes, we've heard of that – some very useful Welsh archers I believe."

"Yes, they were," said Henry. "Where is Megan? Oh, there she is. Hello, Megan. She likes you, you know." Fortunately Henry is almost as drunk as I am.

Then I look at Henry and slur, "Do you reckon I'm well in there, then?"

"Uhm, I certainly think she likes you."

Lord Burford continues to wax lyrical about Edward of Woodstock and I chip in, "Do you know that Cemetery Junction Station isn't really in Woodstock? It's just that Woodstock looks a lot better than Reading does."

No-one takes any notice of me.

"He is a wonderful prince and will make a very good King,", Lord Burford continues to extol the virtues of Prince Edward.

"I bet you he doesn't!" I opine.

The hubbub dies down and the Lord speaks again. "I think you jest too much, Sir Edmund."

"I bet you a King's ransom he doesn't!"

This is close to treason and nervous laughter runs around the table.

"And his son will be a bit of an iffy character when it comes to the peasants' revolt."

"Peasants' revolt?" the man at the end of the table asks. "Why should the peasants revolt?"

"Ah well, that's all to do with the Black Death as well. You see, the plague will decimate the population so badly, as I have told you – or should that be bicimate? Hee-hee, haa-ha! – that there will not be enough peasants to work the land. So the fields will remain unsown and unharvested, and homes will remain empty, so there will be no rent imposed on them. Therefore, some Lords will allow peasants from a different manor, and even serfs, to work on their land and not send them back to their original manors."

More nervous laughter follows, but I just blunder on drunkenly. "Lords will even be prepared to pay money for their work. This will embolden the peasants and they will revolt for social, legal and political rights."

"Rights for peasants and serfs? Haa!" says another man whose name I've forgotten.

Much raucous laughter follows.

"Give him some more wine, Megan," says Lord Burford.

This Megan does and I drink it with relish.

After a few courses of the meal the atmosphere changes and it seems it's time for a little entertainment. First, Henry's younger sister, Anne, gets up and sings a little song. A nice little tune and very simple. Sounds like the sort of thing I used to listen to on Children's BBC. When she has finished, Lord Burford raises his hand and Megan leaves the room only to reappear with three jugs and an uncooked broad bean on a tray. He lines up the three jugs and puts the bean under one of them, inviting people to tell him which jug the bean is under. I've seen this trick done many times on television and by street entertainers but had no idea it was around in the Middle Ages. I suppose it's so simple it would likely be very old. I have no idea how the trick is performed so I watch in great admiration as the Lord of the Manor performs like a troubadour. Fortunately my fascination with the trick means I keep quiet for a while.

Then it seems it's my friend Henry's turn to entertain. As he stands up, Scabbard picks up an instrument from the corner of the room and hands it to Henry. This has clearly been planned and I can see it's one of the instruments Henry showed me in the music room. As far as I can remember it's called a viol.

Henry sits down, puts the instrument between his legs and begins to play, with a bow, a tune that I don't recognise. Of course not! It seems pretty complicated to my rather uneducated musical ear. I just can't get the time signature but it certainly isn't in 4/4 time. I suddenly became aware that the room is silent. Is this out of deference for Henry's social position or is it because they're appreciative of his musical skill? When he has finished, the audience shows its appreciation as do I. Once more Henry has displayed his musical abilities and I'm filled with the thought that I wish I could play like that!

Then comes the moment I've been dreading – my turn to perform. What am I to do? I can't sing, I can't play any of their medieval instruments and I can't do party tricks. There's just one thing I can think of; recite a poem, But which one. Once more that little gremlin gets on my shoulder and I decide to do one of Geoffrey Chaucer's, so off I go.

> "Experience, though noon auctoritee
> Were in this world, is right ynough for me
> to speke of wo that is in mariage:
> For Lordinges, sith I twelf yeer was of age-
> Thank be God that it is eterne on live-
> Housbondes at chirche dore I have had five
> (If I so oft mighte han wedded be),
> And alle were worthy men in hir degree
> But me was told, certain, nat longe agoon is,
> That sith that Crist, en wente nevere but ones
> To wedding in the Cane of Galilee
> That by the same ensample taughte he me
> That I ne sholde wedded be but ones."

At this point I lose track of where I am and pause. This is taken to be the end of the poem and I thankfully take the opportunity to stop. Applause ensues and as I'm making my way back to my seat Lord Burford asks, "Did you write that yourself, Edmund, as I don't recognise it?" Again the gremlin materialises on my shoulder and I reply, "No, it's written by a man called Geoffrey Chaucer and it's from 'The Wife of Bath's Prologue'.

Oh, I've never heard of him, is he a new poet?

How should I answer this one? "Well. Sort of, but I'm sure you will hear a lot of him in a few years' time"

"Mmmm, I shall try to remember his name. Geoffrey Chaucer you say?"

"Yes, sir, that's right. Geoffrey Chaucer." I hammer the point home to make sure he remembers. Chaucer is only a young boy during the Black Death so it appeals to my sense of humour, even if I were sober, to introduce his work a few years before he wrote it.

Whilst the celebration is in full swing, Father Mackenzie arrives at the Bishop's Palace in Gloucester and is brought before the Bishop. "Your Grace, I am your humble servant."

"You are well come, Father Mackenzie. What brings you here in such difficult times?"

"There is much evil abroad, Your Grace, and I believe the Devil himself has come in the guise of a young man to Burford. His name is Edmund de Covny."

"Go on, my son."

"He speaks of causes for the pestilence other than God's retribution. He gives commands as if he were a Lord or even a King."

"And what does Lord Burford say of this?"

"Well, Your Grace, he seems enthralled by the Devil's words. He gives this, this, er, heretic every assistance."

"Does he indeed?"

"In fact, Lord Burford's son, Henry, accompanies him in all he does."

"Mmm."

"He has even been into the Abbey where two of the nuns are sick. They seem to be recovering, Your Grace."

"Obviously it's the work of God upon his servants."

"Yes, Your Grace, but this young man seems to wish to take the credit for the Lord Christ's work."

"Does he indeed?"

"His behaviour at Mass is less than pious, Your Grace, and once he seemed to suggest that we could get the disease from Holy water. He has even told a family with a child, known to be possessed by devils and spirits, that he is not possessed at all"

"Has he indeed? Mmm. His actions must be curtailed. But it will be difficult if he has the protection of Lord Burford."

"There the good Lord may have sent us a sign of encouragement."

"Go on?"

"Lord Burford is going to Windsor tomorrow to see the King and he is taking his son and the young man with him. But he may stay in Windsor and send his son and Sir Edmund home whilst he stays in Windsor. Maybe we could, er...?"

"Yes, I see." The Bishop drums his fingers and then says, "I shall prepare a warrant for the arrest of both of them on charges of blasphemy and heresy."

"Thank you, Your Grace. I have prayed for such assistance."

"I will send some men with you and they will wait for the two young devils to return. You have done well, my son. God go with you."

At the celebration, the party is winding down and the guests are leaving. Once everyone is gone, the residents are making their way to bed but I've been slumped in a chair for a while and am probably snoring loudly. Henry pulls himself to his feet and looks at me. "Megan, help Edmund to bed," he says with an impish grin on his face.

"Yes, sir," responds Megan and rouses me as she helps me to

my feet. A few minutes later she drops me on my bed and is walking towards the door.

"Oh, don't go, Megan," I slur.

She walks back towards me.

"Sit down and talk to me."

She sits and I pull myself into a sitting position.

"You do look tasty, Megan."

"Tasty, sir? What does that mean? Are you going to eat me?" She giggles.

"It means this," I say as I lean forward and kiss her.

She doesn't seem to object and the little gremlin appears on my shoulder once more. "Are you on the pill?"

"The what, sir?"

"Oh, never mind!"

CHAPTER TWENTY FOUR

WINDSOR

"Sir! Sir! Sir Edmund! It's morning, sir. Time to get up."

"Huh? What? Who? Who are you?"

"It's Scabbard, sir."

"Hooray! Can you bring me some water?"

"I have brought you some, sir. Here it is and there is honey and bread waiting for you for breakfast."

"Ooh. My tongue is sticking to the roof of my mouth."

"It will do. Come on, drink this, sir"

"Thank you."

"Everything is prepared for your journey, sir," Scabbard says and leaves me to my own resources. I'm thankful for Scabbard once more but feel his waking me is becoming a bit of a habit.

I swill the water around my mouth and the memory of last night slowly enters my consciousness. Then, wham! It all comes flooding back. Oh my god! What did I say? What did I do? And Megan? What happened? Whilst all this is going through my head I wash and dress before making my way to the dining room. Henry is already there, as is the bread and honey Scabbard promised. It seems the 14th century knows as much about hangover cures as does the 21st century.

Henry greets me with, "Hello Edmund. How are you?"

"Er, a little shaky. How about you?"

"About the same."

I'm rather pleased to hear I'm not the only one with a hangover. We chat a little and slowly I edge the conversation around to last night.

"Did you enjoy yourself last night?" I ask Henry.

"Yes, I did. How about you?"

"I did, but I think I got a little carried away."

"Didn't we all! That's what celebrations are for." Henry reassures me.

This makes me feel a bit better and then Lord Burford walks in.

"Good morrow, gentlemen," he says brightly. "How are you both?"

"Oh, fine!" we chant, both trying to pretend we do not have hangovers.

"All is ready, so as soon as you are, we shall leave."

"We will be out soon," assures Henry.

Lord Burford leaves and we finish eating before I run, rather painfully, back upstairs to clean my teeth.

A few minutes later, I have my foot on the mounting block and I have to use all my strength to throw my other leg over and pull myself onto the horse. Off we go and every hoof fall makes me feel as if I'm being bounced up and down from a great height. We've gone out of the back of Burford House, on a route I only know in theory, and make our way through Swinbrook and across a little bridge. I'm struck by the thought that the village will change little in the next nearly 700 years. Then we ride up the hill, over the Oxford road and down again towards Bampton, which is blocked off, so we have to ride around the outskirts of the town and along the Buckland's road. By now I'm feeling like death cooled down and am sure I cannot continue the ride to Windsor. When will we stop for a rest? On we go and I feel I want to just die on horseback. Up ahead is the river Thames and I wonder if there's a bridge there like the Tadpole bridge, which will still exist in the 21st century. As we approach the river, Lord Burford and Scabbard slow down, as does my horse, without any instruction. Good, I think, we're going to stop for a while. Imagine my ecstasy when it becomes clear that we're going to transfer to a boat for the rest of the journey to Windsor. There's no bridge at all – just a few boats on the river.

At the riverbank there are a few men and as we approach I think I've seen one of them before. I soon dismiss this thought as silly. How could I have seen a man from the 14th century before? Suddenly I realise it's Knut, one of the two men who picked me up the first morning. Immediately my eyes scan the other men for Edgar, who had been with Knut, and there he is. Without these two men I wouldn't be where I am now. I can't decide if that's good or bad. When the horses stop, there's the usual forelock tugging and what feels like a special welcome for me from Knut and Edgar. I had hardly noticed the large saddlebags on my horse, and on Henry and Lord Burford's horses and the even larger ones on Scabbard's horse. Now they're being unloaded, as soon as we have dismounted, and put into two boats. The boats look pretty large and I do not really relish the thought of rowing all the way to Windsor even if I am a member of the school rowing team. However, this does seem preferable to riding all the way to Windsor.

Once more, I'm delighted to find that Knut and Edgar are to accompany us as oarsmen. Lord Burford, Henry and I get into one boat whilst most of the bags are loaded into the other. Finally, Knut gets into our boat and Edgar and Scabbard get into the other. Knut and Edgar pick up their respective oars. I had wondered if these boats are for hire to anyone who wants them and this is confirmed when Lord Burford leans towards the shore and hands a purse of money to a man who I assume is in charge of the quay. Soon Knut and Edgar are pulling on the oars and I'm pleased to lie back and rest as the two servants do the work. This is what is expected, and what they are paid for – if they are – so I decide to make the most of it and rest my hangover. The movement of the boat is very restful and the sound of lapping water on the oars adds to my sense of relaxation. This is so much better than bouncing up and down on horseback.

After a couple of hours, Oxford is in sight. It's a city I know well in the 21st century but this place is a lot smaller and all the landing stages are closed, making it clear strangers are not welcome. The same goes for Abingdon, but at both places Lord Burford announces himself and enquires as to the progress of the plague. It's in both Oxford and Abingdon and spreading fast. I feel compelled to try to do something but know I would have to start from scratch and I cannot be everywhere. My next task is to have my ideas put to the King by Lord Burford, which will be far more effective overall than trying to change every town.

On we travel through Long Wittenham and onto Streetley, both little more than a couple of dwellings next to the river. Eventually, it begins to get dark and all of us are very tired, Henry and I mainly because we're nursing hangovers. A riverside hostelry called the Riverside Inn, where Lord Burford has rested before, comes into sight.

We moor the boat and Lord Burford approaches the inn alone and knocks on the door. After a while a window opens and a head emerges. "Who is it"? asks the landlord.

"Lord Burford," comes the simple reply.

"Oh, my Lord, I'm afraid we are closed due to the sickness."

"I understand that, my man, but you know me and none of my party have the sickness. Come and see for yourself."

"Oh, but, sir, I really shouldn't, I..."

"I will pay more than usual for the night." A long wait ensues and the Lord can hear the landlord whispering to his wife.

"How much, sir?"

"Twice the usual!" More whispering can be heard.

"Very well, sir, but we will not meet you and we will put your food outside your rooms."

"That is quite acceptable to us, Landlord."

The Lord then comes back to the boat and explains the situation to the other five of us, adding, "I knew that with the lack of travellers recently they would really be desperate to earn some money."

Early the next morning, we are up and out again, having eaten the food left outside our doors. The day is cloudy with the odd break of sunshine which, at its low angle, makes the river look like a silver road up ahead.

"We must follow the silver brick road to the land of far, far away," I say and the others just look at me blankly. On we row, making good progress on the smooth water, towards Windsor. At a long, straight stretch of the water there's a track running along the riverside and I ask, "Where are we now?"

"This is a place called Pangbourne," replies Lord Burford. I remember driving along the riverbank here with my Dad a few times on our way to Reading to visit the Makro store. That means Reading won't be too far ahead. An hour or so later we pass the confluence with another river and pull in at an inn called The Jolly Fisherman. As Scabbard approaches the door, it's opened and a woman says loudly, "I can provide a meal but I can't let you in."

"That's fine," replies Scabbard and soon a tray of food and beer is left on a nearby table, on which Lord Burford has left some coins. I look across the river and back towards the confluence and ask what the adjoining river is called. The pronunciation has changed over the near seven centuries but I manage to make out that it is the Kennet river.

"But there's virtually nothing here!" I exclaim in another unguarded moment.

"What were you expecting?" asks Henry and the word 'Reading' passes through my mind. Fortunately it doesn't come out of my mouth. Instead I just shrug.

Soon we're back in the boat and on towards a place where we have to get out of the boat and hire some waiting locals, who keep their distance, to carry the boat around what will later become the weir at Marlow, which is a distinct, if small, settlement. Now the river is much broader than I remember it being in the 21st century – if 'remembered' is the right tense for the verb. It stretches from chalk scarp to chalk scarp. I find this a little confusing for a while and then realise that these are the days before the Thames was channelled. Soon we're under the cliffs at Cliveden and I think about Profumo and Christine Keeler but it would mean nothing to my fellow travellers so I keep my mouth shut. The same procedure of having the boat carried is necessary at Maidenhead as well, and I marvel at the speed and efficiency with which the labourers carry the goods and the boats separately around the rocks. Payment is made into a bowl with vinegar and very soon we're back in the boat.

By now the castle at Windsor has been in sight for some time and this gives Knut and Edgar an impetus to row hard the last few miles. At this point the river is very broad and looks more like a lake. The downstream current, which has helped us all the way from what I know as the Tadpole Bridge, is now so dissipated it's virtually of no help. As we come up alongside the jetty by the hill upon which the castle is built, I look across what seems about a mile and can see nothing on the other side. I'm thinking that those shallow, muddy waters will later become Slough. No wonder it was called 'Slough'!

There's a guard on the jetty but before the boat reaches it, a cry goes up,

"It is Lord Burford!"

We are welcomed and helped out of the boat with no sense of fear, unlike our experiences elsewhere along the river. I wonder if they recognise us because we are expected or because the Burfords are well known at the castle. As with many things, I keep my mouth shut again but I do wonder if I'm being too careful. After all, a person from the far off land of Saxony would ask all sorts of questions. I look up at the castle towering over me. It looks smaller than the time I toured it with my parents, but it's still recognisable as Windsor Castle. We climb up the steps, but with no baggage to carry as it is being carried for us. Being inside a royal castle, rather than being on a guided tour, gives me a strange sense of unreality – but then again, my whole adventure in the 14th century has a sense of unreality to it.

On the way, Lord Burford stops to exchange words with a few nobles we've met and by the time I'm shown to my room my bags are already there. It's an upper room and I look out of the window onto the town of Windsor. The town is not very large and I can't remember what it looked like the couple of times I've been here, but it's now partially obscured by a haze of smoke that hangs over the town. The smell of burning wood is not an unpleasant one and I wonder if it's a particularly poisonous form of pollution. Then I remind myself that the concept of pollution would mean nothing at all to those around me now.

It's dusk by now and the setting sun is to the west side of the castle, casting long shadows across the town. I'm caught up in a dream as there's a knock on the door and I instinctively answer, "Come in, Scabbard."

The door opens slowly and a stranger says, "It is not Scabbard, sir."

"Oh!" I respond, looking at the stranger and realising he must be a castle servant.

"I have come to tell you there is food prepared for when you are ready, sir."

"Oh, I will come now," I say, and follow the man to a large room where a table has been set out with food. Henry is already waiting. A chair is pulled out for me opposite Henry and as I sit down, Henry says, "Eat up, Edmund. We have a night of entertainment ahead of us."

I look at Henry and think, Oh no, I can't stand another heavy night! Then I look down the table to both ends and feel incongruous sitting in the middle of a table so large that it could seat twenty to thirty people. Bringing myself back to Henry's comment, I ask, "Oh yes, what's happening?"

"There is badger baiting arranged in the town for tonight."

"What?" I exclaim loudly.

"Badger baiting."

"What? You mean in a pit with dogs?"

"Yes. All is prepared and the dogs have not been fed for days. Unfortunately, because of travel restrictions, they could not get a bear but the fights should be good anyway."

Oh my God, I think. I am expected to watch dogs tearing a

badger to death! This is just too much. I have tried to fit in with medieval society but to watch that is too much to ask.

"Oh really? Okay... er...Would you pass the salt please?" I say, trying to change the subject. Henry passes the salt three inches across the table.

"Er, has Scabbard eaten?" I ask, trying to move things along.

"I don't know," replies Henry in a rather confused voice. "If he has, he'll be in the servants' quarters."

The meal passes with Henry doing most of the talking, telling me how his father is already with the King and telling him what's being done in Burford and the surrounding areas to prevent the spread of the plague. Once we are full, Henry stands and says, "I will come along to your room when it's time to go."

At this point, I realise that I was led to the dining room and have no idea of how to get back. Turning to Henry I ask him, "How do I get back to my room?"

Henry laughs and says, "Follow me. My room is not far from yours."

Off we go and it's clear Henry knows the castle well so he has obviously been there many times.

"Here we are!" exclaims Henry, throwing open the door to my room. "I will be back soon."

I stand in the semi-darkness. Candles have been lit for me in my absence. I'm deep in thought. Eventually I conclude that I really cannot go to watch badger baiting and pretend I'm excited at the sight of blood and suffering. I've seen bits of bull fights on TV and it sickened me. Not only the sight of it but the thought that humans get kicks out of animal suffering. What am I to do? I pace up and down, look out of the window many times at the lights in the town, and when there's a knock on the door, I quickly throw myself on the bed.

"Come in," I call in an affected groggy voice.

"Come on, we're all ready," calls Henry

"Ooh, er. I really don't feel very well."

"What's the matter with you?" Henry asks as he enters and sits on the bed.

"My head aches."

"Well, come on, you'll feel alright once you're awake and down the town," Henry encourages me.

"No, no. I really can't. I feel dizzy as well. I can't stand up straight."

"I know you were ill yesterday from too much wine but you seemed fine today. Come on, get up!" Henry proceeds to coerce.

"No, I really can't. I will join you later if I feel better."

"Alright. If you really can't, you softie! But if you feel better, come and join us. We will go around the town hostelries later," Henry says rather despondently.

"I will certainly try," I promise lamely.

Henry stands to go but turns and says, "You are to be presented to the King first thing tomorrow, so make sure you're better by then."

"I will," I say as Henry closes the door behind him.

I lie on my bed and think about my new friend's love of animal suffering. I tell myself that this is to be expected in the 14th century but even so, it upsets me greatly. Although feeling ill was an excuse, it's true that I'm very tired, having ridden at least ten miles with a hangover and spent two days on the river over what must have been about 80 miles. I have aches in muscles I didn't know I had. As I lie there, filled with a mixture of sickness at what's happening to the badgers and sadness at the behaviour of my friend, I slowly drift off into a deep sleep.

CHAPTER TWENTY FIVE

THE KING

Suddenly I find myself wide awake and quickly think that I may be able to join them in the hostelries. Then I realise it's getting light outside. It must be morning. I've been asleep all night. Before 5 o'clock I guess. What to do now? It's too early for the others to be up even though Henry had said "first thing tomorrow". So I lie there for a while. Soon it's fully light outside and I get out of bed and dressed. Opening the door I look down the corridor. There's a man at the end, apparently asleep on his haunches. I walk towards him and the man regains consciousness, jumping up pretending he's been awake all the time.

"What can I do for you, sir?" he stammers.

"I'd like something to wash in." I'm hoping to take on the mantle of authority and the right to being served.

"Certainly, sir," he replies and hurries away as I return to my room.

A few minutes later there is a knock at the door and in walks the servant with a bowl of steaming water. He puts it on a table and exits. I merely nod. I wash and look through my bag for the change of clothes that Henry has given me for my presentation to the King. Finally, I begin to clean my teeth with the chalky-jelly Cook made for me. As I'm doing this, the door flies open and in rushes Henry.

"You're up early! What are you doing?"

"Cleaning my teeth. What's it look like?"

"Cleaning them? With what?"

I spit out the toothpaste and rinse my mouth out before washing the toothbrush. "Toothpaste! What else?" I say, pointing to the little bowl with the paste in it. "You ought to try it. It'll help those mouth ulcers you seem to have."

"Ulcers! How did you know I had spots in my mouth?"

"Because you keep wincing when you eat." "Oh, alright," say Henry, taking me at my word, picking up the toothbrush and dipping it in the jelly before beginning to brush his teeth with it.

I look on thinking about my toothbrush in Henry's mouth. What can I say except, "I'm sure Scabbard could have one made for you."

During breakfast the inevitable subject comes up as Henry tells me, "You missed a really good night last night. The badgers fought well."

"Oh did they? Never mind."

"Yes, one of them was dug out with two of her cubs. They were put into the pit with her, so she fought extra hard trying to protect them."

Although trying to avoid talking about it, I can't resist asking, "And did she succeed?"

"Well, they lived a little longer but she fought and fought until both cubs were dead and then she seemed to give up. Certainly the best fight, though!"

"What time do we see the King?", I ask, trying to change the subject.

"I think my father gave him details of your ideas and what we have done, so we shall go to court and wait to be called."

I haven't given a lot of thought to meeting the King but now the time is upon us I'm filled with trepidation. How am I to behave in front of King Edward III? Soon we are walking towards the great hall where the King is holding court. Inside, Lord Burford and many other people are standing around waiting. At the front of the great hall is an empty throne and another empty, smaller chair next to it. Lord Burford explains to me that he spoke to the King last night and persuaded him of the efficacy of my ideas, so there will be little for me to tell him, but that the King wants to meet the man with the strange ideas.

We stand around waiting for literally hours, which annoys me, but doesn't seem to bother either of the Burfords. They probably just accept their lowly position of waiting for the King. Eventually, the herald announces, "His Majesty the King and the Prince of Wales!"

Silence falls, and the King, and the Prince of Wales – later to be known as the Black Prince – walk in. This is the man I had, foolishly, bet would not make a good King. I wonder if anyone will ever remember my words when Prince Edward is to die just before his father dies. A great deal of business is conducted by the King as everyone else waits. This makes me even more bored but what can I do? Then the herald announces, "Sir Edmund de Covny."

I freeze, and Lord Burford gives me a gentle push forward. I approach the throne and do as I've seen others do. I bow my head and say, "Your Majesty."

"Ah, de Covny!" I raise my eyes apprehensively. "Burford has told me about you. You are the young man from Saxony, aren't you?"

"Yes, Your Majesty."

"I have been there!" Oh no, I think. He probably knows more about the place than I do!

"Good hunting!"

"I'm glad you think so, Your Majesty." Then I wonder if this sounds too cocky.

"Well, I have listened to what Burford has to say and your ideas certainly seem to have merit to them."

I smile and keep my mouth shut.

"I have ordered the vinegar cleaning regime, set up the quarantine area of the castle, ordered the killing of the rats and sent out orders to surrounding towns and villages to bring back any cats and dogs."

"This is a good start, Your Majesty." Once more, I'm wondering if this is too presumptuous.

"We shall see how the plague progresses in the town" he adds, presumably rhetorically.

"Your Majesty, it is important that such things are done everywhere to avoid the spread of the disease."

The King looks at me and I realise this is probably overstepping the mark.

"All that is necessary shall be done," responds His Majesty with a finality in his voice.

I lower my eyes. "Your Majesty."

The King makes a slight movement with his hand and I realise I've been dismissed. I back out in the same way I've seen others doing, and when I reach the surrounding audience, I turn and walk, heaving an audible sigh of relief as I hear the herald announce, "Lord Burford and Sir Henry Burford"

This comes as a surprise to me and Lord Burford passes me with a smile which makes me feel better as he approaches the King. Henry doesn't catch my eye.

"Ah, my Lord Burford!"

"Your Majesty," comes the obligatory response with a low bow.

"So, you will be staying here for other matters of state but your son and, er, er, the other one, may return to Burford."

"Majesty."

Another slight movement of the hand from the King and Lord Burford, along with Henry, backs away, as I had done, so I assume I got it right. As they reach the audience the two Burfords join me. Then we all proceed to the back of the great hall and exit.

"Well done, Edmund!" exclaims Lord Burford and I realise that despite my nervousness, I've passed the test.

"Go and eat before you go out to the town tonight but do not get carried away. You must be up early again tomorrow to return to Burford. I am staying here for a few more days and Scabbard and Edgar are staying with me but Knut will go with you."

Once more a sumptuous meal is presented, fit for a King – literally. When we have finished it is late afternoon and I wonder what I have done with the day. The obvious answer is that I waited to be spoken to for a couple of minutes by some bloke with a metal Christmas hat on who was holding a ball, while some other bloke supported his hand. What a way to live! Henry and I return to our respective rooms and I wait for Henry to come and get me. Whilst I'm pleased to have avoided the blood bath last night, I'm sorry to have missed out on the pub crawl, so I'm looking forward to going out this evening.

Early in the evening, Henry comes for me and as we approach the castle gates, we meet two other young men who Henry clearly knows. Henry introduces them to me: Sir John

Fitzroy and Sir Richard Grosvenor. Immediately I wonder if this is an ancestor of the 21st century Grosvenor, the richest man in Britain, and I think about how the family of one of William the Conqueror's hangers-on could end up being the inheritors of the world's most valuable piece of real estate nearly a millennium later. The town is not very big and there seem to be only three inns worth visiting, which is just as well, as we have to be up early tomorrow. The craic is good but I feel uncomfortable each time we enter an inn and everyone falls silent, as if we were intruding on something. Obviously the locals feel intimidated by the presence of their 'betters'. The town is far from empty but Henry observes, "Windsor is usually a lot more lively but people are afraid to go out more than is necessary for obvious reasons."

I add to this observation, "It probably doesn't help that we are from outside the town and may be infected."

"No, it doesn't," adds Grosvenor, and he and Fitzroy fall into drunken giggles.

I realise they had already consumed a lot of beer before we met up and look at Henry. Catching his eye, I motion towards the door.

"Oh, just one more, Edmund."

"Alright, but don't forget we need to be up at dawn."

"Yes, but it is still early evening."

I just stare at him and eventually respond, "Oh well, just one more. I don't want another bollocking from your Dad."

"A what?" asks Henry and I ignore him.

Fortunately he is too pissed to pursue the matter.

"More beer, Innkeeper," calls Grosvenor and more is produced.

We chat, but I have to say it's a little boring being sober with two well-oiled people, and although Henry is not that far gone he manages to get into the swing of things – behaving drunk even if he isn't. I feel the same way as I did when I was the driver in the 21st century; not really part of what was going on, but I certainly don't want to feel the same way I felt travelling down from Burford. I've learnt hangovers are not pleasant things! I drain my tankard and look at Henry again. "Sorry to be a party pooper."

"A what?" enquires Henry.

Amidst more drunken giggles, Fitzroy adds, "I was also wondering about that."

"Oh, alright. We shall leave now," says Henry, producing some coins which he places on the table as the two of us leave, bidding goodnight to Grosvenor and Fitzroy.

Back at the castle Henry and I go to our separate rooms. I lie in my bed for a while thinking of having been 'presented' to the most powerful man in medieval England. Soon I'm asleep.

As the sun begins to rise, Scabbard is standing over me with a bowl of hot water in his hands.

"Good day, sir. It is time to rise."

"Mmm. Er. What? Oh yes, thanks Scabbard."

"Your water is here, sir. Do you need anything else?"

"Umm, no. I didn't have much to drink last night."

"As you wish, sir. There is food waiting for you and Sir Henry," he says and leaves the room.

I wonder why I'm being woken and served by Scabbard in the castle and conclude that because we're all leaving for Burford early this morning, he's 'back on duty' again. I wash and dress quickly, glad that I got to bed early before another couple of days on the river. Outside my room the same servant as yesterday morning is waiting and he shows me through the maze that is the castle, to the breakfast room. To my surprise, Henry's not there and I ask the servant, "Where is Sir Henry?"

"I do not know, sir, but I believe he is just not ready yet."

"Alright," I reply and sit down to eat.

It's not long before Henry turns up and we both chat a little about the day ahead as more and more food is brought in for us, presumably to prepare us for the long row ahead, even if we're not doing the rowing. After we've eaten, I say,

"I'll just pop back and clean my teeth before we go."

"I'll do mine too. I enjoyed that yesterday." I wish I hadn't mentioned it!

How long will it take before Scabbard can have one made for Henry?

Outside my room the servant is waiting once more to carry my bags but I make sure I take time to wash my toothbrush again before I clean my teeth. Not that this makes any difference because I will still have to use it again after Henry has cleaned his teeth. It just seems a little better. Henry watches me brushing my teeth and asks, "Don't you have to do it for a long time?" The gremlin appears on my shoulder once more. "Five minutes if it's not an electric one."

Henry doesn't ask. When I've finished he picks up my toothbrush without asking and proceeds to clean his teeth. I try not to notice but my stomach turns. I'm sure it's 99.9% a psychological thing as it will be washed before I use it again.

Having finished cleaning his teeth, Henry opens the door and motions to the servant, who picks up the bags and walks down the corridor. We follow the servant down and Scabbard is waiting for us at the back gate with another man. Scabbard explains, "Sirs, this is Matthew. He, along with Knut, will be accompanying you to help with the rowing to where you change to horses. He will be in a slightly smaller boat as you have less luggage than when Lord Burford was with you on your journey to Windsor. Then he will bring the boat back."

"Good day, Matthew," I say, acknowledging the man.

Henry seems to know Matthew.

At the quayside Knut is waiting and I say, "Good day, Knut."

"Good day, sir," he replies.

As Henry and I start down the steps to the boats, followed by Scabbard, Knut and Matthew carrying the luggage, we hear, "Henry! Henry! Wait, Henry!"

It is Lord Burford.

"I just wanted to say farewell," he pants as he approaches the quay.

"Oh, thank you, father, and farewell to you," Henry replies, going back up a couple of steps.

"The journey back will take you longer because you are going upstream, so I suggest you stay the first night where we stopped yesterday near the river confluence and the second night, well, I have stayed at an inn at Wittingham a few times. The landlord will know me."

"Alright, father. Fare you well."

"Fare you well, Henry. Fare you well, Edmund."

"Fare you well, sir," I respond.

It seems as if Matthew, and even Scabbard, don't exist.

CHAPTER TWENTY SIX

THE BISHOP'S MEN

We board the boat and push off, waving to Lord Burford. It hadn't occurred to me that the return trip would take longer because it's upstream. The only rowing I've done before was on the Cherwell river in a hired boat or with the school's rowing team on a lake. I don't have to row now, as that's what Matthew and Knut are for, but I like the idea and tell everyone, saying, "When it's convenient, I would like to do a bit of rowing."

Silence falls, except for Henry who gives a little giggle.

I look at him and say, "I enjoy rowing! I do it in the school team and I'd like a bit of practice."

Knut and Matthew say nothing. What can they say? Eventually Henry says,

"Well, if you want to."

It's settled.

Even against the flow we seem to make good time and soon we are at the rocks near Maidenhead. The same men are there to carry the boat and soon we are on our way once again. The same procedure follows at Marlow and we eat whilst the boats are being transported past the rocks. By early evening, we're at the Fisherman's Inn once more. Henry and I approach the inn and a window is opened. "You want the same as before, sir?"

"Yes, but we'd also like to stay the night."

"Ooh, well, sir. I don't know about that? I, er..."

"We will have no contact with anyone and will pay twice the normal amount."

"Well, sirs, I think we could allow that."

We eat our food and find our beds as night falls.

Today we're up, have an early breakfast and get into the boat as quickly as possible. It's an overcast day and there are a few spots of rain in the air. Matthew and Knut share the rowing but I do insist on rowing sometimes. Henry, to my surprise, also joins in on the other oars. I think he just wants to accompany me. Knut and Matthew seem to be uncomfortable. Why keep a dog and bark yourself? They must be worried they're becoming redundant. We're through Pangbourne and by now the spots of water have turned into continuous rain. There's nothing we can do and we eat as we row to save time so that we can get to the Riverside Inn again where we can rest. We round a bend in the early afternoon and there it is. By now it's raining quite hard and Henry and I run towards the inn leaving Matthew and Knut to moor the boat. Once more a window opens and a voice calls out, "You want to stay the night again, sirs?"

"No, just something to eat and a fire to dry ourselves by," replies Henry.

"Oh, sirs, we have no fire lighted it being summer and all."

"Then light one man! You know we will pay well!" comes the rather short reply, as Henry is getting tired of the negotiating in the pouring rain.

We soon hear the sound of bolts moving, and the door opens as the innkeeper steps back saying, "Please wait here whilst I light a fire, sirs."

The two of us begin to remove our outer clothing as the

door opens again and Matthew enters with some of the bags. "Good man," says Henry.

"Scabbard is bringing some more and I will get the rest of the bags, sir," replies Matthew and disappears again as Knut pushes past him.

As he returns, the innkeeper comes back as well saying, "Follow me please, sirs."

He takes us a few steps down the corridor and points to an open door with the glow of a fire emanating from it.

"Thank you," says Henry, a little less irritably this time.

"I will bring you food, sirs." Then he closes the door.

We place our wet clothes on the backs of chairs around the fire and try to dry ourselves. There's a knock on the door and instinctively I say, "Come in!"

There's no reply and Matthew opens the door to find two trays of food waiting. We eat slowly, as we are in no rush to go back out into the rain, but as we are eating the rain seems to be easing off. A couple of hours after we arrive, Henry puts some coins on the table, and we make our way towards the boats again. By now the rain is merely a light drizzle as we push off from the jetty. A voice rings out from the inn, "Thank you, sirs! We hope to see you again."

On we row again, through Streetley and towards Wittenham. I now remember that I've been here once before when I was about 12 years old. My father took me and a friend to one of the music sessions he goes to in a pub, but instead of a stage with microphones and amplifiers, there were just a load of old men sitting around strumming guitars. I can't remember the name of the pub and it certainly didn't look nearly 700 years old. As night begins to fall we approach Wittenham. Lord Burford was right, it will take us three days to get back and we're only just making

Wittenham before nightfall. It must be nearly 10 o'clock. Again Henry and I walk up to the inn, leaving Matthew and Knut to tie up and unload the boats. It's a few hundred yards to the inn and Henry knocks on the door.

"Good day," I call as by now I've learnt that 'hello' just gets me strange looks.

There's no response, so Henry calls out, "I am Sir Henry Burford, son of Lord Burford. My father said you would give us shelter for the night."

We wait and then a door opens. A man stands there saying, "I am sorry, sir, but we need to be careful these days."

"I understand," replies Henry.

This man seems less frightened than the last landlord was. Perhaps it's because he knows Lord Burford, and it makes us all feel more human and less like lepers. The food is good and the beds soft. Early the next morning, I go out to the front of the inn before breakfast to look at the village. There are just a few little houses and a couple of larger ones. I distinctly remember the sharp speed bumps as we drove through the village in the 21st century but, of course, there are none there in the 14th century. When I'm back in the inn I say nothing to Henry about my little nostalgia trip as we eat breakfast. There's no need to make life more difficult than it already is.

After breakfast we get back in the boats for the final leg of the journey and we make good progress through the morning towards Abingdon. Again it's not a sunny day but at least it's not raining. We row through Abingdon and around the city of Oxford. People watch us from the river bank as we pass but we take little notice and no one in the boats speaks to the spectators. As Oxford fades in the background I think it won't be long now until we're back at the Tadpole bridge. But the last few miles seem much further than I had expected and soon after we have passed Oxford, Henry speaks to suggest, "One last stop to eat before we get to the horses?"

Matthew catches an overhanging branch and ties the boats up before he opens the last of the food and drink. Henry and I both get out of the boat, but only really to stretch our legs. From the brief appearance the sun has made from behind the clouds, it looks as if it is early afternoon and I'm overcome with a desire to become and have a watch to look at. Apart from the worry of my parents I'm simply homesick. When, and how, will I ever get back to the 21st century? Having filled our stomachs and stretched our legs we are back in the boats and Matthew and Knut are rowing hard. On we go but the two rowers begin to slow their pace.

"We will take over for the last stretch, Matthew," offers Henry.

Matthew says, with some embarrassment, "Thank you, sir." He looks very uncomfortable once more.

Why has Henry done this? Is he just taking his cue from me or is he as eager as I am to get back?

Both of us are rowing now and, although we are both fresh, we're not much faster than Knut and Matthew, who had been rowing for many hours. Half an hour later we round a bend and the tethered horses come into sight. My heart jumps and I put a final spurt into my effort. We slide onto the river bank as one of the men catches the rope thrown by Matthew. Henry and I sit on a couple of stones on the bank, as the grass is wet, and we rest as Matthew and Knut transfer the bags to the same horses we came down with a few days ago.

"Will Matthew have to take the boat straight back today?"

"No, he will stay the night in Chimney and go back

tomorrow. It will be a lot quicker without us and the baggage in the boat and, of course, it is downstream."

Before long the horses are packed and Henry pays the men. As he returns to me and the horses he says, "There have not been many travellers recently so I gave the men a little extra. Why should the innkeepers be the only ones to get extra?"

This shows Henry's kindness but I cannot help but think of the badgers and the cubs being torn to pieces for his entertainment.

"Farewell, Matthew," calls Henry.

"Farewell, Matthew," I call. "And thank you."

"Oh, thank you, sir."

Henry kicks his horse into life and my horse follows without encouragement.

I remembered how painful the journey out was when I had a hangover. The journey back is much easier but, even so, my muscles are complaining about the work they have had to do over the last few days. We ride through Chimney and the small village, just a few houses, appears to be deserted. Beamtoon, as Henry calls it, appears up ahead and, as before, we have to go around the town. As we come into Brize Norton I desperately want to turn left and go home, but know I can't. I'm thinking of home more and more. Is this just because I'm so tired? How will I feel tomorrow? Then we ride up the hill and I look back to where Carterton should be. My heart aches but Henry is up ahead and I have to follow him. We ride over the Oxford/Gloucester road on the crest of the hill and down the other side into Swinbrook. A man is walking by the roadside and stands aside to allow us to pass. As we do, the man waves, probably recognising Sir Henry.

With a sense of great joy we turn into the back of Burford

House. Henry is pleased to be back home and I'm pleased to be back - even if it isn't home. We dismount and I look at Henry who's clearly less exhausted than me. Living in the Middle Ages is perhaps fitter and healthier in some ways.

Knut doesn't look at all tired and he immediately begins to unload the horses.

Lady Burford emerges from the house saying, "Henry! Henry, you are back!"

"Yes, Mother, we are."

"Oh, I am so pleased to see you." Then she adds as an afterthought, "And you, Edmund!"

One by one Henry's siblings, Anne, Marion, Stephen and Joan, appear to greet their brother and his friend. We enter the house and Lady Burford disappears to organise a meal for the returnees. As Henry and I go upstairs together, leaving the four younger Burfords behind, Megan appears at the top. "Sirs! Sirs, you must get out immediately!"

"Oh, Megan, good to see yo..."

"Sirs! Sirs, you must get out immediately!"

"What are you talking about!" exclaims Henry, and I just look confused at Megan's distressed state.

"The Bishop's men are in the church and waiting for your return without the Lord so that they can arrest you both for blasphemy and heresy," she gabbles.

"What? That's ridiculous!" I exclaim loudly.

"No, no, no, sir. It is true. I am friends with one of the altar boys and he told me."

"Aah, that's silly," I add.

Then I look at Henry who has turned white. There's a brief silence and then Megan starts again.

"Someone in the town will have seen your return and word

will soon reach the church. The Father has made a complaint about you both to the Bishop and they are waiting for you. My friend overheard them talking and told me at great risk to himself. If Father Mackenzie finds out he will..."

I look again at Henry, who is still white and apparently dumbstruck. Eventually he says, "She is right. We must get out and hide until my father returns."

My jaw drops and Henry turns to Megan.

"You haven't told my mother, have you?"

"No, sir, I haven't told no one. I didn't dare."

We all stand there in silence for a few moments as we think. Then I say to Henry, "Well, I know where I can go, but I can't take you with me, Henry.", I say, thinking of my laptop and my safe home in the 21st century.

"Why can't you?"

"I can't."

"Why?"

"I can't explain why but I can't."

"Where?"

"It's not far away, but I can't take you, Henry," I say more forcefully.

"Why not?"

"Because..."

Just then, we hear a loud knock at the door.

"That'll be the Bishops' men! That'll be the Bishop's men," Megan screams in a hushed voice. "You must go!"

"You must take me with you, Edmund."

"I can't."

"Go now. Go now!" presses Megan.

Henry looks at me.

"Alright, come with me but I don't know what will happen."

"Good man, Edmund" Henry says with much relief in his voice.

The banging on the door continues, louder this time, and we can hear footsteps coming towards the door.

"I will try to hold them whilst you get out the back," says Megan as she turns to run down the stairs.

"Megan," I call and she turns around.

I bound downstairs, grab her and kiss her full on the mouth before she turns and runs down the last few stairs.

Henry and I run through the house, down the back stairs and out into the yard again. The horses are still standing there steaming, with a man just about to take them into their stables to be brushed down.

"Leave them," shouts Henry and the man reels around in surprise.

We jump straight onto the mounting blocks and kick the horses off into an immediate gallop. Henry is in front but I draw alongside and shout, "Let me lead the way; I know where to go."

Henry slows slightly and I shoot ahead. Into Swinbrook we speed and over the bridge. Then we climb the hill as fast as the horses can gallop and I, being extremely tired, hang on for dear life as the adrenalin of fear gives me that extra bit of energy I need. We reach the top and cross over the Oxford road in the direction of where Carterton will start to grow in 550 years' time.

"Where are we going?" shouts Henry, but I don't reply.

Now I can see the rough track to our right and turn to follow it.

"Where are we going?" shouts Henry again, but I have no time to explain.

Now I can see the crossroads ahead, and as we cross over it, I turn my horse slightly to the right heading south east. Then I slow and start looking around for the blue windmill.

"Where are we going?" Henry asks again, but I just keep riding slowly back and forth.

"What are you looking for?" asks Henry.

Still, I give him no response.

"What in God's name do you seek?" Henry asks again, more exasperated this time.

"A blue windmill," I reply.

"A blue windmill! Why would a windmill be blue?"

There's no response from my side.

"The Bishop's men will soon follow our hoof marks and catch us."

I continue to ride back and forth.

"Why are you wasting time, Edmund? Please, Edmund!"

But I'm engrossed in my search.

"We must go on, Ed..."

"There it is!" I 'whoop' and trot a few yards. Then I dismount.

Soon I find the hedge under which I'd hidden the laptop in the plastic bag and pull it out. As I'm opening the plastic bag and taking the laptop out of its case, Henry screams, "There they are!"

I press the power button and the screen comes to life.

"What are you doing, Edmund? We must go now!"

The screen starts to load the icons and now we can hear the hooves of the approaching Bishop's men's horses. I hadn't turned the laptop off so it's only in hibernation state, and is quite quick to come back to life. Even so, it seems like hours.

"Come on, Edmund! What are you doing?"

I just sit there crossed-legged with the laptop on my thighs.

"You'll get us both killed, Edmund!"

"Get off your horse and come here, Henry."

"Don't be silly, Edmund. It's the stake for us it they get us!"

"Don't argue, Henry, just do as I say. It's our only chance."

We can hear the horses' hooves slow as the men came closer.

"Now, Henry, or I'll have to go without you."

"Go where?" asks Henry as he finds himself dismounting but not really knowing why.

The horses' hooves stop as Henry reaches my side.

"Sit in front of me and hold onto the other side of this."

Henry says nothing, as it's too late to ride away, and puts his fingers and thumbs around the bottom of the laptop lid. I move the pointer to the 'undo' button as the Bishop's men dismount, swords drawn.

"Hold on tight," I command, "and don't let go no matter what happens. This may take me, it may take us both or it may take neither of us" I say, as I press the 'enter' key.

The letters in the address bar move and mist swirls around us as the Bishop's men see us both disappear into thin air.

THE END